THE RAVEN CORONET

CHRISTINA BRILEY

THE RAVEN CORONET

Misenchanted Press

This is a work of fiction. None of the characters and events portrayed in this novel are intended to represent actual persons living or dead.

The Raven Coronet

Published by Misenchanted Press

Cover art by Ruth Evans

Dedication

The author would like to dedicate this book to her friends and family, for they have consistently encouraged her endeavors and embraced her quirks.

In particular, she believes any dedication *must* mention her beloved husband, Charles, who inadvertently influenced so much of the story – especially with his joking comment that the plot should include a member of WWE.

PROLOGUE

High upon a parapet stood the gaunt and aged wizard. Around him the wind danced and surged, as if pleased to be part of what was to come. The old man raised his arms, and the gale caught the sleeves of his ebony robe until the fabric billowed and flapped like the wings of a great bird. At his summons, black specs appeared on the horizon. These could soon recognized as ravens, each of them carrying a dark, silver-flecked feather in its beak, and each moving to take its place in the living torrent of feather and sinew that now began to circle the magician. When a hundred coal-black wings flapped overhead, the wizard spoke again. The birds opened their beaks and let go their offerings, but the loosed feathers sank only slightly before gathering speed in a tightening ring of their own. Faster and faster this magical construct spun as both circlet and plumes contracted. When at last the apparition stopped spinning, a shimmering wreath the size of a man's head dropped gently into the wizard's outstretched hands.

CHAPTER 1

CIRCUS

"Now, girls," Calista called out as she strode calmly through the commotion in the upstairs hallway, "you obviously can't go out in just corsets and panties, and time off is time off, but that doesn't mean you can't do a bit of advertising for future business."

A traveling carnival had come to town, and Calista had decided to close the house for the afternoon to let the girls take in the show. Even under normal circumstances afternoons were slow; today would be even slower with most of their potential clients out at the far edge of town. There seemed no harm in letting the women have some fun. Besides, Calista knew that a bit of fresh air and time off for the girls would result in a livelier, more cheerful group of women to pleasure the customers that evening. The women hurried about as they searched their closets for clothes that would cover a touch more skin than their usual working attire.

Calista stopped a girl rushing past and placed her hands on either side of the young woman's ribcage. In an abrupt and well-practiced motion, Calista brought her palms up and in, thus unceremoniously hoisting the girl's breasts upwards so that several more inches of flesh towered above the neckline.

"Cleavage, everyone! If this afternoon is going to be 'Look, don't touch!' time, let's give the gentlemen plenty to look at!"

Overhead, Thaedra could hear Calista's voice clearly through the floorboards of her attic bedroom.

1

"Oh, Callie," Thaedra muttered to herself. "Everything you do is about how many coins it will bring in!"

Thaedra sat on the edge of her bed wearily and pulled on one of her boots. It had been a bad night. Scenes from her past had filled her sleep, disturbing scenes made more grotesque by a dream-world mix of real life trauma and make-believe legend.

Thaedra! Are you coming?" Calista's pounding on the bedroom door put a welcome end to thoughts of the nightmare. "Hurry along now! I can't have my girls parading around town without their bodyguard. And those carnies – who knows what that motley band of gypsies might try to do to my sweet charges!"

Now shod, the house bodyguard snorted and stood up. "Hah! 'Sweet charges' indeed! I wonder who's more likely to take advantage of whom!" Thaedra strode over to the dresser mirror to splash some water on her face before yanking open the door.

"Good morn, Calista. You may stop pounding now; my head aches quite enough already, thank you."

The madam caught herself just in time to avoid accidentally rapping on Thaedra's oft-broken nose. Calista lowered her arm and chided snippily: "Well, I'm sorry about your headache, but the day's half over, and you do have a job to do."

Calista turned on her heel and headed for the stairs with the younger, more-muscled woman close behind. The other occupants of the house were already gathered out front on the veranda, chattering eagerly about the circus.

Upon spotting Thaedra, one of the courtesans smiled and sidled over. "Why such a sour face, sleepyhead?" Artella threaded her arm through Thaedra's and leaned close. "The weather is beautiful, and we're off on an outing!"

Thaedra grinned reluctantly at Artella's eagerness. She still would rather have spent the day at home nursing her headache than attending some ragtag carnival, but she was truly fond of the girls. Perhaps the distraction would do her some good.

2

Although the walk across town was a long one, the late spring day was pleasant and sunny, and the girls chattered and laughed along the way. By the time the group reached the field where the tents had been hoisted, even Thaedra's dour nature had brightened a bit. Her headache had eased, and she began to look forward to seeing the show.

"Ooh, look!" cried out one of Thaedra's charges. "They have a magician!"

Thaedra looked, and in a nearby, roped-off area, spotted a man in a long, deep blue robe. The robe was covered with garish gold trim, as well as large, gold moons and stars, and the whole thing struck Thaedra as being somewhat clichéd. The robe had obviously seen better days, and the frayed hem was caked with the mud of a hundred fields.

"Mud?" Thaedra wondered out loud, for the weather had been dry, and the walk across town, dusty. Then she saw that the ring in which the man stood had clearly been drenched with water, and several half-full buckets still stood along the perimeter. A moment later the reason became obvious.

Regardless of what she might think of his attire, she had to admit that the shower of sparks that suddenly shot from the magician's fingertips was impressive. At first, he merely held one hand out in front of him while thousands of tiny gold sparks cascaded from the ends of his fingers to fall harmlessly on the wet ground. After the first wave of "Ooohs" and "Ahhs" had died down, he brought up his other arm. Now the murmurs began anew; the size of the golden waterfall had doubled with all ten fingers streaming bits of fire.

The wind changed abruptly, and some of the sparks flew into the man's face causing him to wince.

"Ouch," Thaedra muttered in sympathy, but the magician's pain seemed to have gone unnoticed by most of the crowd, mesmerized as they were by the ongoing, fiery shower. The man shrugged off the discomfort and regained his composure.

Gradually, the crowd again grew silent, and again the magician changed the composition of the torrent. Now each finger poured out sparks of a different color. Red from the index fingers, then orange, yellow, and blue moving outward. This time the crowd's cries of amazement were even louder.

Soon, though, the rainbow of fire began to die out, and Thaedra could see that the magician was struggling to stay on his feet. As the last spark faded, he held up his shaking hands dramatically so that everyone could see the wisps of spoke that rose from his fingers. The audience applauded wildly while the man made one exaggerated bow after another until finally he excused himself to collapse on a nearby stool. A pretty, young colleague, with long, blond hair and a revealing outfit, circulated among the crowd holding out a hat and suggesting that perhaps the crowd might wish to show their enthusiasm in a somewhat more concrete manner.

"One trick pony," Thaedra said to no one in particular. But when she looked around her, she realized that everyone else was enthralled by what they'd just witnessed. She caught snatches of conversation:

"That was wonderful! I couldn't take my eyes off of him!" exclaimed one of the girls.

"Did you see how the sparks just *poured* out of his hands? They just kept going and going..." chimed in another.

"...And the finery he wore, and his courage to stand amid those burning embers!"

The comments went on. Thaedra resisted the urge to point out that his finery wasn't all that fine anymore, and that it was a pretty useless trick other than looking pretty, and that there was enough water around to make it a fairly low risk stunt at that. But the girls were the only family she had, and she couldn't bring herself to spoil their fun.

A twinge of jealousy struck her. Here was a group of women who made their living flat on their backs, a despicable occupation that Thaedra had literally fought her way out of – for she preferred being bouncer to being whore – yet these courtesans could still have enthusiasm for life. Was her own soul so hardened that she could have enthusiasm for absolutely nothing?

After a bit, the crowd moved along, and Thaedra and her housemates went with it. The next roped off area they came to had a muscular man some years older than Thaedra pacing about it and taunting the crowd.

"Does no one dare to fight me?" he called out. "Younger men, stronger men, hardy farm boys who plow alongside their oxen – *none* of you? Surely now, one of you must have the courage to face Falmund the Fearless!" He slapped his chest with his fist.

"Why should we?" yelled out one of the onlookers. "If you break my arm the way someone broke that nose of yours, I'll not only be useless for the plowing, but I'll hardly be fit to pass time with the wenches either!" The man gestured toward Thaedra's little group. Several people in the crowd chuckled and nodded – though a few of the more righteous turned up their noses at the prostitutes' presence.

"Why fight me? Why, to prove you're a man, of course!" replied Falmund. "I'm sure there are plenty of women with the imagination to make you forget about a broken arm," he went on with a smirk, "and I'm sure they'd rather tend to a man than a mouse! Fight me, and you'll have your pick of this lovely lot over here!

"Besides," he added slyly, "somebody managed to break this nose before; perhaps you'll be the one to do it again!"

"Promising my ladies without asking me?" cried out Calista indignantly from the back of the crowd. Thaedra watched as the irate madam pushed her way through the spectators to stand at Thaedra's shoulder near the ring. "How *dare* you?"

"Begging your pardon, Ma'am," Falmund spoke with a mocking bow, "I wasn't meanin' to be promising anyone to anyone, merely suggesting the ladies might be more willing with a gent who'd already proved his manhood in the ring."

Calista didn't miss a beat, and suddenly Thaedra was certain this exchange was more about the madam's sales than the fighter's salaciousness. Thaedra looked down at her brassy employer, a full head shorter than herself, and wondered with amusement what would come out of Calista's mouth next. The answer turned her amusement to dismay.

"Manhood?" Calista mocked. "My girls can bring any fella's manhood to full blossom, be he lover or fighter. As for breaking that nose of yours again, are you man enough to give a woman a shot? Or would that be too great a threat to your own puny manhood?" She put a hand on Thaedra's shoulder blade and shoved her roughly forward. Calista's smile oozed charm at Falmund, but her eyes were all challenge and cold calculation.

Thaedra started to protest: "This isn't part of my..." but she stopped at a glare from her boss.

Thaedra recognized Calista's your-job-is-what-I-say-it-is look. And she understood the logic of the madam's actions. Humiliate the big, strong stranger and every man in the crowd would feel more manly by comparison. Do it via a hot, sweaty wrestling match with a woman, and they'd be thinking of doing some hot, sweaty wrestling of their own. Logical or not, Thaedra wasn't happy about a fight, but she knew that neither this Falmund person nor she herself was in any position to refuse.

As the crowd waited eagerly for Falmund's response, Thaedra began sizing up her opponent. His nose had indeed been broken at least once, and his face had little about it that one could call handsome. Thaedra smiled wryly to herself when she thought of all the times that someone had made that same judgment of her own visage. Falmund's short, open vest was of battered brocade, the worn gold trim barely still attached in

6

spots, and it did little to cover his broad chest. He was clearly muscled, but not overly so, and Thaedra was sure those muscles of his had been oiled for effect. The beginnings of a paunch were visible just above his leather breeches, and below them bare, muscled calves led to mud-caked moccasins. She realized that this ring, too, had been watered down, and wondered if it was merely an overzealous attempt to keep down the dust.

"So be it!" Falmund called out at last to the audience's applause. "And if I win the battle – which of course I will – do I get to bed the wench?"

"*If* you win the fight," Calista replied, "you may bed any woman in my house, myself included! But first you must win the fight!" The crowd roared its approval, while Thaedra felt a flush of rage at the thought that she might once again be forced to bed a man on someone else's say-so. Nonetheless, she ducked under the rope to face her opponent. Perhaps, she mused, her anger would give her the edge she needed.

"So, lass, you'd best make your move first," Falmund spoke loud enough for the crowd to hear. "I won't hit a woman unprovoked, and I expect to have you down on your back in two shakes of a mutt's tail anyway!" He grinned at Thaedra, and she heard the whistles and catcalls from behind her. Angry and overconfident, she lunged at him. He calmly sidestepped her and let her momentum and the slick footing land her face down in the mud. Mentally, she kicked herself. She knew better.

The reason for watering the ring was now all too clear. Falmund was used to fighting in the mud and could use that to his advantage. Not only that, but judging by the crowd's enthusiasm, the slimy, slippery goo made the action that much more entertaining. Thaedra pushed herself up onto her hands and knees and from there raised herself to a kneeling position. As she did, she glanced down and saw her wet, muddy shirt plastered revealingly to her ample breasts.

"I have to give that woman credit," she muttered ruefully, as she looked at her own protruding contributions to Calista's advertising campaign, "she does know what will excite the men and bring in the business!" The rage faded a bit and a smile tugged at the corner of Thaedra's mouth.

Falmund looked down at her and extended a hand. "Done so soon?" he asked.

"Oh, not quite." she replied nonchalantly, reaching up to grasp his wrist as he in turn clutched hers. Halfway up from the mud she tugged on him hard. It was an old, obvious move, and he merely staggered a bit rather than go down as she had hoped. But it did pull her up far enough, and him down far enough, that he found himself suddenly face to cleavage with her. His surprise at being smothered in female flesh threw his balance off further than any hackneyed wrestling trick could have, and with a shove of the shoulder from Thaedra it was his turn to go down.

Now the fight began in earnest as first one and then the other would seem to get the upper hand. From his position flat on his back, Falmund reached up for Thaedra's hand; she stepped forward to straddle his legs and generously offer her aid. But instead of gripping her outstretched hand, he abruptly swung his legs sideways to trip her – and so she joined him down in the mud once again. On their knees they came together, each struggling to rise, and each struggling equally hard to make sure the other went down. Face to face, dripping mud and sweat, they clenched their teeth and stared at each other as muscles strained. Thaedra found herself looking into his eyes, deep blue eyes that seemed to draw her in, and it suddenly occurred to her to wonder if she had ever actually looked into a man's eyes before.

The distraction of the thought was enough to break her concentration, and suddenly Falmund was up and she was down. Lying beneath him, she swung her leg up to strike him in the groin, but checked the blow in amazement when she realized

8

the size to which her target had swollen. There was nothing puny about *his* manhood! Despite all her years in the brothel and all her stone-cold bitterness, she began to muse about his potential in bed.

"Focus!" she chided herself under her breath. "He's just another horny, sweaty bastard like every other man out there." She cautiously pulled herself up out of the mud again, watching him warily as she struggled to keep her footing.

But he, too, seemed to be losing interest in battling; he stood staring at her and breathing heavily. Thaedra wondered if losing and being Falmund's "prize" would mean more time gazing into those delicious eyes, or whether it would be just another quick and dirty roll in the sack.

Halfheartedly, she made another lunge for Falmund. But though she was aiming a blow for his chest, her arms instead seemed to slide around his waist of their own accord. Startled but willing, he clasped her to him. Hands that a moment ago had been those of an opponent now seemed the hands of a lover.

Thaedra was surprised to realize she wanted to kiss him. Still, not only did they have an audience, she wasn't sure that even this man's kiss would be worth the mouthful of mud that would come with it.

So she settled for staring into those eyes, and he stared back, and the crowd began to get restless and murmur.

"Hey, what's the deal here? Finish it!" one man called out in disgust.

Thaedra heard the man's words and knew they could not end the fight this way. She nodded her head imperceptibly to Falmund and he bent slowly as if to kiss her. The crowd held their breath, not knowing if they'd be witnessing a fight or a rape, but happily enthralled either way. Falmund's hands moved to grip Thaedra's shoulders, his lips brushed hers... And he promptly threw her unceremoniously into the mud. Laughing,

Falmund leapt down on top of her and pinned her shoulders to the dirt.

"Do you yield now, wench?" His voice was mocking but his eyes appeared to be telling her something different.

This man intrigued her. Were she and Falmund fighting or playing or something else entirely? Did she even know how to play anymore? In spite of her confusion, she managed to fill her voice with the sullen resentment the situation seemed to require as she replied: "I yield, bastard!"

He climbed off her, with evident reluctance, and this time offered his hand genuinely to help her up. Yet, once she was up, he grabbed her by the waist, slung her over his shoulder, and climbed over the rope and out of the ring. The crowd parted for them, applauding and cheering as the pair made their way quickly through the mass of people. When Thaedra squirmed a bit for effect, a few onlookers loudly offered lewd suggestions of what he might do to tame his reluctant prize.

As soon as they were free of the crowd, Falmund broke into a swaying lope, still bearing his opponent. The wrestler kept up his bruising pace until at last they entered the outskirts of Cobbleton and could duck out of sight behind the nearest building. Breathing heavily, he gently put Thaedra on her feet.

For a moment neither of them could talk, worn as they were from the exertion of the fight and the jarring trek that had followed. Thaedra waited for the flush to leave her cheeks now that she was upright. But the longer she stood staring at Falmund, the less likely it seemed that her color would return to normal anytime soon. Falmund, it appeared, was having equal difficulties in getting his breathing to slow to a more relaxed rhythm. The moment grew more intense.

It was too much. Thaedra started giggling. She wondered how long it had been since she last laughed. "What," she asked between giggles, "just happened?"

"What are you laughing at?" Falmund exclaimed indignantly, still wrapped up in the fervor of his desire for this woman. But then he took a good look at the mud-encrusted object of his desire and, as he reached to push Thaedra's matted hair from her face, he felt himself began to chortle also.

Thaedra's giggles became gales of laughter, and she slumped against the building clutching her stomach and beginning to hiccup. Years of bottled up mirth seemed to at last have found a chink in her emotional armor and out the silliness tumbled. "Gods!" she gasped between hiccups. "Are you ever *hung*!"

Falmund glanced down at the bulge in his pants and then at Thaedra's blouse, a blouse that was barely containing its own treasures, and his own laughter grew louder. "Well," he replied, wiping a muddy tear from his eye, "those ain't nothing to sneeze at either!"

Falmund sat down beside Thaedra and for some time neither could speak. Each time their mirth died down, one of them would catch the other glancing sideways at their respective protuberances and the laughter would begin anew. Finally, sheer exhaustion put an end to the hilarity, and the need to wash and to sleep began to be overwhelming.

"If we can make it to the far side of town," Thaedra offered, "there's a little pond up in the woods where we can bathe and wash our clothes. And I can grab a few blankets from home on the way to wrap ourselves in while our clothes dry."

Falmund nodded mutely and stood up. Together they started off toward the whorehouse and the lake beyond, leaning against each other like a pair of old drunks, chuckling and staggering on their way.

CHAPTER 2

THE LAKE

It took Thaedra and Falmund quite awhile to get to the pond in their tired, befuddled state. And all along the trek, one or the other of them would periodically suggest that perhaps they should just take a nap right where they were.

"How about the gutter?" Thaedra asked only half joking. "Can't we just take a nap right here in the gutter? Somehow it looks amazingly tempting right now. Is it really so much filthier than we are?"

Falmund eyed the gully along the edge of the road. It was a view that he'd been staring at for some time now, given that he and Thaedra had been hanging on each other's shoulders, heads bowed, for the entire walk.

"Nay, my sweet..." Falmund replied, although he was interrupted by Thaedra snorting loudly at the thought of being referred to as "sweet," especially in her current state. Falmund ignored her and went on: "You are far too sweet to lie among the refuse we've been passing. I, however, should find myself right at home there, a home I believe would be quite comfortable just now."

Thaedra snorted again and reached up to rap Falmund gently on the side of the head. They staggered on.

The stop at the deserted brothel was brief. Thaedra didn't dare invite Falmund in the house to smear dried mud on the brocade chairs and red velvet couches, so she left him standing on the lawn while she ran inside for blankets. She came out and led him around back to begin trudging up the hill behind the house to the pond.

Last autumn's leaves crunched under their feet as they walked through the woods. Out of the hot sun at last, Thaedra felt some of her energy return. The forest around her was lush and green; the ground speckled with sunlight. The cool, clear lake that she knew lay up ahead seemed to be calling out to her. The urge to run and skip and laugh, pleasures absent from so much of her childhood, came over her now.

Her steps grew faster, and Falmund's strides lengthened with her own. Finally they crested the hill to see the water sparkling in front of them. Thaedra paused but a moment to drop the blankets and to yank off her boots before racing for the water's edge.

Her long legs kicked up great sheets of cool water as she ran, laughing, into the lake. Over the splashing of the water, Thaedra heard Falmund behind her cursing, and she turned to see him still standing on dry land.

"Bloody hell!" he grumbled as he struggled to unfasten his pants. He looked up at Thaedra. "I can't get me good leather britches soaked, now can I? A little mud is one thing, but a complete dousing? What if they shrank? Why, I'd strangle!"

She laughed again and turned her back on him, not wanting to make him uncomfortable by staring as he undressed. Although, she thought, there was probably not much that would embarrass this particular man. As she strode further into the water, she began to think that she, too, should have shed her pants, for her woolen knickers felt increasingly heavy. Quickly, she reached under the surface of the lake and a moment later she tugged the soggy garment off over her feet.

"Here, catch!" she called out as she turned and flung the sodden woolens at an unsuspecting Falmund. She had misjudged the distance badly, as he had come up behind her while she struggled with the pants, and the pair of dripping knickers flying

14

at his face from so near caused Falmund to attempt a dodge, lose his balance, and plunge headlong into the lake. Concerned, she strode to where he'd gone under, but just then she felt strong hands running sensuously up her bare legs, and her concern turned to something else entirely.

For a moment she froze and savored the sensation. But then she caught a glimpse of her pants sinking under the water's surface, where she was sure they'd be caught in whatever current there might be and disappear forever. Thaedra pulled away from the inquisitive hands and lunged after her trousers.

A great form rose up out of the lake behind her, flinging back its head and spraying water from its hair in the process. "Ah, lass!" Falmund called out. "Do ya seek to escape me? 'Tis not wise to toy with the denizens of the deep!"

Her hand closed over the wayward pants. This time she wrung them out a bit before throwing them. And when she flung them it was not at Falmund but at the shore, upon which they landed safely in a heap. When she turned back toward her companion he was already upon her.

Her loose blouse floated about her in the water, and his hands found their way under it easily. "Oho," she laughed, "Two can play at that game." For the first time in memory, she found her skilled hands applying their expertise for no reason other than her own desire.

The mix of sensations overwhelmed her: soft lips and muscular bodies, hot flesh and cool water, lust and laughter and longing. All these eddied and swirled and came together.

When their desire was sated, each set about helping the other remove the mud that still clung to their hair. And, in between fresh giggles and kisses, each gently scrubbed the last remnants of soil from the other's face. Exhausted, they finally climbed out of the water. Whatever garments the pair still wore, they removed and spread in what little sun they could find to dry. Together the two curled up in the blankets.

15

"You are a strange and wondrous creature, Lass." Falmund murmured sleepily.

"No stranger than you, sir, for you make me feel as if I'm melting into your body. Just where is it I end and you begin?" Thaedra queried. A part of her longed to say more, longed to stay awake and go on savoring the idea that a man's touch could be something to enjoy rather than to endure. But sleep overcame her.

*   *   *

When they awoke the sun was low in the sky. As if by unspoken agreement, the pair confirmed that sex on dry land could be as pleasurable as in water – perhaps, even more so. When they were done, Thaedra and Falmund reluctantly got up and dressed. They gathered the blankets and started down the hill.

"How long are you in town?" Thaedra asked Falmund with feigned indifference.

"How long would you like me to be?" he replied.

"Oh?" she stopped walking and looked at him skeptically. "Would my answer really matter to you? Surely you had plans for the next few days when you arose this morning, and I am quite certain they didn't involve such damaged goods as myself."

Irritation crept into her voice as competing impulses warred within. Cut loose this traveling stranger or embrace him?

"My lady!" Falmund exclaimed melodramatically as he reached for her, "I wouldst hardly call thee damaged! Thou art the sun to my moon..."

"Falmund," Thaedra growled. "You know nothing about me, so do not tease." She took a step back, out of his reach. "I asked you a simple question."

"I wasn't teasing..." he began to protest, but thought better of it. After a moment's consideration, he answered carefully,

16

"When I got up this morning, the plan for our group was to remain in Cobbleton for one or two more days and then move on. However, *if* you find me as interesting a companion as I find you, then perhaps I could find a way to extend that stay. Which brings me back to my original question: 'Would you like me to stay?'"

"Yes," she answered simply. "That would be very nice." Her wariness tempered her words.

Falmund looked at her curiously. "'Nice' is not the word I would have chosen." Seeing Thaedra smile in agreement, he relaxed and reverted to his usual jovial manner. "I would have said 'stupendous' or perhaps clapped and danced at the thought." He executed a quick little jig interspersed expertly with rhythmic clapping.

Thaedra chuckled.

Encouraged, Falmund stopped dancing, struck a pose, and proclaimed emphatically: "And if you are what constitutes damaged goods, then may the gods eternally spare me perfection!"

Arm in arm, the pair strode onwards.

When they reached the foot of the hill, the house that Thaedra knew as home was aglow with lights. Lanterns hung along the front porch, and men lounged there awaiting their turn with the girls inside. It seemed Calista's advertising had, in fact, worked a bit *too* well. Calista herself was circulating through the men trying to amuse them and see that no one became overly impatient. Every so often she would glance around, obviously looking for someone, and it was clear that she was none too pleased when she didn't find the person she sought.

"Oh, damn!" Thaedra spoke under her breath to Falmund. "It appears I'm much needed. Duty calls, and all that."

Falmund looked at her askance.

"Not *that* duty! I'm the house *bouncer*. I thought you would have guessed after Calista set me up to fight you."

17

"Of course, of course. You shall have to tell me more about how that came about sometime."

Just then Calista caught sight of them. "There you are!" she exclaimed in annoyance. "Get your sorry butt up here and see that things don't get out of hand. If you were here doing what you're paid to do, I could be seeing to some of these gentlemen myself." She smiled sweetly at a fellow who'd just planted a kiss on her neck and helped himself to a handful of breast.

Falmund stepped forward. "Might I be of some assistance, Madam?"

"Well, if you're through running off with the help, you might pitch in with some crowd control." Her voice still carried an annoyed edge to it. "And given how full up we are, if *you're* doing crowd control then perhaps your little 'prize' there might take up her former duties..."

Thaedra stiffened and frowned, but Falmund leaned in close to his companion and commented quietly: "Aha! So the job as bouncer was a promotion from '*former* duties.' Well, let's see if I can sooth your boss and keep you for myself this evening."

He redirected his attention to Calista. "But Madam," he proclaimed in his practiced, carnival barker's voice, a voice designed to reach the ears of every onlooker, "I haven't collected my prize yet at all! I merely conquered my opponent and dragged the brute off into the woods with me where I demanded she wash the mud off every inch of my body. Of course, this was done merely that she might show deference to the superior fighter, and brought me no pleasure *what*soever!" His voice took on an over-exaggerated tone of innocence, and he shook his head emphatically. He made sure to step forward into the light from the porch before offering his audience his best lecherous smirk.

Behind him Thaedra winced. For an instant she was appalled that he should speak of her so. But an instant was all it took for her to see he was merely playing to an audience and trying to get her off the hook. Still, it was with some satisfaction that she assumed the role of the resentful bitch, and landed her boot firmly on his backside.

"Bastard!" she cried out.

Falmund whirled to face her and grabbed her arms, pinning them to her sides. He rubbed his body against hers lewdly, like a bear scratching an itch by rubbing itself on the trunk of a tree. Their audience applauded and whistled in appreciation.

Thaedra looked at Falmund worriedly. She could play the game all right, but she was finding it hard to know what was fact and what was farce with this man.

"Trust me," he mouthed to her. Then, much more loudly: "Mmmmm! That whet my appetite!" He abruptly let go of her and turned back toward the house. "Now, I need me some real lovin'! Where are all those pretty, little things you promised I could choose from?"

"You'll have to wait your turn," Calista called out, "I've got a full house already!" Calista had seen what was going on, and she had to concede that Thaedra would probably be more good to her right then entertaining the customers by sparring with Falmund than by tending to them individually in the sack. "In the meantime, you'll have to settle for amusing yourself with my bouncer there." She gestured casually toward Thaedra and turned to escort one of the waiting men inside.

Falmund turned again toward Thaedra. She saw his head drop in dismay, his broad shoulders droop in despair. She saw him heave a deep sigh of disappointment that seemed to come from the very tips of his toes and could hardly be missed by the onlookers behind him. She also saw the sly wink he gave her, the one that those same men would indeed miss, the one that said how pleased he was that they were now under orders from her boss to spend the rest of the evening together.

"Well, wench," Falmund brought his head up and spoke cheerfully, obviously striving bravely in the face of his so-called disappointment to make the best of a bad situation. "What pleasures do you wish to offer me?"

Thaedra paused to consider her reply carefully as any number of possible answers, both true and false, came to mind. She held her head up and looked him straight in the eye.

"Why, sirrah..." she purred. Her weight shifted to one leg as she thrust the other hip toward him. She slid her foot forward and took a slow, sensuous step closer, the way a cat would stalk its prey. At the same time she placed her hands upon her shoulders, from where they began to slide seductively over her own curves. Shamelessly, she smoothed the thin fabric of her blouse tight over the generous circumference of her breasts, proudly presenting them for her audience's admiration. She took another step closer to Falmund. Her hands continued their leisurely journey down her body, her waist, her hips, her thighs. From her own thighs, they slid to those of the man in front of her. Now her hands began to travel upwards again. As they came to rest in the center of Falmund's chest, she heard his breath grow faster, and she felt herself sinking into those eyes once more.

She quickly shook off the sensation and continued her response: "...What pleasures do I wish to offer, you ask? Why, I wish to offer you the pleasure of *planting that self-absorbed ass of yours in the dirt!*" Her voice was no longer a purr; it had grown to a roar. She pushed Falmund hard, and he went down at her feet, surprise on his face. "Perhaps such plantings are the best chance you have of growing little Fearless Falmund seedlings! For what woman would want such a braggart as you?" she taunted him.

"Oho!" crowed one of the men on the porch. "I knew there was a reason I never tried to bed that bitch! She's a feisty one, ain't she?"

"Ha! I like my women soft and eager," called out another to Falmund. "Better you than me, buddy!"

Falmund's lips seemed to disappear completely as he bit down on them trying to keep from laughing aloud in delight. Here was a woman after his own heart, a woman who could both take it and dish it out. She was not one of the mewling, delicate women that other men seemed to want to warm their beds and ornament their homes – but from whom they expected no hint of independent thought. *This* was a woman Falmund could respect.

Thaedra looked down at him and watched him prop himself on his elbows. His efforts not to laugh did not go unnoticed, and she squelched a chuckle of her own. As she pondered their next move, she found herself thinking how exhausted she was and just how much she didn't want to stage another brawl. Glancing up at their audience on the porch, she was relieved to see that the last few men were being escorted inside by some of her prettier, but surely equally tired, housemates. Smiling, Thaedra held out her hand to help Falmund up.

"It seems our fans have abandoned us," she told him.

He glanced over his shoulder. "Alas," he said in mock sorrow. He grasped Thaedra's hand, but instead of letting her help him up, he pulled her down to him. "I simply cannot stand another moment without feeling your glorious body pressed against my own," he muttered before bringing his lips to meet hers.

Mere seconds later, Thaedra felt a familiar bulge pressing against her nether regions. She sighed and reluctantly drew away. "Perhaps we might consider finding a bed this time?"

"What a novel idea!" Falmund exclaimed. "A bed it is then! Lead onward, Lass! Actually, perhaps you might lead us to a bed via the kitchen? It has just now occurred to me that I seem to be starved for more than simply your sweet self, delectable though that may be."

A bit awkwardly, they climbed to their feet and brushed themselves off. Grabbing Falmund's hand, Thaedra led the way to the side door of the house, where they could stop by the kitchen before continuing on to Thaedra's waiting bed.

CHAPTER 3

THAEDRA'S STORY

Thaedra awoke to a gentle kiss on the tip of her nose. In the instant between sleeping and waking, she thought herself a happy child once again, a child who still considered her stepfather to be her savior, a child whose mother still lived. Little Thaedra felt safe and cared for. She opened her eyes to see Falmund watching her and remembered how far astray her life had gone in the intervening years. Yet, looking at Falmund, she found that the warm and happy feeling from her dream stayed with her.

"Good morning, lass," Falmund said gently.

Still half asleep, she lifted her head to kiss him on the cheek before falling back on the pillow and muttering: "Good morning, sirrah."

But as she came more fully awake, the contented feeling faded and doubts crowded in. She looked up at Falmund questioningly. "Is there any particular reason you're staring at me so? Has the cold light of morning revealed me to be some sort of muscled freak, perhaps?"

"Nay, lady!" He shook his head emphatically. "I have never quite understood so many men's fascination with fragile women; a woman such as yourself is of far more interest."

"Oh good. I'm 'interesting,'" she replied a touch peevishly.

"You are a good deal more than that," Falmund said seriously, "and I am lying here wondering how you came to be that way, *and* in this occupation. I can't say as I've encountered another female bouncer anywhere."

Thaedra sighed and wondered how much she should tell him. "The short version of the story would be 'destitute young widow turns to whoring and then battles house bouncer for his job.'"

"A very short version indeed. Perhaps you might fill it out more?"

"Where shall I begin?"

"At the beginning, I suppose. I hear rain starting to tap on the roof overhead; I doubt there will be a show today, so I'm in no hurry."

Thaedra slid out from under the covers and grabbed a robe. "For a story that long, I shall need some nourishment. Let me run down and get us some breakfast. I'll bring it up and we can eat and talk at the same time." Before Falmund could respond, she was out of the room and closing the door quietly behind her.

By the time she returned with buns and cider, Falmund had put on his britches and was sitting propped up at the head of the bed. She sat down next to him and took a bite of roll before commencing her tale.

"I never knew my father – he abandoned us when I was an infant. My earliest memories are of poverty, of begging for food, and of trying to vanish silently into the dark corners of friends' houses where Mama had begged shelter. 'Don't run, don't make noise,' Mama told me over and over, 'or they will surely throw us out in the street.'"

Falmund looked sympathetic. Yet he remained silent and let Thaedra continue.

"Then my mother married a member of the guard, a captain, and for awhile I had the perfect childhood. We had a home, and food on the table, and Josnah treated me as his own." Thaedra remembered her wakening dream that morning and added: "And a puppy, I even had a puppy. Your wet kiss on my nose

24

first thing this morning made me think of that for the first time in years."

"Not sure I appreciate my kissing skills being compared to those of a dog. Still, I *am* glad I could bring back pleasant memories." Falmund grinned and leaned over to kiss her somewhat-crooked nose again. "But you said you had a perfect childhood 'for awhile…' What happened?"

"Mama died having Josnah's stillborn child, and I never really forgave him for what he did."

"For begetting a baby? That hardly sounds like a bad thing."

"It wasn't that… it was… it was the whole day she died." Thaedra had never talked about that day before. She wondered why she was even talking about it now.

Plunging onward, she said: "Josnah wanted me out of the way while everyone was trying to tend to Mama. So he dropped me off with some of his men at their rooms over the tavern…"

"They didn't!" Falmund looked horrified. "How old were you?"

"Oh! No! Not that exactly. I was six… and they wouldn't have dared; he was their captain after all. But they *did* have women in their room, and I was in their way, so they put me out on the roof outside their window so they could have some privacy."

In an instant, Thaedra could see herself on the roof again, huddled against the side of the building. Daylight was waning, and the nearby houses metamorphosed into dark, mysterious giants threatening to reach down and grab her or, worse still, to sweep her into the black nothingness at the roof's edge.

"*Mama*," the adult Thaedra whimpered in unison with the child in her memories. She remembered crawling to the window in hopes of rescue – but all she had seen through the crack at the edge of the curtains were writhing silhouettes that moaned and panted and frightened her even more.

Falmund put his hand on Thaedra's arm. "Lass?"

25

She dragged her thoughts back to the present and cleared her throat. "Sorry. I got distracted. In any case, I couldn't believe that my beloved papa had abandoned me in that place. And then when Josnah finally returned and told me that Mama and the baby had died..."

"I can imagine..."

Thaedra doubted he actually could, yet she let it go. "After that he did his best to raise me but he had no idea how to raise a child, much less a girl, and he was truly devastated by Mama's death himself. It was a difficult situation for both of us."

"And you escaped it by marrying the nearest farm boy?" suggested Falmund. "Who proceeded to die in some gruesome accident involving farming tools or angry bulls?"

"Hardly." Thaedra recognized his words for a playful effort to lighten the somber tone. Still, Falmund had wanted to hear her story, and she was going to give him the unvarnished truth. "He married me off to one of his fellow guards. Somehow Verin, the other guard, convinced Josnah that he knew something that could make them both rich and famous. And if Josnah would make Verin part of the family by giving him my hand, then he would share the secret."

"And I suppose it wasn't just your hand he wanted," Falmund broke in wryly.

"No, it was not."

* * *

She had been in the midst of cooking Verin's breakfast when he came up behind her and wrapped his arms around her waist. "Good morning, luv." He kissed her neck. "Something smells good. Is it you or the eggs?"

Thaedra reached up to pat his cheek affectionately. She had finally become accustomed to his touch, to the warmth of his body, the musky smell of his skin. "Good morning, husband.

Nay, I can't imagine you refer to my unwashed self just now. 'Tis your breakfast then." Thaedra started to pull away so as to put his meal on the table, but Verin gripped her tighter.

"You're mistaken, lass," Verin replied with amusement, "I do believe that you and breakfast are one and the same this morning." He pressed his bulging crotch against her backside. "And I'm sure you'll both be delicious."

"Surely you need some *real* nourishment to keep on as you do!" Thaedra replied teasingly. It was flattering that he wanted her so, and better than having him spend his money on the whores over at Madame Calista's, but Verin's lovemaking was hardly the delight to Thaedra that it obviously was to him. It was, in many ways, just another chore on a long list of daily chores. "Aren't you on duty today?" she went on hopefully.

"Aye, but not for a few hours; I walk the late guard today." He nudged her toward their little bedroom where it lay just off the kitchen. "Come back to bed for a bit."

"But your breakfast is ready, and I need make a trip to the market!" Thaedra squirmed in his grasp. Frustration welled up in her, and she wondered whether anger or humor would best serve to deflect her husband's attentions.

"Leave the breakfast," Verin insisted. "Come take care of me and then we can both go to the market, and I'll help you carry your bags home before I have to leave again."

Thaedra sighed as she accepted that neither tactic would be sufficient. Verin grinned, for he knew he had won. He let Thaedra pry his hands from her waist and watched contentedly as she took the pan of eggs from the stovetop, covered it with a lid, and placed it upon the stove's upper shelf where it would keep warm but the contents would not burn. The pot of coffee she left where it was; it wouldn't hurt it to perk awhile longer.

"You *are* a pretty one, you know, Thaedra," Verin said admiringly.

Thaedra did not respond to the compliment from her husband. Instead, having seen to the breakfast, she turned toward him and placed her hands on her hips. "Now, sirrah, you wanted something?" She spoke jokingly, but there was a hint of irritation in her voice that anyone who chose to listen would have heard.

Verin didn't catch it. Instead, he put his arm about Thaedra and guided her toward the bedroom door. He leaned his head close to Thaedra's and spoke gently, as one might speak to a child who needed help with their lessons, "My sweet, young Thaedra, it's time you learned some of the special things your husband likes."

Thaedra wondered what he meant. He seemed to like very much what they'd been doing in the bedroom. Thaedra had to admit that it felt nice to be able to please her husband, and it made her feel powerful that he wanted her so. She might be at his mercy in most things, yet, when he was inside of her, she could lie there aloofly and know that for those few moments she was in control and he was not.

Now Verin kicked closed the bedroom door and pulled off his britches. Thaedra began to unlace her bodice but Verin didn't wait. He stepped up to her, put his hands on her shoulders, and pushed her down. Confused, Thaedra dropped to her knees on the hard wood floor.

Verin lifted the hem of his blouse and urged: "Kiss me."

Blushing, Thaedra turned away. "Verin! That's disgusting!" She couldn't imagine what he was expecting of her. Surely this was some sort of stupid joke!

He placed his hand on her head and pulled her face against him. "I want to feel your mouth on me," he insisted. "Please?" he added belatedly.

"Who would do such a thing?" Thaedra again drew back. Smells of sweat and urine and the stale scent of last night's sex engulfed her. While the kitchen had been full of the cool air of early morning, the bedroom seemed to contain only the stifling heat of a long summer. Thaedra felt as if her face were afire as she asked angrily. "Where did you *get* this idea?"

"Every whore I've ever had would do such a thing! Surely a woman can do as much to please her husband as a woman can do for a few coins!"

"I'm not your *whore!*" Thaedra burst out in fury as she started to rise.

"Just *do it!*" Verin exploded, shoving his wife back down none too gently.

His push caught Thaedra off balance, and she fell sideways, hitting her head on the corner of the dresser before catching herself with one hand. Her eyes filled with tears and she let herself sag the rest of the way to the floor.

"Oh, gods! Thaedra! I'm sorry!" Verin had gathered his wife in his arms and lifted her onto the bed. "I never meant to hurt you!"

Thaedra had lain silent. Anger, pain, humiliation, and fear all churned inside of her. Verin lay down beside her to hold her but she was stiff in his arms. Like a puppy begging for forgiveness, Verin nuzzled his cheek against his wife's.

After awhile Thaedra's rage had subsided, and her feelings had coalesced into a hard, helpless, numbness. Gradually the desire to scream at her husband, or spit in his face, or run from his bed were all crushed beneath the overwhelming weight of her own impotence. And so she had done nothing.

* * *

Falmund was silent after Thaedra had finished explaining her husband's first "lesson." He put his arm around her and pulled her close. After a time, he asked softly, "I suppose that wasn't the last time he hit you?"

"Well, things were all right for a time after that. I coped – and I learned my lessons *really* well! That young, sweet, innocent me would *never* have admitted to anyone what I was doing in the dark with Verin, but I was actually kind of proud that I could please a man so well." Thaedra reached over and patted the crotch of Falmund's britches playfully; now it was she who was trying to lighten the mood. More somberly she admitted, "But yes, you're right. What really pushed things over the edge was that damned stationing he and my stepfather got themselves up north for six months as part of their great quest. Apparently, the trip didn't go as planned and... well, neither did his homecoming."

* * *

Thaedra was leaning over the kitchen sink, her back to the door.

"Thaedra?" came Verin's voice from behind her. The tone had seemed almost shy; he had been away a long time.

At the sound of his voice, his wife turned towards him. The full curve of her belly was immediately obvious in the high-waisted shift she wore. "Hello, husband," Thaedra said. Knowing her condition would be quite a surprise to her spouse, Thaedra smiled, a funny little half-smile, proud and uncertain and rueful all at once.

For a moment Verin was dumbfounded, but only for a moment. In two strides he was across the room and standing in front of Thaedra. But rather than offer the happy kiss she was expecting, he slapped her across the face with all his strength. "*Whore!*" he spat at her, shaking with anger.

Thaedra struggled to keep her balance, and her hand flew up to her cheek. She was stunned at her husband's response. "But you wanted a child..." she stuttered. Abruptly she realized

30

the cause of his fury. "But Verin, it's *yours. By all the gods, I swear...*"

"Do you take me for an *idiot?* How many times did I lie with you that first year? *How many?* And there was no baby! So now I leave you for six months and come back and find you with... with... like *that!*" He gestured at her stomach.

Fear and indignation battled for control of Thaedra's tongue. "If," she spoke uncertainly, and then again with a growing vehemence, "if I am a *whore*, I learned everything I know *from you!*"

This time Verin didn't use the flat of his hand. His knuckles connected firmly with his wife's face, and Thaedra's nose broke at the impact. A wave of power washed over Verin's countenance as his anger fed upon itself and grew. Thaedra became the target for the disappointments of his quest, the disappointments of his entire life. A target that had no prayer of fighting back.

"*Slut!*" he hissed. "You're *my* wife! I *own* you! You'll do as I say and like it! But only with *me!*"

Thaedra slid to the floor clutching her ruined face. Blood ran between her fingers and down her wrists to stain the front of her dress. The blood seemed to catch Verin's attention; perhaps somewhere deep down he knew he didn't really want to hurt her. But then he looked past the blood to the full belly on which it fell, and any mercy was lost in a flood of rage. He drew back his leg and swung his booted foot at Thaedra's abdomen.

Thaedra made a strangled noise as his boot connected. There was no air left in her lungs with which to scream. She gasped for breath and in so doing got a lung-full of blood from her broken nose. Choking and writhing on the floor, Thaedra was barely recognizable as the mother-to-be who had moments before greeted her husband with a proud smile. At last she drew in enough air to satisfy her aching lungs and stopped squirming, curling instead into a bloody, defeated ball. She said nothing,

31

even when she realized that there was warm liquid trickling between her legs.

Verin's rage started to ebb.

"I... I... Thaedra..." he began. He fell silent again. There were no words to undo this, no apology existed that could take away the pain. Verin knelt down and reached to touch his wife's hair only to have her cringe in terror.

Desperate to escape this horror, Verin turned back to his anger to protect him from the onslaught of guilt. He spoke softly to the cowering figure on the floor: "Well, bitch, I doubt your bastard will ever leave his mother's womb alive now. Perhaps next time you'll know better than to betray your lawful husband."

Verin turned on his heel and left the house.

* * *

"By the time the neighbors found me," Thaedra explained to Falmund, "the baby was dead, and I was in a bad way. I think my poor friend. Arienne, had to use up a month's grocery money to pay a healer to save me – though even the healer couldn't save me from becoming barren. Arienne had her husband bury the baby and fetch Josnah, but no one saw Verin again until the next day."

"Where had he gone?"

"Here, actually. He spent all night whoring and then came home as if nothing had happened."

CHAPTER 4

ESCAPE

"So you said you ended up a widow," Falmund commented from his position next to her on the bed, "just how *did* Verin die?" By this time the pair was stretched out on their sides, with each propped up on an elbow to gaze at the other.

"I killed him," Thaedra stated flatly. "He had told me he would kill me if I tried to leave him – I believe his exact words were, 'I'll be in your fuckin' face for the rest of your fuckin' life.'" She sighed heavily. "I stuck it out a long time. My ability to appease him seemed like the one smidgen of control I had over the situation. The thought of giving that up was terrifying. But eventually, I decided that staying with him was even *more* terrifying. So I ran."

* * *

The younger Thaedra stood looking in the mirror ruefully. She gently touched the rapidly swelling bruise below her eye.

She thought back to Verin's promise to Josnah to take care of her. "It's a shame," she muttered through swollen lips, "that men don't put half the weight behind their promises that they do behind their punches." She started to laugh at her sad joke, but promptly stopped as the action proved too painful.

"By the gods!" she exclaimed. "He's robbed me of my peace, my freedom, my children, and now, even my laughter. Enough is enough."

Thaedra turned and looked at Verin as he lay passed out on the bed, that bed where he expected her to satisfy his every whim on command or suffer a beating such as she had this night. But she resolved that from that moment on she'd do it no more. She muttered softly: "At least if he kills me for trying to leave him, I'll finally be at peace. 'Twould be better than going on with my innards knotted in terror day after day."

Thaedra looked around the room and tried to think if there was anything she needed to take with her. Money? Clothes? They'd certainly be helpful, but if he awoke and saw her taking them he'd know she was trying to leave again – and she had a feeling that killing a runaway wife was one promise he'd keep.

A knife, she'd take a knife. Perhaps it would give her a fighting chance when he came after her. She shivered at the thought, and almost lost her resolve, but the spasms made her bruises ache down to her bones, and reminded her that more of the same lay in store for her if she stayed.

"I can't go on like this," she whispered. "Better to die fighting." She took a knife from the kitchen drawer and let herself out of the house as quietly as she could.

Once in the street, Thaedra felt as if there were eyes behind every window, eyes waiting to give her up to her murderous husband. A stray cat rubbed up against her ankles and she started in terror. The animal began to meow plaintively. Desperately, Thaedra scooped it up to silence its wailing. Clutching the squirming, scrawny animal to her breast, and thanking all the gods and goddesses she could think of for the noiselessness of her soft-soled shoes on the cobblestones, she ran.

Thaedra flew soundlessly through empty streets. Yet her pace soon flagged – not just because she grew short of breath or because her passenger dug its claws in with the jarring, but, more

34

importantly, because she feared her mad dash for freedom would catch the attention of Cobbleton's night patrol. The guards, she was sure, would be Verin's allies, not hers. Her movements became stealthier, and she stayed to the shadows.

Eventually, Thaedra reached one of Cobbleton's main roads. There she paused, firstly to put down the now-quiet cat, and secondly to choose her path out of town. The stray sat in the street contentedly washing his paw; his ride under Thaedra's cloak had warmed and consoled him even if it had done nothing for his empty stomach. After a moment, the beast set off one way searching for food while Thaedra decided to go the other.

Of her options, the easterly route seemed the wisest. Thaedra had spent all her life in Cobbleton and knew that it marked the northwest corner of the kingdom; nothing but wilderness lay beyond in those two directions. Nor did traveling south appeal to her since it would take her right by Josnah's house. Thaedra couldn't bear the thought of passing the home where she'd had her few happy years – nor of facing Josnah should he happen to be awake. For all she knew, he would send her back to her husband to die.

So she headed east. Gradually the houses grew farther apart and the open spaces more plentiful. Thaedra looked at the road ahead of her, lit by a sky full of stars, and felt joy welling up within. The terror was still there; the thought of Verin awakening and pursuing her was ever in her mind. But freedom beckoned. She knew it would be hard, knew she might go hungry, but she would be alive, and she would manage somehow.

The stars began to wink out as the new day approached, and the road took Thaedra into a patch of forest. It was just as she entered the stand of trees that she realized someone was following her. All around her the countryside still slept – and in that lull before dawn, Verin's voice reached his wife's ears easily, though he was yet some distance away.

"Leaving me again, eh? How can you keep doing this to me when I love you so? Stop and look at me!"

Thaedra kept her head down and continued walking. She pulled the knife from her belt and gripped it anxiously under the folds of her cloak.

"Ignore me, will you?" he called, his voice rising. "How *dare* you! After all I do for you? Damn it, *bitch, listen to me!*"

His tone suddenly dropped again and turned pleading as he begged: "Please, Thaedra, just come home and all can be as it was. Don't make me drag you."

"*As it was...!*" Thaedra wanted to scream. But she bit her tongue and merely walked faster.

The fury returned to Verin's voice. "You will *not* humiliate me," he snarled. "You are my wife and my woman. The law, the gods, and *I* say so. I'll see you *dead* before I see you with another man!"

Now Thaedra could hear him striding up behind her. Her stomach was so knotted in fear she thought she would surely vomit. Then his hand was grasping her shoulder... She whirled round.

In one smooth motion, and without conscious thought, the knife swung up under his breastbone and into his chest, driven deep by years of pent-up rage. The expression on Verin's face turned from rage to astonishment, and finally to death's vacant mask. He sank to his knees, and Thaedra went with him, too stunned herself to release her grip on the knife. Even as she became aware that her husband was dead, she couldn't bring herself to let go. It seemed as if somehow the move was not final and could be taken back just so long as she didn't remove her fingers from the playing piece. She hadn't meant to kill him. She'd only wanted to escape the pain and fear that had haunted their marriage for so long.

His head fell forward limply against her shoulder, and the sticky warmth of his blood traveled over the knife and ran down her sleeve to pool at the elbow. But still she knelt in front of him, keeping his lifeless body upright by her grip on the blade. Finally, deep within her, another bit of her soul turned cold and hard, and she could focus on what needed to be done.

Gritting her teeth, Thaedra lowered the body to the ground and pulled out the knife. She set the weapon aside and gingerly set about searching Verin's pockets, struggling to avoid feeling his still-warm flesh through the cloth. Bile collected in her throat, and she gulped it back down. Thaedra knew that searching the corpse was necessary, partly because she needed any money she could get and partly to make it look as if robbers had killed him. The law was not kind to women who murdered their husbands, no matter what their reason. The hardened, practical side of Thaedra overcame her desire to run from the scene, and she began to nervously scold the corpse as she went about her task.

"Ah, you've more beer money on you than you gave me for food for the both of us, you cheap bastard!" She pulled a handful of coins from his vest. "You won't be needing these anymore." Thaedra had the urge to throw them in his face. But dead was dead and she needed them more than he now. She pocketed the coins and then picked up the knife, wiped it clean on some leaves, and tucked it back in the waistband of her skirt. Thaedra took one more look at what had been her husband before grabbing the body by the wrists and dragging it off the road into the bushes.

With that done, Thaedra could at last escape the scene. "I'd best get back to town quickly," she told herself, chewing her lip anxiously. "If I run from Cobbleton now, everyone will know I did this. She pulled her hood up until it hid her face. Wrapping the cloak tightly about her so as to hide her bloodstained clothing, she hurried through the wakening streets in order that she might reach home before word of her husband's demise.

* * *

"And no one ever connected you with his death?" asked Falmund.

"I think Josnah eventually figured it out, but he kept it to himself. I can thank him for that much, at least," Thaedra replied ruefully.

"And you aren't in the habit of randomly murdering husbands...or lovers?"

"Only if they try to murder me first!" Thaedra suddenly sat up and climbed atop Falmund to kneel straddling his hips. "Or beat me excessively!" she teased.

"Well, I can promise not to try to murder you," Falmund said with a grin, "but this beating each other up has been rather rewarding..."

Thaedra rapped her fist gently against his jaw before continuing her tale. "When the money ran out, I realized that there was a single, particularly marketable skill set that I'd gained from my marriage. So I gave up my reputation and my friends and my home and I joined Calista's household."

"But how did you become bouncer?"

"I didn't much like making my living on my back, and I liked Thorpe, the piggish lout of a house bouncer, even less. So I worked out a plan to replace him. I would learn to fight."

With a smile, Thaedra explained further: "Suppose you were a client lying there, just sated and recovering from round one. What if I sat here atop you, nude..." Thaedra shrugged out of her robe. "...and wiggled my hips..." She demonstrated suggestively. "...and promised you another round, off the books. You need simply teach me a few fighting moves on my day off." Thaedra felt a familiar twitch beneath her. "See?" she gestured at his crotch. "I'll wager you'd be happy to race around the woods with a half-naked courtesan, alternately instructing her with a steel sword and ravishing her with a flesh one."

Falmund sucked in his breath. He reached up and grasped Thaedra's shoulders. "I do see the appeal. But I think we should save the rest of this story for later – I believe I've got the gist of how you came to be you." He pulled her down towards him. "And a very enticing you, you are..."

CHAPTER 5

BELTON

Many towns away from Cobbleton, Captain Josnah Farmson rode down the lane that led into Belton's magic quarter. Almost two years had passed since Josnah's first visit to Belton, but he remembered the previous trip well.

Josnah nudged Windweaver's sides with his heels. "Today I will not be dissuaded. Today that witch, Nazera, will tell me what I need to know."

He passed Palagonia's hitching post, still topped with two slender, wrought-iron hands cradling a glass globe. Above it, her sign swung gently in the breeze: "Palagonioa: Professional Prognosticator."

"Now *there* was an obliging magic-worker. And an extraordinary artist as well!" Josnah mused aloud.

He recalled his surprise when he had he entered Palagonia's shop on his earlier trip. The usual hangings and mystical decorations had been absent, and he had found himself in a well-lit room whose walls were covered by paintings. The scenes they depicted were eerily distorted ones, some of them quite beautiful, others thoroughly unsettling. There was a certain similarity to them, although it had taken Josnah a minute to put his finger on what it was. The paintings all curved away from the viewer at the edges as if seen through a convex lens, or, more likely under the circumstances, seen inside a crystal ball.

Absorbed in the artwork, Josnah had been caught off guard when a voice next to him inquired, "Do you like my paintings?"

When he turned to look, his heart had fallen. The seer in Cobbleton had said that he must seek out a psychic with raven hair in Belton; Palagonia was a redhead. But when he questioned her, she had been most helpful.

"Well, I suppose I could insist that you pay the regular fee and join me while I consult my crystal to find your raven-haired seer, but it really isn't necessary. If you'd said 'dark-haired' there would have been a few possibilities. But mention 'raven,' and it has to be Nazera."

"Nazera?" Josnah had queried hopefully.

"Nazera is an apprentice who clerks at her mistress' magic shop down the lane. The shop you want is called Zephyrs and Flora."

He had tossed her a coin and ridden off. There had been no problem finding the shop.

"The problem," he muttered now, as he dismounted once more in front of Zephyrs and Flora, "was getting Nazera to tell me what I wanted to know. I had had such high hopes! And when I entered the shop and spotted the tip of a raven tattoo peeking out from her collar, I was sure that the Raven Coronet would soon be mine.

"But that was months ago, and here I am back in Belton empty handed."

Josnah fell silent before yanking open the shop door and striding in. An unfamiliar woman stood behind the counter.

"Where is Nazera?" he demanded.

"Gone," the woman answered simply, raising her eyebrows in surprise at his audacity.

"Gone where?"

The proprietress looked displeased. "I have no idea where! And even if I did, I see no reason to answer to such rudeness."

Josnah swallowed his irritation and spoke more soothingly. "Forgive me. I was here some time ago in search of information. She told me that the answer could be found in the Royal Archives at Azenburg."

"And have you looked there?"

"Yes! I spent almost *two years* looking there!" He struggled to keep his frustration in check. "It took me a month just to convince the scribes and keepers of the kingdom's history to give me access. It's a wonder the United Lands function at all with all the forms and foolishness the government puts their citizens through!"

"And once you gained access," the shopkeeper pressed him, "did you learn anything?"

"I learned a great deal. I learned about the founding of the United Lands, about King Dargason and his chief wizard, Aza. I learned about how they had agreed that the squabbling fiefdoms and constant bloodshed were a sorry waste of life and resources and how they longed for a way to unite the lands under one rule and end the incessant battles. I learned – down to the last detail – about the creation of the Raven Coronet and about how its potent effect gradually spread outward from its wearer across all of the known lands of man. I learned that after the spell took effect, the only arguments between the warlords centered on how best to please Dargason."

"That sounds like quite a bit. So, just what was it that you did *not* learn?"

"*What happened to the Coronet after all that!*"

"Why, it was destroyed, of course!"

The woman's answer caught Josnah by surprise. "Destroyed?" he echoed. "Nazera dismissed it first as a child's fairy tale, and then admitted that it was real but tried to convince me that it was dangerous. But destroyed?"

Patiently, as if to a troublesome child, the shopkeeper explained: "It's generally accepted among those versed in magic that Aza must have destroyed the Coronet once the kingdom was united. It would be hard to keep it hidden and dangerous to risk it falling into hands that would abuse its power. I can't imagine why Nazera didn't tell you as much herself."

"I don't believe you, and I wouldn't have believed her either," Josnah protested. "I have reason to think it still exists."

"Think what you like. I have told you all I know."

"But you have not told me where Nazera is! Nor precisely who you are, for that matter."

"I am Gaylith," she declared haughtily. "Nazera was my grown apprentice turned clerk. But she up and ran off quite awhile back. Now I, one of the most *accomplished* of Belton's witches, must tend shop myself and forgo those pursuits more worthy of my skills!"

Gaylith swung her arm wide, gesturing dismissively toward the door through which Josnah had entered, as if to indicate that he had exhausted her forbearance and should now depart. This movement brought her robes to his attention. Although Josnah took her claim of fame with a grain of salt, the designs on the cloth did indeed confirm that she was a guild witch. Absorbing this new information, and still filled with determination, Josnah was oblivious to her dismissal. He stood waiting for her to somehow produce Nazera for him.

Seeing him make no move to leave, the witch spoke again: "Sir, I have answered your questions, despite your rudeness, and have had quite enough of you. Would you kindly remove yourself from the premises?"

Josnah scowled at her but realized she either could not, or would not tell him more than she already had. It would be unwise to try pressuring a trained witch, and so he stormed out of the shop without further comment. Remounted, Josnah adopted a sullen slouch as he turned Windweaver's head back toward the main part of town.

THE RAVEN CORONET

There was one particular bit of information in the Royal Archives that Josnah had *not* mentioned to Gaylith. The capital had not always been in Azenburg; it had been moved there well after the United Lands' formation so as to be centrally located. No, Dargason's original fortress had been at Raven Keep, near the town of Belton, and it was Belton that had originally been the seat of government. All this had made Josnah more certain than ever that the raven-haired witch, Nazera of Belton, was the key to obtaining the Coronet.

"Damn," he blurted out. "How will I find her now?"

Just then, Palagonia's signboard caught his attention. "Perhaps *she* could help me track down Nazera," he mused.

When he entered Palagonia's shop this time, Josnah could see that many of the paintings from before had been removed and replaced by new ones. He hoped that they had all been sold rather than merely cycled into storage, for Josnah had been favorably impressed by both the art and the artist.

Palagonia turned from the painting on the back wall that she had been straightening. "Good day, sir!" she said pleasantly. "May I help you?"

"Hello again," replied her visitor. "Remember me?"

The seer looked intently at Josnah and then shook her head. "You'll have to forgive me, my mind is quite a sieve sometimes. I find it's just as well. If all my customers and all my visions just accumulated in my head it would be quite crowded in there, and soon there'd be no room left for any new thoughts whatsoever!" She smiled apologetically.

"My name is Josnah. I stopped by here about two years ago looking for a seer with raven hair; 'Nazera' you told me."

"And did you find her?" Palagonia asked, without admitting whether or not she recalled their previous encounter.

"I did," Josnah replied, "but I have more questions for her."

"Ah," Palagonia nodded sagely. "'Tis very common to think of more things one should have asked after a visit with a prognosticator. But I'm afraid Nazera's left town."

"So I've been told. You wouldn't happen to know where she's gone, would you?"

"I'm afraid not," the seer replied.

"Might I avail myself of your professional services then?" Josnah asked with a bit of a bow.

"A prognostication? Why, certainly!" Palagonia responded. "Right this way, sir."

She led her customer through an archway in the rear wall of the gallery, into a smaller, less well-lit room. An easel stood in one corner and numerous canvases, both bare and painted, rested on edge upon the floor around the room. These were stacked five or six deep against the wall in some spots. In the center of the clutter sat a table draped with a midnight blue cloth. If Josnah hadn't already surmised the source of subject matter for Palagonia's artwork, he certainly would have known it now; upon the table sat a carved cherry-wood base cradling a foggy crystal orb.

Palagonia drew back one of the chairs from the table, being careful not to poke a hole in the surrounding canvases with an errant chair leg. "Have a seat, Josnah," she offered, nodding to the chair before her. When Josnah had seated himself, she slipped around to the other side of the table and settled into her own chair.

"Now," she began, "just exactly what is it you want to know?"

"I want to know where I can find Nazera."

Palagonia said nothing but drew the orb and its stand toward her. One arm rested on the table loosely enclosing the crystal in her embrace – whether to protect the orb or to hold it captive, Josnah could not tell. The other hand started to stroke the crystal's surface, as one would caress a cat, first sliding languorously over the curve of its crown and then slipping around beneath to fondle its "chin." The movement was hypnotic and sensual. Josnah felt himself grow warm watching this woman, and his face flushed with both desire and embarrassment. It seemed as if he were a peeping Tom intruding upon a pair of lovers.

Gradually, the long, graceful fingers slowed their circumnavigation of the orb. But the glass itself no longer seemed opaque; its foggy quality now lay not in its surface but beneath it, and the mists contained within the globe were shifting. The churning fog followed the path Palagonia's fingers had traveled, much the way a cook stirring a pot of soup starts a whirlpool that will continue on its own for a time without further prompting.

From where Josnah sat, he could see the movement of the mists but nothing else. Yet for Palagonia there were breaks in the clouds, and through these gaps she saw images of Nazera.

"She is with Falmund," offered Palagonia in an emotionless voice as she recognized figures within the glass, "...and Hargot."

"Falmund? Hargot? Who...?" Josnah began.

"Not now," she silenced him. "Ah," she continued, "I see Nazera has a crystal orb of her own now. She stands before a large crowd and offers them their fortunes. There are walls around them, walls of canvas."

Josnah longed to ask just *where* these "walls of canvas" were but did not dare interrupt the seer again.

Palagonia continued to watch the orb in silence, and Josnah continued to watch Palagonia. At last the fog's movement slowed, and it seemed to again become one with the glass. Palagonia blinked twice, shook her head as if to clear it, and looked up at her client.

"Well?" Josnah demanded, "Where is she?"

"I'm afraid I can't give you her exact location," the seer said biting her lip.

Josnah seethed with frustration, but he hadn't yet given up on Palagonia's vision. "Can't you give me *some* information?"

"Why yes," she said in surprise, "certainly." Palagonia could never quite get accustomed to clients who expected a specific answer to a specific question and were ready to dismiss the whole process as useless when the answer didn't materialize.

"So?" Josnah's impatience grew.

"So she's with Falmund, a former guardsman here, and a very congenial one I might add, and Hargot, a two-bit wizard, also formerly of this town."

"And they are where?"

"If I knew *that* I'd know where Nazera was, wouldn't I?" replied Palagonia, getting a bit irked herself. "But I can offer some suggestions as to how to find out where they are. To begin with, it appears they have formed some sort of traveling circus together, so if we can just get you headed in the right direction it shouldn't be hard to find a group that's actively trying to draw attention to themselves."

"Makes sense," conceded Josnah.

"You should talk to Falmund's former comrades in the guard. And Hargot used to be a regular at Aily's."

"The guard is easy; I'm a retired captain of the guard. I've no problem asking around the barracks." Josnah agreed. "But Aily's? What, and where, is it?"

"Up With Aily" is the real name," explained the redhead. "It's a pub, named after some girl the owner was smitten with whose name conveniently sounded a lot like 'ale.' But everyone just calls it Aily's. If you continue up this street out of the magic district and towards the center of town, you'll find it on your right."

"All right, then! Pubs are no problem either," Josnah said with a grin. With his hopes of finding Nazera, and hence the Coronet, restored, he was out of the side room and halfway across the gallery before he felt Palagonia's hand on his arm.

48

"Aren't you forgetting something?" she asked firmly. She stepped in front of him and held out her free hand.

"Oh. Forgive me, I'm terribly sorry," Josnah apologized for the oversight. "I'm afraid my eagerness to follow up on your suggestions made me forget myself." He dropped a generous payment into the seer's hand.

Palagonia closed her hand over the coins and stepped aside. Without another word, Josnah was out the door and pulling himself up onto Windweaver's back.

Josnah urged his mount into a trot, much to the annoyance of the slower traffic that was forced to step aside. Sitting his mount easily despite the jarring gait, Josnah made his way quickly up the lane.

There ahead of him was the pub's signboard. Accompanying the words was a picture of a hand holding a tankard raised as if toasting someone. "Probably Aily," thought Josnah smiling.

He dismounted and tied up his steed. At the door of the pub, he stopped to gather himself. Looking over-eager might bring questions he had no interest in answering. Taking a deep breath, Josnah pushed open the door and walked calmly between the round oak tables that filled the room to make his way to the bar. He leaned forward on the counter and said casually to the barkeep: "A mug of the house ale, if you please, sir."

The man drew the ale as requested and placed the mug in front of Josnah remarking: "Can't say as I've seen you about here before."

"No reason you should have; I'm just traveling through. Someone told me awhile back that if I was ever in Belton I should stop by Aily's and catch the wizard Hargot's little performance."

"'Fraid Hargot's gone," the bartender said ruefully.

"Gone?" Josnah raised his eyebrows as if this were news to him.

"Yep. He and a few friends got themselves a couple of wagons and set off to travel town to town putting on a show. It's been a year or two now since they left."

"Now *there*'s a show I'd like to see," said Josnah, lifting his mug for emphasis before putting it to his lips. "You wouldn't know where they went, would you? Perhaps I could catch up with them."

The barkeep eyed him suspiciously. "Yer not the law, are you? You're not out to collect a debt from poor Hargot or something?"

"Nothing like that," Josnah assured him. "I only heard tell of what a nice display the man put on with his magic. Can't say I'd relish trying to collect a debt from a man armed with magic anyway!"

The two men chuckled together and any tension ebbed away. The bartender offered what knowledge he could to Josnah. "Can't tell ye exactly where the group of them went. Don't know if they'd precisely decided themselves when they left town. But there ain't much to the south or west o' here so you can forget those. The nearest town lies slightly north of due east from Belton, and I'm pretty sure that's where they went. Had a few customers mention seeing the wagons heading out the old east road." A thought occurred to the barkeep. "But all that was awhile ago. You're not going to be able to just ride out and catch up to them as if they'd left yesterday. Just how important is this to you anyway?"

"Oh, I'm simply traveling about these days seeing the world. Having a specific goal for a time, the goal of setting my eyes on this circus for instance, might be fun," Josnah spoke lightly. He sat trying to digest the information he'd just been given. The barkeep probably knew all there was to know about finding Nazera's group; there seemed little point in questioning the men at the barracks. Chances were half of the guard patronized Aily's anyway, and any useful gossip they knew had already been passed along to the fellow standing here behind the counter.

Josnah placed a gold coin on the counter. "You've been kind, sir, and the ale was excellent. Keep the change." Draining the last bit of ale from his mug, Josnah stood and left the pub.

CHAPTER 6

CHOICES

Back in Cobbleton the morning was already past, but Thaedra and Falmund were in no rush to leave their cozy, attic room and go their separate ways.

"So, Sirrah," Thaedra spoke, tracing little circles with her finger in the hair on Falmund's chest. "What is *your* story?"

"Mundane childhood. Grew up in Belton. Became a guardsman. Wasn't impressed with the boredom – which was alleviated only by the occasional need to kill someone – or by the macho morals of my fellows. Figured I was good at fighting, and a fight always seemed to gain an enthusiastic audience, so I got together with a few magic-wielding friends and formed a traveling circus that would incorporate my brawling skills."

"An interesting tale, but so short. Or is there more to it?"

"Not really. We've added a few more members to our troupe since it began, but there are no scandalous secrets of which I'm aware." Falmund suddenly had an idea. "Perhaps you could join us, too." The instant the words were out of his mouth, Falmund realized they might be a mistake. He barely knew this woman. And if everything she had said was true, she was hardly a woman with whom to trifle.

"Ah," replied Thaedra coolly, without looking up from drawing patterns on his chest. "And when I have given up my security here and you have tired of me, you shall leave me by the side of the road in some strange town, penniless and alone?"

Falmund took her by the chin and looked her in the eye. "I find it hard to imagine tiring of you."

Thaedra pulled away and focused on her tracings once more. "And I suppose you will say that I am the first woman you ever invited to join you and your friends?"

"No," Falmund said with a chuckle that shook Thaedra's drawing surface. "Beyond the members of the original troupe, the first woman I invited would be Faylah, but she is a centauress, and my motives were business and friendship only. You are the first *lover* I have asked, yes."

"A centauress?" Thaedra murmured idly. "I must have missed her yesterday." But in Thaedra's head, her thoughts were racing. The idea of leaving the brothel behind to travel with Falmund and the circus appealed to her, more than she cared to admit even to herself. Still, she took pride in being practical and in being nobody's fool; running off with a bunch of strangers could hardly be called wise.

Having already broached the idea, for better or for worse, Falmund realized that he genuinely did not want to leave this woman behind. "You'd like Faylah," Falmund encouraged. "She is *almost* as unique a female as yourself. And we could most certainly come up with an act for you. Or perhaps I could include you in my own routine and 'suffer' wrestling you everyday." He broke into a broad grin at the thought.

"Perhaps a change is in order..." muttered Thaedra. "What is the worst that could happen? I could end up bouncer somewhere else?"

"I can hardly picture you as the helpless victim you say you once were," offered Falmund. "Even if things don't work out with the troupe, I am sure you'll manage wherever you land." He sat up and looked down at her earnestly. "But regardless of what happens between you and me, I genuinely believe you would do well as a circus player, and you would fit in wonderfully with our little band of misfits."

"Little band of misfits..." Thaedra repeated. "A misfit, that's me. I would be right at home there, wouldn't I?" She suddenly felt as if she would suffocate should she allow this window of opportunity to close and trap her at the brothel forever. "Prudence be damned! Why not?"

* * *

It was not long after that that an excited, but somewhat nervous, Falmund set off alone on the long walk across town to the carnival. He might have convinced both himself and Thaedra that she should join the troupe, but now he had to convince his fellows. The plan was for him to go win them over while Thaedra packed up her few belongings and settled things with Calista. Thaedra would head after the strongman as soon as her business with the madam was done.

The meeting with Calista was brief. Thaedra found her in the kitchen going over the previous night's receipts.

"So, did your new friend finally leave? You two seemed a mite smitten with each other," Calista asked brightly. Thaedra suspected that Calista's cheerful chumminess was due more to the substantial pile of coins on the table in front of her than any real interest.

"Yes, he's left."

Before Thaedra could continue, Calista cut in: "Are things back to normal now? I hardly expected you two to run off for the entire afternoon! I've never known you to be the flighty type before." She looked at Thaedra curiously.

Thaedra snorted. "Now, that's hardly fair! It was your idea that I fight the man in the first place. And I certainly couldn't go wandering around the fairgrounds any longer after the mud bath I took," she went on defensively. "But in any case, no, things are not back to normal. I believe you'll be needing a new bouncer."

Thaedra began casually searching the pantry for lunch, as well as for a little something to take for the road.

Calista's eyes widened. "You mean my tough, hard Thaedra is running off for the sake of a man? Ha! Who'd have thought *that* would ever happen?" Somehow her voice managed to convey both sarcasm and affection simultaneously.

Thaedra wondered which emotion was stronger in Calista: her pleasure at hearing that Thaedra yet had a chance at happiness, or her annoyance at losing her bouncer. It had been some time since Thaedra had driven off Thorpe, but she still felt a bit guilty about leaving Calista without a peacekeeper.

Thaedra finished her search of the pantry and turned back to her employer. "I've taught the girls a few tricks about handling rowdy customers themselves," she offered trying to be helpful, "and you might want to talk to our friend, the blacksmith, and see if he could temporarily keep an eye on things until you find a permanent replacement for me."

"Oh, I'll manage," Calista declared with deliberate nonchalance. "I always do."

Even as Thaedra watched, Calista's earlier chumminess seemed to fold in upon itself and her expression took on that imperturbable, sweetly defiant look she always wore for business dealings. Thaedra remembered the first time she had met Calista – Callie, as she had been known then – for Callie was one of the whores young Thaedra had seen squirming in the darkness from her perch on the tavern roof. Callie had been reluctant to let the men put the girl out on the roof in the first place and had been very kind to the child when Thaedra had finally been allowed back into the warmth of the inn bedroom.

But now they were both toughened survivors – and they would both do what was needed to protect themselves.

"Here," Calista pushed a small pile of coins across the table to Thaedra. "You weren't much use as a bouncer yesterday, but you managed to be damn good for business all the same." She went back to noting the profits, her business with Thaedra done.

"Thanks," Thaedra spoke to the top of Calista's bowed head. She gathered up her coins and tucked them in the purse that hung from her belt. Thaedra left the room awkwardly, still thinking she should say more in the way of goodbyes to the woman whose house she'd shared these past few years. She glanced back at Calista to speak, but the madam sat studiously ignoring her. Thaedra shrugged and muttered: "So be it."

In the hallway, Thaedra hesitated again. What about the other women of the house? Should she make her goodbyes to them or sneak out quietly and let them find out about her departure after she was gone?

The question abruptly became moot when someone sidled up from behind and squeezed Thaedra's buttock suggestively. "Seems your blood can run hot at times after all," Artella purred in Thaedra's ear. "He was something of a charmer in a coarse sort of way, wasn't he?" She pushed past Thaedra in the narrow hall and turned to her with a smirk.

Thaedra smirked right back at her. "You wouldn't happen to have been eavesdropping on me a moment ago, would you?"

"Sweet little me? Eavesdrop?" Artella pouted for only a moment before her smile returned bigger than ever. "Of course I was! Congratulations! At least *someone* is getting out of here!" Artella gave Thaedra a quick hug and then made a dash for the stairs. Thaedra could hear Artella making her way down the upstairs hall, pounding on doors and calling out: "Get your lazy butts out of bed! Thaedra's leaving! Come say goodbye!"

"Don't you *dare* call me lazy," a sleepy voice floated down the stairs. "After last night, no one better ever call me lazy again!" The voice suddenly sounded more alert. "Wait a minute, did you say Thaedra was leaving? What's going on?"

A half dozen females in various states of disarray started straggling stiffly down the stairs. Amid the groans of discomfort came a series of questions, questions that Thaedra did her best to answer:

"After my little performance with the strongman yesterday, I was invited to join the carnival," Thaedra explained, not bothering to mention that the invitation was thus far hardly unanimous. "I've lived in Cobbleton all my life, and this will be my chance to see more of our vast United Lands."

"And more of our vast strongman, I'll bet!" giggled one of the women.

As they all caught sight of the color rising in Thaedra's cheeks, the others realized the truth of the matter. Excited voices filled the air with affectionate teasing and heartfelt wishes for a bright future. While there might be some competition and cattiness among the working girls, their staunch bouncer was another matter. Thaedra was the big "brother" for whom they all wanted to find a paramour – and for whom they were now genuinely happy.

"Now you be careful," Artella scolded. "You hardly know this vagabond. You tell him to treat you right, or he'll have to answer to us! And if he thinks we girls can bring pleasure, just wait until he sees what we have to offer for pain!"

"Do you think he'll view that as a threat or a promise?" Thaedra chuckled.

Another of the prostitutes chimed in teasingly: "She has a point, Artella, honey. If all this started with that brawl, you gotta admit he likes it rough!"

"Oh, for goodness sake!" cried out a third woman from the stairs, "Just tell him we'll come cut his balls off if we hear he's mistreated you. That should be clear enough!"

"What a *waste*!" Thaedra couldn't help blurting out with great feeling. At which point the whole group dissolved into laughter.

Somehow, amid the hugs and the fuss and the giggles, Thaedra managed to gather up her belongings and make her way out the door, but only after promising that she'd get word back to them all on a regular basis as to how she was faring.

Outside at last, Thaedra discovered that the previous day's bright sunshine was nowhere to be seen; the drizzle she and Falmund had heard on the roof earlier was now a steady downpour. None of this darkened Thaedra's mood, though she did wonder how Falmund had felt walking clear across town in such weather with nothing but a vest and breeches to cover him.

"So much for keeping his britches from a good soaking!" she spoke to herself. She smiled at the memory of him peeling them off in haste up at the lake, and her steps grew faster with the thought of joining him again. Still, she had no idea just what her reception would be, either from Falmund – now that he'd had time to think over his rash invitation – *or* from his colleagues.

CHAPTER 7

WELCOME

By the time Thaedra reached the fairgrounds she was drenched through, even with an oilskin covering her shoulders. The grounds appeared deserted except for a few wagons from the caravan scattered here and there, and one large tent that Thaedra believed had housed some of the exotic animals and a few of the acts the day before. It was from this tent that Thaedra could hear voices arguing.

"She's another mouth to feed!" spoke a female voice angrily. "How's she going to earn her keep? Set up a little tent for whoring?"

"Nazera..." A male voice spoke warningly. Thaedra recognized it as Falmund's.

"Oh, don't mind Nazera," another man broke in. "My darling little wife just wants to keep the object of her desires – I mean the other 'object,' the one she hasn't already bed and wed – focused on her own bewitching self. She doesn't relish any extra competition for dear Falmund's attentions."

"I never said...I don't...! How dare you!" exclaimed the woman. There was a quiver in her voice and, even through the canvas wall, Thaedra thought she could hear tears of humiliation threatening to break through the outrage.

"Now, now, dear, we all know that you want as many appreciative males in your orbit as..." her husband began.

"Save it!" This was a new speaker, female, Thaedra thought. But the voice was pitched low for a woman and it gave the command an air of authority. More calmly it continued: "Falmund is one of the original members of this group and is a real crowd-pleaser. If he says he wants her to join the troupe and that she'd do well with us, then I say she comes. I'm sure there are plenty of ways for the woman to earn her keep without resorting to Nazera's rude little suggestion. In fact, given that her fight with Falmund yesterday brought in a good bit more than we usually get from his act, she could be a very profitable addition to our ragtag group."

Thaedra smiled to herself that that little roll in the mud had worked out so well for all involved. Well, except maybe for this faceless "witch," Nazera. Thaedra longed to step into the tent and out of the rain, but she hesitated. She hoped to get an idea how the rest of the group felt before making her entrance.

"Now, there's the spirit!" she heard Falmund announce enthusiastically. "Companionship for me and a few extra coins for everyone else! What more could you want?"

"A little consideration," grumbled Nazera sullenly.

But apparently everyone else ignored her as a few more voices called out their agreement with Falmund. With that encouraging sign, it seemed to Thaedra that this was as good a time as any to get somewhere dry.

Taking a deep breath, she lifted the tent flap and stepped through. "Falmund?" she called out questioningly.

"Here, lass!" The delight in his voice was unmistakable, but she noticed a bit of color in his cheeks when he realized she'd most likely heard some of the discussion. She smiled at him and shook her head ever so slightly to let him know it didn't matter. Even this minimal movement was enough to send drops of water flying; it was obvious to all that she was soaked to the bone. Falmund grabbed a nearby blanket and strode to her side.

"Let me help you off with that wet jacket," he insisted. He took her bundle of belongings and set it aside. Everything she carried would have to be lain out to dry at some point, but that could wait for now. Thaedra shrugged out of her wet coat and Falmund bundled her in the blanket with a happy kiss on the cheek.

He turned to the group around him. "May I introduce to you the subject of our discussion? This is Thaedra, everyone, although she seems to end up in need of fresh clothing every time she ventures into our neck of the woods," he teased. His arm slid around her waist, and he squeezed her affectionately, ignoring how the move dampened his own garments.

"Hello there, Thaedra," spoke one man, as he ambled up to plant his own kiss on her cheek. She recognized the voice as that of Nazera's husband and realized that he was the magician with the waterfall of fire from the day before. He wore no fancy robe today, just leather pants and a simple linen blouse. "I'm Hargot," he offered.

Over Hargot's shoulder, Thaedra could see a woman dressed in black glaring at her angrily. She took this person to be Nazera and, judging by the pentagram the woman wore round her neck, it appeared Nazera might actually *be* a witch. Thaedra made a mental note to do her best to win the witch over; she had no desire to invite vengeful magicks.

"Hello Hargot," Thaedra said pleasantly. She tried to sound friendly, but not so friendly as to further antagonize Nazera. "I saw your act yesterday – very nice. My companions were quite impressed." Hargot looked at her expectantly. Belatedly she added a diplomatic half-truth: "As was I."

"Thank you, my dear. I try." Hargot turned toward his wife and nodded. "This is my wife, Nazera, our resident witch and fortune teller. To the public she is 'that purveyor of potions, that maker of magicks, that foreteller of the future: *Nazera the seer!*'" His voice had momentarily taken on the same carnival barker's tone to which Falmund regularly reverted. Now it dropped back to normal: "To me, she is my bane or my beloved; it varies from moment to moment." He smiled sadly.

There was an awkward silence as everyone in the tent waited to see how Nazera would react to such an introduction. To Thaedra's surprise, a warm smile spread across Nazera's face, and the witch rose to greet the newcomer.

"Thaedra, how nice to meet you!" Nazera clasped Thaedra's hands, and Thaedra wondered just how sincere the woman's words were. Perhaps Nazera meant what she said, but Thaedra suspected that the witch was more concerned with getting in Falmund's good graces than welcoming an extra troupe member. "It'll be nice to have another woman among us, and one who can hold her own with the boys at that." Her voice was smooth as silk but Thaedra caught the malice in Nazera's eye and recognized the remark for the putdown that it was.

Falmund, however, did not. "Thank you, Nazera," he broke in, the relief in his tone obvious.

Everyone listening knew that the strongman was thanking Nazera for not making a scene as much as for anything else. The tension eased somewhat, and Falmund went on with the introductions: "The centauress here is Faylah."

As Nazera and Hargot stepped to one side to allow Thaedra a clear view of the rest of the tent, the first person that drew her attention was indeed the centauress. Centaurs generally kept to their own and chose not to dwell in the towns of men; still, Thaedra knew one when she saw one. But even so, she'd never imagined a creature quite like the one before her!

To begin with, Faylah's rump looked like that of a piebald pony. Most of her pelt was a soft brown color – no surprise there – yet, near the tail, a large patch of white fur flecked with chocolate spots marred the uniform coloring. As far as Thaedra had ever heard, such markings on a centaur simply didn't happen. Thaedra was further surprised to see that Faylah's human body appeared as muscular as Thaedra's own. Though it was clearly a woman's torso sprouting above the equine forelegs, and a generously endowed one at that, it lacked the soft and graceful curves that were known everywhere to be the glory of centaur women.

But it was Faylah's face that really grabbed the attention. Long, rich, waves of auburn hair surrounded what would have been a lovely feminine face, were it not for the full reddish beard that graced her chin! Thaedra wished she had seen more of the carnival the previous day so that she would be better prepared for some of the surprises that now greeted her eyes. She hated to be rude and gawk, but it was hard to avoid.

Faylah chuckled warmly, a deep, rich, not-quite-human laugh that hugged Thaedra like a summer breeze. "Greetings, Thaedra." Thaedra recognized the husky female voice as the one who had supported Falmund in having her join the group. "Feel free to stare if you must, it's part of what I get paid for, but I'd much rather be friends than gawker and gawkee." The centauress gave an amiable nod that reminded Thaedra of her stepfather's stallion, Windweaver.

Thaedra marveled that such a noble creature traveled with this somewhat shabby group – and then promptly realized that the proud centaur clan would never accept the odd, masculine mare as one of their own.

Stifling an absurd urge to kneel and confirm Faylah's equine gender, Thaedra brought her eyes up to her hostess' face and stepped forward to shake hands. "Forgive me. I saw very little of your group yesterday given the course of events, and you can hardly deny you are an unusual looking woman." Thaedra flashed a smile of her own. "I, too, would very much like to be friends."

Falmund again stepped to Thaedra's side. "Faylah is the voice of reason around here. She is also our exotic animal wrangler, seeing as she has a bit more in common with our four-legged friends than the rest of us," he teased the centauress affectionately. "Seriously though, she's the only one around here who can outrun all of them if she has to, even Crystal over there." Falmund nodded toward a snow-white unicorn standing at the far end of the tent.

Thaedra gasped. The unicorn had escaped her notice until now. "How in the world...? I didn't think they existed in captivity!"

"Oh, she's not really in captivity," Falmund clarified. "She's taken a liking to Faylah and just sort of follows us around. Which is certainly a convenient bit of luck for our business! Right now, I think she's more interested in being in out of the rain than in hanging around with us."

Falmund leaned closer to Thaedra and whispered in her ear: "Unicorns are attracted to madmen and virgins, you know. While none of us is any more mad than the next fellow – at least, not so far as I've noticed – the unicorn seems to be drawn to Faylah because, well, because she's viewed as repulsive by her own kind so she's not exactly in demand as a mate." Falmund hurried through these last words. Then he shrugged and looked apologetically at Faylah, who could hardly help but guess what he was saying. Firmly he proclaimed: "The more fools they!"

"Excuse me," spoke up a small, wiry man. "But could we finish introducing the humans, uh, *people*, before we go on with Crystal and the other animals?" He gestured grandly: "I am Marcus, knife-thrower extraordinaire!" Marcus walked over to Thaedra and took her hand to kiss it. She felt his well-waxed mustache brush against her skin. This fellow certainly didn't lack for vanity, she mused; it must have taken a great deal of both wax and effort to achieve and retain such a curl in this humid weather.

"Sorry about that, Marcus. 'Twas not my intention to snub you," Falmund apologized. He turned to Thaedra and began to explain: "Marcus used to be..."

Here Marcus cut in dramatically: "Let *me* explain, lest our friend here besmirch my noble intent." Thaedra suppressed a smile at the man's eagerness to impress her favorably. Marcus

66

continued, "I am a trained assassin, schooled in the countless ways of the guild to bring death to those we choose. Yet, in spite of the many rigorous years of training, I chose life instead of death!"

"He couldn't do it," Falmund broke in mischievously. "He was too soft-hearted to find killing palatable despite all those years of training."

"Of course I could!" Marcus denied indignantly. "I *chose* not to."

"Be that as it may," Falmund spoke soothingly, "He's a damn good knife-thrower and keeps the crowd mesmerized with throws you're sure are going to draw blood. Yet he never does, and here is Desirée to attest to it!" Falmund turned to the one person present who hadn't yet been introduced.

"Hai." spoke Desirée shyly.

"Hai." replied Thaedra. She looked at Falmund. "This is Marcus' target?"

"I wouldn't call her a target, since he's aiming *not* to hit her and does a very good job of it, but she *is* his assistant, and his girlfriend, and a wonderful exotic dancer in her own right. When she joined us she was called Desarah, but 'the delightful Desirée' has more of a ring to it."

Thaedra turned back to Desirée. "Nice to meet you. I hope we can be friends." Desirée's youth and quiet demeanor made Thaedra uneasy; the girl reminded Thaedra a bit too much of her own younger, more vulnerable self, and Thaedra wondered if Marcus had any of her late husband's nastier traits. The age difference between partners looked disturbingly familiar, and an image of Verin's face distorted in anger crept into Thaedra's head, but she pushed it aside.

"I hope so, too." Desirée replied simply, and Thaedra found herself determined to learn more about the mismatched couple. Perhaps Thaedra might save someone else from acting out her own sad story. But that could wait; now was not the time.

"Anyone else here I should meet?" asked Thaedra brightly.

"Me," came an odd voice from the far end of the tent. Thaedra thought it sounded more like a large, deep-throated bullfrog attempting speech than anything else.

"Hello?" she asked.

"Hullo," the voice answered.

Thaedra looked for the speaker, but saw only Crystal the unicorn, a two-headed goat, and a sorry-looking mule. She started when she saw the goat, as she'd missed seeing him earlier, but despite the unusual number of heads he bore, she was convinced the words hadn't come from him. She was quite sure it had not been the unicorn, either. That left the mule. Thaedra looked at Falmund questioningly.

"That would be Marlon," he offered. "Marlon, the mule."

"He talks?" Thaedra asked.

"Obviously," Falmund replied. "But I wouldn't try holding a conversation with him. He's not very bright, and he has the attention span of, well, of a mule. See? He's already forgotten you and gone back to his pile of hay."

"Where'd he come from?"

"Oh, he was one of our regular draft mules that Nazera decided to try a new spell on. She could have made them all talk if she'd wanted, but we discovered one was quite enough, thank you. Besides, one talking mule is a novelty; eight would be unbearably annoying."

Thaedra smiled at the thought of a whole clique of mules drawling to anyone who'd listen about absolutely nothing. The smile soon faded, for the curiosity that had sustained her through all the introductions was at lasted sated. She started to shiver with cold and exhaustion. It had been a long day, and she'd had little sleep the night before.

"Soon, my sweet," Falmund said, "we need to talk about how you're going to fit into all this." Again he hugged her and kissed her cheek. He was concerned to find her skin was cold to his touch. "But first, if you can brave one more brief trip through the rain, we need to get you into dry clothes and a warm bed. If everyone will excuse us...?"

Falmund glanced at the rest of the group, grabbed the bundle Thaedra had bought with her, and started steering his new bunkmate toward the tent flap. Much as Thaedra hated the idea of going back out into the rain, the promised bed was too strong an attraction to resist. The fact that that bed would also contain Falmund managed to overcome any last bit of reluctance she had about exiting the tent.

Once outside, she could see that the dark, rainy day had given way to an even darker, wetter evening. Together, she and Falmund raced through the downpour to one of the wagons that stood in the field. Built of colorfully painted wood, with shuttered windows and an arched roof, the wagon appeared to be a cozy little house on wheels. Falmund had left a lantern burning inside, and the golden glow through the slats of the shutters beckoned invitingly to them.

Moments later, they were up the pair of steps, through the entrance, and the door was closed behind them. By this time Thaedra was shivering so badly that she barely saw the clutter and the scattered laundry that were the marks of a man accustomed to living alone. She and Falmund both stripped off their clothes hurriedly and dropped their sodden things in a heap by the door. The strongman led Thaedra over to his bed, slipped in under the covers next to her, and wrapped his arms about her in an effort to share his warmth.

Thaedra felt Falmund's body respond to her own and dutifully turned toward him to offer her services. "I could manage to stay awake a bit longer if you'd like..."

"Nay, lass, I can wait." Falmund smiled and rubbed his stubbled cheek tenderly against her own, smoother one. "We've plenty of time for that later, and right now you need rest."

CHRISTINA BRILEY

In the last few moments of consciousness before sleep overcame her, it crossed Thaedra's mind that this refusal of sex was probably the most romantic thing anyone had ever done for her. Her dreams that night were sweeter and gentler than they had been for many a year.

CHAPTER 8

AZA'S KIN

As the night wore on the storm worsened. While some members of the troupe slept soundly through the tempest, others were not so fortunate.

Among those were the witch and the wizard. Hargot's slumber was fitful, disturbed mostly by his restless wife, but Nazera could not sleep at all.

Gloomily she gazed into the darkness. A flash of lighting tore through the sky outside their wagon's window, and for some minutes thereafter, images of it floated before Nazera's eyes. When she blinked away these phantoms, she blinked away tears too.

"I should be happy for Falmund," she chided herself silently. "I have my Hargot, why shouldn't he have his Thaedra?"

When the three friends – Hargot, Falmund, and Nazera – had first left Belton almost two years ago as a fledgling circus, Nazera had thought it might be Falmund who would eventually move from the men's wagon to her own. Imperturbable Falmund: always pleasant, always considerate, her rock in a sea of emotional turmoil. But she could never get past that unflappable façade. Whatever flirtatious suggestions she might offer, they rolled off his good-natured banter without effect.

So she had turned to Hargot. In truth, she had much more in common with the wizard than with the strongman, and he understood her better than a mundane man ever could. And she loved him, she truly did.

" 'But the thing one cannot have...' Mother used to say, '...retains a special attraction.'" Nazera muttered to her pillow. "Especially if one sees it every day!"

What rankled most was simple jealousy. "How *did* Thaedra do it? Why did Falmund take her into his bad and not me?" Nazera wondered. And it was so easy to attach a particular epithet to this particular woman. "*Whore!*" the witch seethed with righteous satisfaction.

But it didn't make her feel any better. It just made her feel guilty.

Eventually, Nazera drifted off to sleep. Thoughts of her mother mixed with traces of guilt to bring dreams from her childhood.

* * *

"Climb into bed Neesa, and I'll tell you a story."

"Is this the fairy tale about the princess and the centaur?" Nazera asked her mother excitedly. "I *love* that story!" Neesa's mother shook her head and Neesa asked suspiciously: "Am I even going to *like* this story?"

The woman gave her daughter an apologetic half-smile. "Probably not, Sweetie. But life is not all sugar and sweet spices, and it's important to pass on some of the not-so-nice legends so that we can learn from them."

Neesa slouched down in her bed resignedly and folded her arms across her chest as if to ward off the words that were coming. It did her no good; her mother told the tale anyway.

"...and then Lady Isalaine put the torch to her home," her mother had recited, nearing the end of the story. "The lady watched the flames leap into the night sky, the fire cavorting and crackling as it consumed the building wherein lay her sleeping husband and children. It mattered not to her now that these innocents had done her no wrong, that they had, in fact, been as

72

kind and loving a family as one could ever have wished for. Nor did she seem to remember that only yesterday she had loved them equally well in return.

"When Lady Isalaine was sure that all that bound her to this place was dead and destroyed, she felt as if a great weight had been lifted from her. Now the lady was free to follow the hunger in her heart and to seek King Dargason, wearer of the blessed Raven Coronet."

"Mama! I don't want to hear anymore of these stories!" cried out Neesa clapping her hands over her ears. "Please tell me this is the very last one!"

Neesa's mother gently pulled the child's hands from her head to take them in her own. "Have I filled your thoughts with too much horror?"

"*Yes!*" Neesa exclaimed emphatically. "You have told me of women burning their children, of men murdering their neighbors for imagined sleights. You have told me of people's heads on pikes and of fathers and mothers leaving their babes to starve in the snow. Enough! I understand! The Raven Coronet brought about great evil when it was loosed upon the world!"

"I'm sorry, sweet Neesa," her mother replied regretfully. "But you must know these things to battle the pull of the Coronet. It will call to you to come free it, as it has called to generations of our family. For every charming promise from the Coronet, you must have a tale of horror to deflect it. If I could spare you of this burden, I would." The woman's eyes filled with tears, and she shook her head in sorrow.

"Why ever did Great-Grandpa Aza *make* such an evil thing?"

"What your Great-Grandpa Aza made," her mother replied bitterly, "was a very serious mistake."

And the young, dream-Nazera wrapped her arms about her mother so as to comfort them both.

Suddenly, as is the way in dreams, the scene shifted and little Neesa was no longer in bed. Daylight poured through the kitchen window as her mother prepared them both lunch.

"Mama?" the child asked.

"Yes, Neesa honey?"

"Is the Raven Coronet itself *really* evil? Or is it just the people who did those awful things who are evil?" Neesa twisted her hair around her finger nervously.

"Have you been having those dreams again?"

Her daughter bit her lip and nodded.

"And in your dreams everything seems so wonderful? All that love that the Coronet would bring if only you release it from its crypt?"

Neesa nodded again.

"I suppose," her mother conceded reluctantly, "that the Coronet itself is not evil. King Dargason and Aza certainly created it with the best of intentions. But that doesn't really matter because you can't separate the Coronet from its effects. And the *effects* of the Coronet are evil, if only because humans interpret love in so many different, and sometimes violent, ways. The magic just makes it all more extreme."

"When you say violent," Neesa inquired, "you mean like the men I hear joke sometimes about slapping their wives around because they have to show they love them by teaching them their place?"

"Well, maybe. Or maybe they're just selfish, stupid, nasty little men," replied her mother in disgust. Then she asked thoughtfully, "Remember the two neighbors and the wooden statue?"

"Ick. Yes," replied Neesa wrinkling her nose.

"Well," explained her mother, "one of those men thought love meant grand gestures while the other thought it meant quiet caring. It's the same with natural love. There are the people who give the object of their love expensive gifts and others who simply help them with the mundane things, like washing the dishes."

"And which do you think is real love, Mama?"

"Oh, it's great if you can have both," she answered laughing. "But I'll settle for your father's help with the dishes. After all, my sweet, love is in the details."

* * *

For awhile after that, Nazera's slumber was peaceful. But then one more recollection came to her. It was a familiar dream, a dream that seemed to worm its way into her sleeping mind from without, rather than arising from within.

"Just this once," Neesa whispered to herself sleepily, "just this once I'll pretend to agree. But I won't – not really."

No human heard the girl's words, for she lay alone in her bed while the world slept around her. But the Coronet understood – and it engulfed her in its warmth.

"Mmm..." the girl smiled as she slept. In her dreams, she saw the Raven Coronet in front of her. She reached out to touch the apparition, and her fingers tingled with its magic. The sensation flowed up her arm to encircle her brow and weave itself through her mind.

"I love..." little Neesa began to murmur happily, but paused in confusion. "Love what?" she thought. "Love the Coronet? Love the person who wears it? Love whom?" And she realized that this was not the warm, safe love she felt for her parents, but a love laced with lust and desire, a desire so strong it made her chest hurt to be unable to clutch the object of it to her bosom.

The child was bewildered and overwhelmed by the urges that welled within her. Still too young to have known mortal passion, she found herself drowning in yearnings far beyond anything she'd ever imagined.

75

Suddenly the warmth was gone and Neesa felt herself grow ice cold – but the drowning sensation became even stronger.

* * *

"What...?" the adult Nazera sputtered. Wind whipped her hair, and her sodden nightgown clung to shivering flesh. The woman's eyes flew open. Behind her, she could hear the banging of the unlatched door as the gale caught it and swung it against the side of the wagon.

"Neesa?" Hargot's voice asked uncertainly, using her childhood nickname as a term of endearment.

Nazera looked toward the sound and could see her husband in the cabin doorway.

"Are you all right?" He leapt down into the mud and came towards her. "It's the Coronet again, isn't it?"

Tears welled in Nazera's eyes, tears of frustration and shame. "Mama always told me that it would get easier. But it isn't; it's getting worse."

"We've left Belton now," Hargot spoke consolingly to the miserable wretch in front of him. "You no longer have an entire kingdom between you and the crypt. Perhaps we should go back..."

"No!" his wife exclaimed angrily. "I will not let it control me. I will fight it and live my life as I choose. I will *not* just walk away from my friends." To herself she thought, "or Falmund."

Taken aback by her vehemence, Hargot merely nodded in agreement and guided Nazera back toward the wagon. "Then I shall do as much as I can to help you. But right now, let us get dried up and back to bed."

CHAPTER 9

MOVING ON

On her first morning with the circus Thaedra woke to the smell of coffee perking and eggs cooking. Prying open her eyes, she found her view blocked by a rope that stretched from one end of the cabin to the other, a rope that bore every soggy scrap of clothing she owned. Her need to use the chamber pot was overwhelming and it seemed the clothesline offered her as much privacy as she was likely to get right now. After quietly taking care of business, she chose a reasonably dry blouse and drawers off the line and slipped them on.

"Good morning, sirrah," she spoke cheerfully, as she ducked under the clothesline to find Falmund cooking breakfast atop a small, potbellied stove. Being careful not to distract him *too* much, lest he burn himself on the hot stove, she stepped up behind him to slide her arms round his waist and snuggle against his back.

"Morning, lass," he replied, playfully wiggling his backside into her hips.

"Mmmmm," Thaedra sighed. "Was that you inside me in the wee hours, or just an incredibly real and delightful dream?"

"Well, you seemed willing and more rested and most decidedly warmer than you had been earlier. Did I take unfair advantage?" Falmund asked innocently.

"Hardly!" Thaedra laughed. "So, what happens now?"

"Now, we get some breakfast into you. Then, although I find it most regrettable, we put a pair of pants on you." He glanced lewdly at her bare legs.

"Cad!" she scolded. She proceeded to wrap one of the long legs in question around Falmund's own two and run her bare foot suggestively up and down his shin.

"Stop it, woman!" Falmund replied in mock irritation. "You're distracting me!"

Thaedra stopped. It would be unwise to endanger either her breakfast or her lover by getting too rowdy around the stove. She'd never had a man cook her breakfast before. She wondered if it would be edible.

"Sorry, I'll behave – for now anyway." She disentangled her leg from his. "What happens after breakfast and pants?"

"After breakfast and pants, you and I shall go join the rest of the crew and help strike the main tent. We've already been in this town four days, and it's time to move on," Falmund explained as he turned to put plates, mugs, and utensils on the small table that sat next to the stove. "Seeing as I am not leaving you behind," he admitted happily, "I have no need to come up with excuses to tarry. After a few days, anyone who's likely to come see us and offer a few coins has already done so. Better to leave them hoping for more than to have them longing for our departure."

He transferred the eggs and coffee to the table and continued: "I trust you don't mind using those delightful muscles of yours to wrestle some tent ropes instead of my own irresistible self."

"Sounds reasonable enough," she said as she sat down to eat. She looked up from her plate at him: "After the tent is down, then what?"

"Then we pack up the wagons and animals and head for the next town," he spoke through a mouthful of eggs. "Along the way, you and I can discuss how to fit you into things around here."

"Speaking of which..." Thaedra hesitated. "Any second thoughts yet about bringing me along? Should I look forward to being dumped by the side of the road at some point?"

Falmund dropped his fork, placed the back of his hand against his forehead, and rolled his eyes heavenward. "Lady! Thou dost cut me to the quick!"

Thaedra ignored his antics. "Seriously, Falmund, this all happened so quickly. I do not want you to feel you have some sort of obligation to bring me along. You are of an age when most men have married, so one might assume you prefer to keep your relationships brief."

He looked at her soberly. "Fair enough. You do have a point. My relationships have tended to be short and shallow of late. Back when I was working as a guard I had a few longer relationships, but they always ended badly."

"How badly?" Thaedra broke in anxiously.

"Oh, not *that* badly," he replied remembering Thaedra's husband. "No one ended up dead, just disappointed." He shrugged. "But this, this is entirely different. At least, I *think* it is. I certainly *hope* it is!" He looked concerned for a moment but then went on more confidently. "No, I *know* it is. You are the most incredibly enticing woman, and you know how to stand up for yourself, too. You are as much my equal as any man I know. Gods, you even *fuck* like a man!" he exclaimed with heartfelt awe.

"Oh," she replied. "Excuse me for asking, but what are you talking about? I mean, have you ever fucked a man?" Thaedra was pretty sure she knew exactly what he meant, but she couldn't resist putting him on the spot.

"No, I haven't – that's not what I mean." Falmund looked a tad flustered. "I mean you're, uh, *enthusiastic*. You don't just *lie* there. You move as much as I do, uh, thrust for thrust, so to speak."

Thaedra laughed. "I do believe you're blushing, my dear Falmund. Thank you for the compliment, which is how I intend to take it. It's very easy to be enthusiastic with you." She grinned at him. "Which, come to think of it, may very well be because you *do* consider me your equal, instead of merely some convenient receptacle for your pleasure."

"You are," he said earnestly, "the first woman I've ever met that I felt I simply *could* not let get away."

Thereafter, the couple went about hurriedly finishing breakfast in a companionable silence; both knew it wouldn't help her standing with the rest of the troupe if they dawdled and held up the whole crew. Despite the rush, Thaedra was pleasantly surprised to discover that a man – well, this man anyway – could cook a breakfast as tasty as any she'd ever had.

* * *

It impressed Thaedra how well the team worked together, despite any differences they might have had the day before. Falmund handed her a sledgehammer and set her about knocking loose stakes around the tent's perimeter. The newcomer enjoyed the feeling that she was playing her part, for now, anyway.

With the group using a combination of muscle and magic, the tent was down in short order. Thaedra had noticed that there were four wagons all told; three of the little house wagons and one plainer, more functional one. The tent that had just been struck was carefully bundled and thrown onto the roof of this fourth wagon, where it was tied down securely. Most of the other props and supplies had been loaded inside the day before to get them in out of the rain.

With the mules all hitched in pairs, and the two-headed goat tethered to the rear of the supply wagon, Thaedra climbed up next to Falmund in the driver's seat of his coach, and they were off. Hargot and Nazera's carriage was in front, Marcus and Desirée's next, and then Falmund and Thaedra with the supply wagon right behind. Marlon was hitched beside one of his mundane brethren pulling this rear cart, and Thaedra could hear him moaning and muttering to himself. Faylah trotted alongside the morose mule, alternately encouraging him and chiding him for all his complaining. Meanwhile, Crystal ranged as she pleased, sometimes disappearing into the surrounding trees for several minutes, but always reappearing eventually to follow the little caravan.

"So," Thaedra asked Falmund once they were moving, "where are we off to?" There was a tinge of excitement to her voice. It had been a very long time since she had made any major changes in her life, and even longer since she'd made any changes by choice rather than necessity. Had she ever made any plans entirely by choice before? It didn't seem so. And now she was leaving town altogether, the only town she'd ever known.

"Wherever," Falmund replied casually. Traveling was nothing new to him, but having a woman at his side was. He took the reins in one hand so that he could use the other to pull Thaedra close to him. "I think the next town along this road is called Skylark, though it doesn't really matter. We simply follow the road wherever it takes us, and most of the towns look the same after awhile. Still, there are always some interesting variations, and every so often we hit a big city with grand sights to see." Falmund began to share some of Thaedra's excitement. "It will be fun to have someone to show them to." He looked at her fondly and kissed the tip of her nose with a loud smack, loud enough to be heard by Faylah behind them.

"Enough, you two!" Faylah called out as she trotted up next to Thaedra. "It seems I'll have to spend as much time breaking up you lovers as I do breaking up those fighters..." She nodded toward the front wagon. Teasingly, she continued, "Aren't you two supposed to be our *fighters* and they're supposed to be our one loving, genuinely *married* couple?"

"In my experience," offered Thaedra ruefully, "'Loving' and 'married' are not synonymous."

"Perhaps some day we might see if we can change that," offered the strongman. Thaedra looked startled at the remark, but Falmund simply gave his companion another loud kiss on the nose and grinned defiantly past her at Faylah. "I suppose that right now we'd better discuss the 'fighter' aspect of our relationship."

"Agreed," nodded Faylah. "We need to fit Thaedra into your act or find her one of her own." Redirecting her attention to the newcomer, Faylah asked: "Do you have any special skills?"

"*Does she ever!*" interrupted Falmund appreciatively. It was obvious to what he was referring.

"Gods!" Thaedra burst out in both amusement and annoyance. "Do you ever know when to shut up? I hardly think such comments are going to endear me to anyone around here!" She shoved Falmund with her shoulder. At this, he made a great show of almost falling off the wagon, until she finally relented and pulled him back toward herself and safety.

"That's a bit better!" Faylah chuckled. "Fighters who actually fight! I wouldn't worry about fitting in, Thaedra; you seem to be doing just fine. And if Falmund likes you, that's good enough for me. Now, can we get back on the subject, please, and discuss any skills Thaedra might have for the enjoyment of the general public?"

"Well, I can fight, you've seen that. I suppose *I* could challenge the public to fight me the way Falmund does," Thaedra suggested doubtfully, "but I fear men would be more inclined to grope me than put up a respectable fight. And I doubt you'll find many women out there who'd even consider a public brawl!" Thaedra smiled sheepishly. "I guess I'm a bit of an exception. Not very ladylike, am I?"

Before Falmund could protest, Faylah responded: "And I am? If unladylike means forthright, funny, earthy, and strong, then may we both revel in our lack of lady-likeness!" the centauress proclaimed with feeling. More quietly she went on: "But you are right to be concerned about a woman offering to wrestle men she doesn't know. It's generally a recipe for trouble."

"Of course, I can always wrestle Falmund," Thaedra said with a smile. "That's certainly fun for us but I'm not so sure about the audience."

"You got a decidedly positive response from the crowd the other day," Faylah admitted. "But would you be acting as a member of the troupe or as a ringer from the audience? Wrestling Falmund has definite possibilities; we'll have to think about it." She looked expectantly at Thaedra: "Anything else?"

"I'm good with a sword," Thaedra offered.

"So am I," added Falmund, an idea beginning to take shape in his head. "We could stage a big, dramatic sword-fight, as long as we can be sure of keeping it safe so no one gets hurt."

"Now, *that* has possibilities." Faylah spoke with satisfaction. "Safety is definitely an issue, though. How about this for a plan? For now, Thaedra will circulate with the crowd. She can check out the other acts, 'ooh' and 'aww' at the appropriate places to get the audience going, and toss a few coins to 'prime the pump.' If Falmund has trouble finding challengers, she can step up to fight. If he's already fought one or two, she can be the grand finale. If he's fighting someone and it's going badly, she can butt in brazenly and say something like: 'Aww, this big-mouthed Fearless Falmund couldn't even beat a woman! Get out of the way and let me prove it!'" Faylah glanced apologetically at Falmund: "Just business, you know."

Falmund put the back of his hand to his forehead and rolled his eyes upward. "Lady, you cut me to the quick!"

The two women looked at each other knowingly. "Seems to me I've heard that somewhere before," spoke Thaedra.

"Uh-hmmm," agreed Faylah.

"Uses it a lot, does he?"

"Oh, quite. Being a ham is part of what makes a good showman."

"Well then, I shall do my best to equal him, ham, bacon, pork roast and all!" Thaedra promised firmly.

"You're making me hungry!" accused Falmund. He went on, "So far, Faylah's plan sounds good to me. I'd rather have a battered ego than a battered body if it looks like someone's getting the best of me. What about the sword idea?"

"I think the sword idea could be a real crowd-pleaser but it'll take lots of work to make sure it's both exciting and safe," Faylah answered. "You two need to spend whatever spare time you can coming up with moves that have maximum flair with minimum risk, and then putting them all together into a whole act. You might want to think about a story line, too. Something dramatic: evil prince battles Amazon queen, or masked fighter defeats great swordsman to reveal after the fight that the mask hides a woman's face – you know, that sort of thing."

Falmund nodded thoughtfully in agreement. Thaedra looked from one to the other and spoke: "As long as we can be sure it's safe, it sounds good to me. It could be fun, all flash and sparring..."

That settled, the three made idle small talk until it was time to stop for lunch. It wasn't much of a stop. Each wagon carried its own food supplies, and when the group was traveling, the mid-day meal generally consisted of something simple. Falmund offered Thaedra and Faylah bread smeared with fruit preserves. After accepting a slab of bread from Falmund, Faylah wandered off with it to check on the animals while the two affectionate fighters ambled about eating and talking.

Aside from the meal and a chance to stretch, the stop also allowed Nazera to cast some promotional spells to alert the residents of Skylark to the group's imminent arrival. Thaedra caught sight of the witch dipping a set of three silver rings into a shimmering solution, and then waving them through the air as she murmured incantations. Great clouds of soap bubbles drifted off toward Skylark.

"What's she doing?" Thaedra whispered to Falmund, being careful not to distract Nazera.

"See those bubbles? They'll expand in size as they approach Skylark and be about the size of a baby's head by the time they get there," Falmund explained quietly. "Inside each bubble is an image of a different act from our group, or an image of the main tent set up in a certain field outside of town. The bubbles will catch people's attention and cause a stir as everyone compares what they've seen in our little 'flyers' with one another. The bubbles themselves will burst harmlessly in a short while, but the crowd's excitement will continue to grow, and they'll be eager to catch the show tomorrow." He looked at Thaedra and then back to Nazera. "It's a nice trick, isn't it?"

"Very. She's quite good, isn't she?"

"Yes," Falmund replied admiringly.

Thaedra drew Falmund further away from Nazera and the others. "May I ask you something?"

"Ask away," Falmund declared bravely.

"Was there, *is* there, something between you and Nazera? I heard her husband imply as much when I was outside the tent yesterday. I don't want to cross a powerful witch and wake up as a toad one morning." Her joking tone did not completely cover the concern in Thaedra's voice.

"Nazera and I have been friends a long time, since before we were part of this traveling circus. We've worked together a long time but we've never had a romance. In the early months of our friendship, one or the other of us always seemed to be attached

85

to someone else. By the time we were both unhitched, I'd realized she wasn't my type: too mercurial, too full of feminine wiles. As a result, we agreed to keep things on a 'just friends' basis. I was happy for her when she married Hargot. So the answer to your question is 'No,' there is not, and never has been 'something' between Nazera and me." Falmund finished his explanation. He obviously thought the matter was that simple.

Thaedra did not. "I suspect," she replied carefully, "that agreeing to be 'just friends' does not automatically erase other needs and wants from the one who might desire more." She put her hand in the center of Falmund's chest and rested her forehead upon his shoulder. "A man does not announce that his wife lusts after another man unless there's something to it."

"Pshaw!" Falmund took Thaedra's chin and drew her face to look up at him. "Nazera no more desires me than I desire Marlon! And you know how I feel about Marlon!" He smiled at Thaedra but she did not smile back. Urgently he went on, "Nazera and Hargot pick at each other constantly; it's the way they are. Hargot's remark was only one more dig at his wife; there's no truth to it!" More gently, Falmund said: "If Nazera lusts after me, it's in the same way she lusts after all men, for attention, to make her feel whole. Most witches are tied to the earth and its magicks and feel fulfilled; Nazera does not. It's as if she were a water lily whose roots had been ripped away from her; she stays afloat but is buffeted by every emotional eddy that comes along. I suspect that it's her neediness that limits her powers and keeps them at mere carnival level."

"I don't get the impression she lusts after Marcus." Thaedra wasn't willing to concede her concerns so easily.

"She considers Marcus a sneaky little toad beneath her notice. What I mean is that she lusts after all men who are anywhere within her range of acceptable." Falmund was beginning to sound exasperated.

"Which, within this group, would be you." Thaedra drove home her point.

"Fine, you win. She lusts after me. This is my fault?" he asked helplessly.

"I suppose not. You can't help being irresistible." Thaedra reached up to kiss him affectionately. "But I still think we need to be wary of Nazera and tread lightly around her feelings."

"I refuse to apologize to a married woman for having found someone of my own to care for!" Falmund burst out. "Nonetheless, I suppose there's something to be said for prudence. I shall do my best not to let the glory of your own self totally drive Nazera from my consideration! Satisfied?"

Resisting the urge to assure Falmund that it was fine with her if he *did* let "the glory of her own self" drive Nazera from his thoughts, Thaedra simply nodded and kissed him again. By the time this kiss ended it was a struggle to pull away from each other. Regaining their composure with some difficulty, the two finally headed back to their wagon to continue the journey toward Skylark.

CHAPTER 10

SKYLARK

It was dusk when the little group reached the field outside Skylark. Thaedra's skin tingled from spending the day in such close proximity to Falmund with no opportunity to satisfy her baser desires. She was sure Falmund felt the same. It was thus a relief when the group decided not to attempt raising the main tent in the fading light, for this decision put her one step closer to bed and Falmund. Still, the mules had to be unhitched and rubbed down, the animals fed and watered, and everyone's presence was expected at a communal dinner and briefing.

Despite Thaedra's eagerness to be alone with her lover, once she'd finished her share of the chores she found the smells wafting from the bubbling cook-pot to be extremely appealing. Thaedra strolled over to the campfire where Desirée was preparing dinner and asked: "What is that you're cooking? Can I be of any help?"

"No, no, you're still a guest," Desirée insisted. "You just relax. Besides, I took care of the nasty part of the job while we were on the road."

"The nasty part?"

"Skinning the poor little rabbits for the stew," Desirée explained. "I took a turn driving the mules while Marcus did a bit of hunting; then he drove while I worked inside the wagon."

"So," Thaedra chuckled, "I take it he assassinated some rabbits for dinner."

Desirée smiled and nodded.

"Given the appetite with which I suddenly find myself," Thaedra declared patting her stomach, "I certainly hope Marcus is as good at *hitting* a target with those knives of his as he is at *missing* you during your act. I could eat quite a bit all by myself!"

"Oh, I'm sure there's plenty for everyone!" Desirée replied. "Here, why don't you find a spot and get comfortable? The stew's about ready; I'll bring you a bowl."

Thaedra heard Falmund's voice behind her: "Thank you, Desirée. We'll do that. The rest of our misfit friends are hereabouts somewhere; they should be here anon."

Falmund slid his arms about Thaedra's waist from behind and pulled her close. Pressed together thusly, the playful couple waddled from the fire in clumsy synchronization as they sought a likely spot to sit. Just as Falmund released Thaedra and both dropped happily to the ground, Hargot, Marcus, Nazera, and Faylah entered the circle of firelight. Faylah was the first to speak.

"Perhaps," suggested Faylah, as the rest of the group began settling around the fire and Desirée's steaming pot of stew, "we might tell Thaedra a bit about how we all came to be traveling together, and she might offer us a bit of her own background in return. There's no need to drag out every skeleton in the closet, but it's nice to know something about the people with whom you'll be working and living." She smiled reassuringly at her audience. "How much or how little you reveal is your own choice." Faylah nodded toward Falmund. "Falmund, would you start? You're not only behind Thaedra's presence here, but that of the rest of us, also."

Falmund got up and stepped forward. As he began speaking, Desirée quietly served the stew to his listeners. "Well," Falmund explained, "I believe everyone here already knows, including Thaedra, that I used to be a guard. I lived in Belton, a good-sized city some leagues from here, and spent most of my days walking the city walls and quizzing traveling strangers as to their intentions. Once in awhile there'd be serious trouble and it was kill or be killed; mostly it was boring." Falmund shrugged. "I grew up in Belton, and becoming a guard always seemed the obvious choice for me. I was big, I was strong, and I loved the idea of fighting and adventure and defending things that were important to me, like home and family. My parents always thought I had enough brains to do better, but with the near-sighted wisdom of youth, I couldn't see spending years in study when joining the guard would offer me an income and 'make me a man' immediately.

"It didn't take me long to find out that my folks were right." Falmund's voice momentarily took on the swaggering tone he used in his act: "Oh yes, me friends, I chummed around just grand with me fellows in the guard, every one of us a man's man." He thumped his chest proudly. "Except, of course, when we be bedding the wenches!" He followed the remark with two sharp hip thrusts and a lusty leer before returning to his normal inflection. "But it was all bluster and bullshit. A lot of them were basically nice guys, but I was unimpressed with men who found fulfillment spending their entire lives walking the walls before spending their off-duty hours drinking, fighting, gambling, and whoring. This included the ones with wives and children. I think some of them would have liked to treat their families better, but they depended on their comrades to watch their back, and they couldn't risk being seen as weak or having divided loyalties.

"In any case," Falmund continued, "it all struck me as a waste of one's life. And in those instances where I was actually doing something useful and defending the city, it usually meant taking someone *else*'s life. More waste. I started to regret having squandered those purported brains of mine, but by then it was far too late to be apprenticed and learn a trade. What could I do? All I knew was how to fight! Then it occurred to me how a fight always drew an audience. Whether it was a drunken brawl, a skilled sword fight, or a bloody battle, people loved to watch the contest and root for one participant or the other.

"So making a show of my fighting skills seemed to hold some promise of keeping me fed and clothed. And if I was going to make my living brawling, at least I could make it interesting by seeing the great wide world while I was at it. That's where the traveling part of the idea came in. I decided to see if any of my friends or acquaintances were interested in joining me." Falmund gestured at Nazera. "I had met Nazera when I'd stopped by the little shop where she sold potions and prognostications, and we'd become friends."

"Ah," broke in Marcus jokingly, "so you were buying love potions for the ladies?"

"No, I was trying to see my future and decide where it would lead me," Falmund replied with a touch of irritation. He knew Thaedra had no illusions about his past, but he didn't need anyone suggesting to his new love that he was sleazy enough, or desperate enough, to go around enchanting his way into women's beds. "Nazera and I became friends after she'd told my fortune a few times.

"And what was your fortune?" This time it was Thaedra interrupting.

A broad smile lit up Falmund's face as he answered her. "Oh, that I'd see the world and meet many people yet still be unlucky in love for a very long time – that is, until the right woman came along."

"Ahem." Nazera cleared her throat. "That's very sweet, and I'm glad you appreciate the accuracy of my predictions, but may I take up the tale from here before you two get distracted?"

"Oh, sorry." Falmund dragged his attention away from Thaedra. "Go ahead. That's pretty much all of my story anyway."

Desirée offered Falmund a bowl of stew as he sat down, his oration finished. Nazera set aside her own nearly empty bowl and sat up straighter as she launched into her tale. Thaedra found Nazera fascinating to observe. The witch tossed back her long, dark hair, sucked air deep into her breast, and opened her eyes impossibly wide as she prepared to speak. It was easy to imagine her mesmerizing a customer with an intense and wondrous recitation of the client's future. As Thaedra watched the other woman slipping into the role of all-knowing speaker, the way one might slip into a silken robe, she was reminded of Faylah's remark about hamming it up being part of the job – and of Falmund's words regarding Nazera's need to be the center of attention.

"I was," Nazera began, "the manager of a small magic shop in Belton. I had been apprenticed to Gaylith, a talented witch, when I was twelve years old, but as her business grew she neglected my apprenticeship. Rather then teaching me enough that I might carry some of the burden, she ran hither and yon doing everything magical herself and leaving me the mundane job of salesclerk. By the time I was seventeen, I rarely saw my mistress, for she was constantly tending to business elsewhere.

"I'd learned a little witchcraft early in my apprenticeship, and over the years I learned more running the shop, either through my own research or advice from my customers. But it was not enough for me to put out my own sign offering my services, or to feel I could compete with the better trained witches in the area. Running the shop wasn't a bad living; it just wasn't what I wanted.

"When Falmund came along looking to hear his fortune told, it was inevitable that he tell me something of what he sought for his future. His frustrations mirrored my own and it was not long before we poured out our hearts to each other."

It seemed to Thaedra that Nazera's words were carefully chosen to remind everyone how long and deep and fated her friendship with Falmund was. The hairs on the back of Thaedra's neck stood on end, and she had the sudden desire to smack the witch across the face. She squelched her irritation and reminded herself that what Nazera thought she had with Falmund was of no importance; it was what Falmund thought that mattered. Thaedra held her tongue as Nazera continued.

"So when he came to me with the suggestion that we travel together as entertainers, I leapt at the invitation." Nazera's self-satisfied smile as she spoke of Falmund's desire to have her join him reminded Thaedra of nothing so much as a cat after a successful hunt. Thaedra bit her lip and threaded her arm through Falmund's to keep herself anchored to him; she feared she might leap up and do or say something she'd regret. Falmund merely smiled affectionately at Thaedra as she took his arm, oblivious to the effect Nazera's words were having upon his woman.

Hargot was much more attuned to his wife's wiles than was Falmund. The wizard glanced sympathetically at Thaedra before cutting in on Nazera's story. "And this is where I come in!"

Nazera glared at her husband in annoyance. He ignored her stare and innocently came forward to offer his own recollections. Nazera's story-telling persona gradually dissipated, and she slouched back into the shadows to sulk.

Hargot spoke. "I first met Falmund in a tavern in Belton. I'd sometimes entertain the patrons there in exchange for dinner and a glass of stout. There was always the worry that I might set the place on fire," he smiled sheepishly, "but the bartender would fill an old half wine-cask with water, and I could do a little display of sparks over it. The water not only kept the sparks from igniting the bar, but also reflected the specks of light and made the display all the prettier.

"Falmund was fascinated by my little show and wanted to know more about how it was done. I'm afraid there wasn't much I could tell him. Like my lovely wife, I had been apprenticed to learn magicks as a youth. In my case it wasn't a neglectful master that held me back; it was my own shortage of natural talent. The only spell I ever mastered was the 'Cascade of Fire' and that had become so ingrained that I no longer knew just how I did it; I only knew that I could will the sparks to appear and there they'd be.

"When Falmund was looking to put together a traveling show, I, too, found it the perfect opportunity. The truth of the matter is that all three of us had talents that were impressive enough to each new, un-jaded audience, but that would wear thin over time. Nazera's fortune-telling was perhaps the one exception to this, as people always appreciate the sort of guidance that knowing the future offers, but she chose to go with Falmund for one reason or another. I like to think she chose to *stay* with the troupe because of me." He smiled a bit sadly at his wife.

This time Nazera smiled back, an open, genuine smile. Thaedra's jealousy cooled a bit when she saw this, for it appeared the witch really did care for her husband. It seemed Nazera simply let her own needs overwhelm her love for Hargot at times.

Hargot continued: "Falmund and Nazera each had some money set aside, and they purchased two wagons and the mules to pull them. At first we men shared one wagon at night while Nazera had the other. During the day we'd spell each other on the driving. After some months, the nighttime arrangement changed. As I recall, Marcus joined us while we were holed up that first winter. That was about the same time Nazera and I made our commitment official." Hargot gestured in Marcus' direction.

Here, Marcus took up the story: "There isn't that much for me to add. I, like Falmund, had trained in a job which involved killing, thinking that it would mean glory and adventure. When I discovered how disturbing and distasteful it was to take a life, I was caught in the same bind as he." Marcus looked around the group and exclaimed in frustration: "Isn't it a shame that we're forced to choose our road in life so young, before we have any idea what truly matters to us?" There were several murmurs of agreement from his listeners.

Marcus returned to his tale. "When Falmund and company took refuge from the weather in my town – doing their little show in whatever indoor venue they could find – joining them seemed the perfect solution for me also: take those talents designed to kill and cripple and use them instead to titillate and astound. Money for a wagon was no problem; I may find being an assassin distasteful, but it did pay well. So I purchased a wagon for myself and, once the snow thawed, off I went with them."

"This was the makeup of the group when I encountered them." Now Faylah had stepped forward to speak. Her rich voice eddied around them, warming them all with it's honeyed tones. "My own kind had tolerated me as a child despite my unusual markings, but they had always looked down those proud noses of theirs at me. When I matured and grew both breasts and a beard, the situation became intolerable. I was an embarrassment to my family and my tribe. So I left them, fully intending to live out my life alone. I would wander the woods and make my own way.

"At some point, Crystal came into my life. Her presence was comforting, but I longed for companionship that included debate and discussion rather than just silent camaraderie. Every so often I would bind my breasts, don a vest to cover me, muddy my white fur, tie back my hair, and stroll into a town at night. In the evening light, I could pass for a man of my race and speak with any friendly souls who happened to be around and about.

"It was on one such occasion, one when spring had barely arrived, that I came upon this small carnival just as they were settling down for the evening in a field on the edge of town. The crowds had gone, and the performers were all tired, but they welcomed me to their campfire and allowed me a chance for conversation. Perhaps they were only friendly because they saw in me a novel new act from the beginning."

"Not true!" Falmund started to protest. But Faylah held up her hand to shush him and went on.

"Be that as it may, I doubt they realized just how novel my appearance was in actuality – or that I might value their friendship as much as they might value my unusual looks. The five of us – Falmund, Nazera, Hargot, Marcus, and myself – all chatted well into the night. By the time I took my leave around midnight, it had been decided that I would rejoin them in the morning and travel with the group.

"I slept in the woods with Crystal as was my custom. When dawn broke, I bathed in a nearby brook and again put on my vest, this time without binding my breasts first. I was tired of skulking about being ashamed of my appearance; on this day I would be myself and make no more apologies! When I cantered off toward their encampment, the markings on my rump shone brightly in the sunlight, and my auburn hair waved loose in the breeze. I entered their camp proud and breathless, my obvious femininity bulging between the fastenings on my waistcoat to be tickled by my long, full beard.

"To my new companions, my appearance was a marvel and a delight, not something to hide or demean. I'm not so fool as to think that there weren't just a few pieces of gold dancing in their vision of me, but there was genuine acceptance too, something that I had never experienced up until that time. When Crystal started shadowing the caravan and I explained that she was my companion, everyone felt blessed to have the good luck of a unicorn traveling with them.

"So here is where I've found my home. While I've no idea why the fates chose to make me an outcast among my own people, I've learned much about the world in my travels, and about the living beings that inhabit it, things that even the centaur elders with all their wisdom cannot fathom."

It was a moment before anyone spoke. Faylah's speech was a hard act to follow. Thaedra finally shook off the effect of the centauress' words and turned to Desirée. "I believe that leaves you," Thaedra pointed out quietly.

Desirée looked a bit like a young doe caught suddenly by torchlight. She drew a deep breath and spoke softly: "Oh, my story is the shortest of all, perhaps that's because I'm the youngest." She smiled at her little joke. "I never had a regular career or apprenticeship like the rest here. I was a flighty, restless child who drove my parents to distraction with my dreams and wild stories. They gave up any idea of an apprenticeship for me; I think they feared that less loving guardians than themselves might beat me to death in the process of trying to make me focus on daily tasks. My parents' plan was to marry me off to a loving, tolerant husband, who they hoped would find me amusing and not too hopelessly inept, and thus insure my future.

"And what was *my* plan for my future? Oh, nothing and everything! I dreamed of being a dancer, and I would dance about the yard stealing my mother's linens off the clothesline to serve as flowing costumes. Or I would use the pilfered bedclothes as veils, veils with which I could sweep the sky and dance to the silent music that coursed through my head." Desirée suddenly looked around embarrassed, as if she had given away more about herself than she should have.

She cleared her throat and went on hastily: "Another youthful plan of mine was to run away and join the circus. Then Marcus came to my town with this troupe last autumn and took me under his wing, and... Well, here I am!"

Thaedra wondered if it would have been more accurate to say "took me into his bed" than "took me under his wing." How old was Desirée anyway? She'd been with Marcus for months, and she couldn't be more than fifteen or sixteen even now. And he was what? Thirty-five or more? Thaedra knew she couldn't change the world, and it wasn't all that unusual for daughters to be married off at twelve or thirteen, but she still didn't think much of men who chose to take young girls to their bed. It was as if they couldn't handle a relationship with a woman their own age, because, gods forbid, an older, stronger woman might actually demand respect! Thaedra leaned her head against Falmund gratefully and wondered why all men couldn't be more like him.

Resting comfortably against Falmund's shoulder, Thaedra suddenly realized how tired she was. She lifted her head and looked around the group to see that they all appeared exhausted, and tomorrow they would have to rise early and raise the tent. "I'm grateful that you've all shared your stories," she spoke up, "although some of them have piqued my curiosity more than satisfied it. I feel very at home among all you fellow misfits!" Thaedra commented jokingly. "But I think I'd best indulge myself asking questions another time; everyone looks tired."

"I have a question myself," replied Hargot. "What about *your* story? Weren't you going to tell us how *you* ended up here?"

"Oh dear," Thaedra cringed at the idea of staying awake long enough to recite her own lengthy story. "You're right, I was. All right, here's the very short version, and I'll fill in all the gory details some other day. I had an unhappy childhood: the first half mired in poverty, the second half motherless. I was raised by a stepfather from whom I am quite thoroughly estranged. Among other sins, he married me off at seventeen to a crony of his who beat me regularly for several years until I killed him in self defense." Thaedra instantly wished she'd been a bit more circumspect about her role in Verin's death, but there was no way to take back the words now.

She hurtled on, "Having no husband and no career, I turned to brothel work to earn a living. I honed my fighting skills with helpful customers until I could convince the madam that I deserved the job of house bouncer, an accomplishment that allowed me to give up my whoring duties. I took Falmund's challenge the day before yesterday at the insistence of my boss who wanted the publicity. The whorehouse got the publicity, I got Falmund, and here I am!" Thaedra glanced at Nazera with a look of triumph, as if to remind her who was Falmund's woman now.

Before anyone could respond to Thaedra's brief summary or venture questions, Falmund made a show of rising as if to make it clear the story was over for tonight. He offered his hand to Thaedra, and she pulled herself up. Putting his arm around his lover, Falmund steered her away from the fire and toward their wagon. "Goodnight, all!" he called back over his shoulder. "You may stay up talking all night if you like, but we're off to bed like sensible people!"

Thaedra, too, called back a "Goodnight!" to those behind her and heard an echo of replies. Someone doused the fire, and with the hiss of the dying flames, the dark of night engulfed the couple.

They walked away from the group. "Do you think there'll be trouble because I admitted killing a man?" she whispered to the figure beside her.

"Hmmm. It had occurred to me too that it might have been best to keep that part to yourself for awhile. But what's done is done," Falmund conceded. He then went on reassuringly, "There'll be no trouble from Faylah; she believes in a woman standing up for herself. And not from Desirée either; she'd not betray any one of us. Marcus has his own killings to answer for, and Hargot can't be bothered making trouble for anyone but Nazera. I doubt Nazera would be fool enough to incur my wrath by making trouble for you, but perhaps I'll speak to her about it."

They had reached the little ladder that led up to their cabin. Falmund paused to turn toward Thaedra in the darkness and pull her to him. "I want a future with you, wench, and I won't let Nazera's petty jealousies or anything else come between us." He kissed her, gently at first, and then long and hard as his hand slipped to her breast. When he paused to search out her face in the velvet night, Thaedra pulled away and took his hand so as to lead him up the few steps to the door – and into the privacy of their new home together.

CHAPTER 11

SHOWTIME!

The morning sun rose to find the group already hard at work hoisting the main tent. Thaedra, Falmund, Marcus, Hargot, and Faylah contributed the sheer muscle it took to haul on the ropes and raise the structure. Desirée scurried about making sure that everyone had something to eat and drink, for there had been no time for the luxury of a hot breakfast in their cabins this day. When the humans were fed, the girl tended to the animals, after which she began pacing off the areas that would be roped in for Falmund's and Hargot's acts. Throughout all this commotion, Nazera concentrated on casting a spell that set pennants fluttering in mid-air without benefit of poles, and at her command a cheerful background tune could be heard about the site with no apparent source.

Marcus and Desirée would perform inside the main tent, as would Nazera, and Faylah would fill duel roles as ringmaster and head exotic animal. Her captivating voice made her the perfect announcer, and her strange appearance and four hooves easily shared the spotlight with Crystal, Marlon, and the goat. Falmund and Hargot were relegated to their outside rings, partly to whet the crowd's appetite, and partly for safety's sake. Should one of Hargot's sparks or one of Falmund's brawls catch hold and spread, the audience could easily escape either the flames or the fists in the open field.

* * *

The sun was well along in the heavens by the time everything was ready. A number of children had already made their way to the field while the tent was still being raised. They threatened to get under foot and cause problems at first but a stern look from Faylah and a prancing rear up onto her haunches, her muscled forelegs pawing the air over their heads, and they stayed well out of the way.

As more people began appearing, Faylah and the exotic animals withdrew into the tent. Thaedra led the mundane mules around behind the tent to tether them out of sight. Hargot had gone to wash off some of the dust and don his blue robe. His wife seemed to consistently dress in a witch's black attire, on duty or off, but she, too, had retreated to their wagon to prepare for the show.

Once Thaedra was done securing the mules, she looked about for Falmund and realized that he, like the others, had gone to clean up and change. Based on what she'd seen of his act, there was nothing special about his costume except for the application of oil to his skin to give him that muscled sheen. Thaedra considered following and offering to help – but after thinking about it she was quite sure that the end result of her rubbing oil on his body would be to delay the show, not ready him sooner.

People were beginning to mill about, and Thaedra had no idea what, if anything, she should be doing to entertain them. Just then Faylah emerged from the tent. The crowd fell silent. Even Thaedra found herself staring in disbelief.

Faylah's coat shown from a vigorous brushing, and her muscles glistened with oil. Black canvas with brass studs had been shaped to form a brassiere that barely covered her full breasts. Above the brassiere, a generous coating of oil made the curving flesh gleam. Matching canvas bands encircled her upper arms and she wore a studded collar, as well. A panel of chain mail hung from the lower edge of the bra as if to shield her abdomen from a sword blow, yet it offered little protection from the crowd's prying eyes. Hair and beard spread wildly about her face. All of this combined to offer a spectacle that was both human and equine, muscled strength and sensuous curves, restraint mixed with wild abandon.

And that was before Thaedra even noticed Desirée. Straddling Faylah's back was the very antithesis of the centauress' version of womanhood. Where Faylah was all muscle and bulk and armor, Desirée was gauze and sparkle and vulnerability. Brightly colored skirts hung from her hips and spread across her mount's rump, their sheer fabric leaving her long, slender legs visible. Bare feet and belled ankles brushed Faylah's sides. Desirée's wide, low-slung belt was covered with gold embroidery and sparkling beadwork and left her young belly bare. Like Faylah, Desirée's top was designed to make the most of her assets, but instead of coarse canvas it was made from soft satin. The bra fabric was covered with the same gold embroidery and tiny beads as was the belt and these embellishments twinkled in the sunlight with the wearer's every breath. It was as different as it could be from the black and studded attire Faylah wore.

"Welcome, all!" the centauress called out. "Welcome to our little display of magicks, marvels, muscle, and mystery!" Her rich voice carried easily to the furthest reaches of the crowd. "See fire and flame pour from a man's hands yet burn him not! Wrestle with Falmund the Fearless and see if you can best the hulking beast!"

Thaedra chuckled quietly at the reference to her dear "hulking beast."

Faylah went on: "Let the delightful Desirée show you how she earned the name, and then gasp in horror as she faces her knife-wielding assassin!" Faylah leaned toward the crowd as if she were telling each of them some dreaded secret. Upon the creature's back, Desirée cringed appropriately, flinging an arm woefully to her forehead.

"See the only unicorn in captivity! A mule that talks! A goat with two heads! And if the present bores you..." Here Faylah paused. The watchers held their breath and leaned towards the two women, waiting for the centauress to finish. Thaedra noticed that Desirée also leaned forward, as if she herself were waiting for the rest of the sentence, but at the same time the young woman grasped the straps on the back of Faylah's top tightly.

"...Let us show you *the future!*" As Faylah bellowed the final words, she rose up and reared, thus lifting her head a few more feet above the spectators over whom she already towered. Desirée not only managed to stay astride the prancing creature, but also smiled fetchingly and freed one hand to wave at the crowd.

"Wow," muttered Thaedra quietly.

Faylah turned, and in one great stride disappeared behind the tent flap. Several minutes passed before anyone dared to lift the flap and peek in after her, but as soon as the first brave soul did, it was as if a great dam had broken. Suddenly the crowd was talking and laughing and fishing in their purses for the coins they knew they would need to enter the tent to see more of Faylah and the wonders she had promised them.

Thaedra tagged along with the crowd. When she reached the entrance, Marcus was collecting admission from everyone, the daggers in his belt discouraging any argument over payment. Thaedra dutifully pulled a coin from her purse and handed it over.

"Thank you, my lady." Marcus tipped his head politely, taking no more notice of her than he had of any of the preceding women.

Thaedra nodded back, happy to remain anonymous and keep her connection to the performers a secret. Should she be called upon to serve as a shill this day, it would be for the best.

THE RAVEN CORONET

She entered the tent and looked around. It wasn't a huge tent, not like some of the royal pavilions she'd heard about, but it was big enough to have an imposing center pole and two quarter poles in a line down the middle of the tent. A number of side poles ran around the outer edge of the enclosure. Where the sidewalls of the tent met the big top, a variety of circles, squares, moons and stars had been cut into the hanging panels of canvas to allow more light to enter.

Also running around the edges of the tent was a single line of benches. Many of the women in the crowd had grabbed seats on these benches while their children sat at their feet and their husbands stood behind. Thaedra could hear squabbling here and there over who would get the limited number of remaining seats. When the majority of people seemed to have settled on a spot from which to view the show, Thaedra noticed Desirée standing near an opening in the far side of the tent and knew that the performance was about to start.

Thaedra redirected her attention to the center of the tent and saw the large section of fence that she'd helped erect earlier. Six feet high and four feet wide, the structure consisted of two uprights and several planks with large spaces between them. A solid wall would have blocked too much of the audience's view; this one did not. Thaedra wondered how it fit into the scheme of things. She didn't have long to wait for her answer.

Desirée suddenly drew back the tent flap, and Faylah cantered in with a whoop. Her back was empty this time but now she carried a lance and shield in her hands. With hair flying, chain mail jingling, and equine and human muscles rippling, she galloped about the ring.

"Not bad," commented Thaedra to no one in particular, "mount and rider all in one." She glanced around her at some of the awestruck faces and knew that the rest of the audience agreed.

Just then, Faylah left her previous path and cut across the dirt at an angle heading straight for the barrier in the center. With a huge leap, she soared over the fence. Landing on the other side, the centauress came to an abrupt halt; a cloud of dust spewed up as she fought her momentum with prancing hops. With a frenzied rear onto her hindquarters and with her forelegs pawing above the swirling sand, she flung her spear into one of the planks she had just vaulted. The lance landed with a thud.

There was a hush in the tent for a moment, and then a great wave of applause.

Faylah dipped her head to the crowd, made a quarter turn to her right, and dipped her head again, repeating the move until all sides had been acknowledged.

Pushing back her hair with her empty hand, Faylah spoke cheerfully to her audience as their applause began to dim. "Now, good people, perhaps a little lighter fare?"

At these words, Thaedra heard a loud crack followed by a familiar voice moaning melodramatically: "Ow, ow, ow. Oh poor me. What did I do to deserve being struck so?"

Thaedra looked across the tent toward the voice and saw Desirée raise her hand to smack Marlon's rump once more. But then the girl changed her mind and threw her shoulder against the mule's hindquarters instead. Reluctantly, Marlon shuffled toward the center of the ring.

The animal had a large, red ruffle about his neck and his ears stuck though holes in an old jester's cap. If the poor, stupid beast had had enough brains to be embarrassed about his appearance, Thaedra might have felt badly for him. As it was, she joined the crowd in a hearty guffaw.

"Hullo," Marlon called out as he spotted Faylah. He walked a little faster toward the only creature present with hooves other than himself.

"Hello, Marlon," Faylah replied. "We have guests. Say hello to the audience." She gestured towards the crowd.

Marlon looked around dully. His ears twitched, as if trying to shake off the cap, but all he did was cause the bells on the hat to jingle. "Oh. Hullo. Who are you?" The crowd tittered, but no one answered the mule's question.

Marlon looked at Faylah. "Are they here to see me?" It was hard to tell if the quaver in the animal's voice was pride or terror, or both.

"Yes, Marlon, they're here to see you." She had left her shield leaning against the center pole while he was entering the tent and now she placed one hand on the mule's neck. "Why don't we go say hello to the children in the tent one at a time? Do you think you might like them to stroke that velvety nose of yours?"

"Really? They'll be gentle, right?"

"Absolutely. And I'll be right here next to you," Faylah reassured him. "Folks," she spoke clearly to the crowd, "if you could all remain where you are, Marlon and I will come around and greet you all properly. And for those of you awaiting your turn, we have another treat for your eyes!"

Just then Thaedra spotted Desirée riding in on Crystal's bare back. The unicorn pranced nervously as Desirée leaned forward and patted the creature's neck reassuringly. Thaedra was sure that Crystal would tolerate only Desirée, the lightest of riders, but it was still quite a surprise that she'd tolerate any rider at all! Thaedra remembered Falmund's words: "*Unicorns are attracted to madmen and virgins...*" Desirée wasn't a virgin; of that, Thaedra was sure. But was she somehow unhinged? Or was Crystal putting up with a rider simply as a favor to Faylah? Thaedra resolved to see what she could learn later. But for right now, she would focus on enjoying the show.

As unicorn and rider reached the tent's center, Desirée slipped quietly off Crystal's back, carefully keeping one hand in the animal's mane. The other hand she raised to her mouth and placed a single finger against her lips.

"Sssssssshhh" she whispered with great intensity. Desirée opened her eyes wide and leaned toward the crowd. The woman stared earnestly at the audience as she began walking slowly around Crystal so that everyone could see her gesture for silence. The hand that had grasped the mane now trailed gently along the beast's hide as if to serve as a constant confirmation of Desirée's presence.

Off to the side, Faylah placed her hand over Marlon's soft muzzle and his latest greeting became a muffled "Hullmmph?"

A few shoes fidgeted in the dirt but the crowd fell silent.

"This," Desirée said in a quiet voice that nonetheless carried amazingly well, "is Crystal. Unicorns can't survive in true captivity – but Crystal isn't truly captive." She lifted her hand from the unicorn's back to demonstrate the lack of physical bondage. Crystal danced nervously to one side and then brought her nose back so close to Desirée's face that the two shared breaths.

This was more than just a favor to Faylah, thought Thaedra with concern.

Desirée smiled and replaced her hand on her companion's neck. Reassured once again, the unicorn swung her head to look at the audience, and Desirée was free to continue speaking.

"Unlike Marlon, Crystal is still a wild thing, and I'm afraid it would be impossible for all of you to pet her. But..." Here the woman paused and widened her eyes again for emphasis, "I will pick two..." The crowd began to murmur and Desirée raised her voice over the noise, "...two very *quiet children*, who may come up and pat Crystal's nose and touch her horn."

Silence reigned supreme.

Thaedra stifled a giggle. She had never seen such a group of yearning, intent, *quiet* children.

Desirée peered about the tent full of anxious young people. At last she picked out a boy from one side and a girl from the other, both of them only five or six years old. Thaedra was

110

reminded briefly of her friend Arienne's children, back in her old neighborhood, and wondered how they had all fared over the past few years. She smiled now as she watched the chosen pair jump up quickly, a sigh of disappointment traveling through the rest of the audience.

Despite the pair's first enthusiastic leap, it didn't take long before the little ones had second thoughts. They approached the center of the ring with some trepidation. Desirée leaned to whisper something in Crystal's ear, whereupon the magnificent animal curled one foreleg and lowered herself onto her knee in an elegant bow. Desirée waved the children forward.

"You may pat her gently," Desirée instructed them in a warm and reassuring voice. "But be careful of the horn! The tip is quite sharp."

The children warily ran their little hands down the unicorn's neck and held their fingers under her warm and velvet nose so that she might accept their scent.

"Now," Desirée told them, "I want you to take your first two fingers on one hand and run them carefully down Crystal's horn, and then I want you to go back to your parents and touch these same two fingers to theirs." She smiled at the children and watched as they obediently did as they were told.

The children raced across the dirt towards their respective seats, waving the fingers that had touched the horn over their heads. Crystal rose up from her bow.

"The children are coming to share the good luck of a unicorn with all of you," Desirée announced to the crowd. "After they touch their fingers to those of their parents, their parents should 'pass the luck' by touching the fingers of those near them, and so forth around the ring."

Thaedra watched as the audience followed Desirée's instructions. Fingers reached for fingers as a wave of smiles and wishes for good luck made their way through the tent. There were chuckles too, for the fingers occasionally took more than one attempt to make contact and would feint this way and that trying to find the hand they sought. Thaedra suddenly realized it was her turn, and she felt herself smile as the woman next to her held out her fingers.

Passing the luck along as bidden, Thaedra laughed out loud when she noticed a certain little scene across the ring. The young girl who had touched the unicorn had hopped out of her seat again to run to Marlon and touch her two lucky fingers firmly to the beast's' nose. Even Marlon seemed to respond, and his ears perked up from their normal droopy pose.

Desirée escorted her four-legged charge out of the ring at a trot, for the increasing noise from the crowd had the unicorn fidgeting uneasily. Faylah and Marlon went on with their meanderings along the edge of the ring greeting the spectators individually. For a time, the audience was content to relax and chatter after the hush that had fallen during the unicorn's appearance.

Soon though, it was time for the show to go on. Faylah sent Marlon out the performers' entrance – after quietly whispering a promise of carrots to him lest he decide to balk at leaving his adoring fans – and then the centauress strode back to the center of the tent.

"Ladies and gentlemen!" She called out. "Friends and sharers of the unicorn's luck! Lovers of wonder, one and all! Let me present to you that mysterious dancer from lands far beyond our own, *Desirée!*"

A cloud of smoke arose from near Faylah's hooves. Thaedra was fairly sure that it wasn't magic but was rather some sort of smoke device that Faylah had flung to the ground. Although, when she thought about it, Thaedra had no idea where the centauress could have hidden such a device in her skimpy costume! Magic or mundane, when the smoke cleared, Desirée had suddenly appeared wearing several additional layers of veils, and posed in a deep backbend with a scimitar balanced across her neck. Faylah slipped quietly from sight.

"Tik-tik-tik-tik-tik-*thwack!*" Marcus strode into the ring with a drum tucked under one arm. With his free hand he tapped his fingers in sequence on the drumhead before striking the rim sharply.

The "thwack" was accompanied by the ping of a pair of finger symbols being struck, and Thaedra realized that Desirée wore zills in addition to the extra veils. Desirée still held her precarious backbend, but now the hand that had struck the note began an undulation that traveled up one arm and across the other. Marcus settled himself on the ground, and the drumming began in earnest.

Desirée gradually straightened up, waiting until she was almost upright, and the sword about to fall, before stopping her snake-like arm movements to lift the sword from her neck and hold it high over her head. Dragging her bare toes sensuously through the dirt with each step, she walked slowly toward the drummer and placed the scimitar in the dirt in front of him. Free for the moment of the sword, she began unwinding her veils teasingly. Her kohl-accented eyes peeked exotically from behind each veil as she held it tantalizingly in front of her before abandoning it. Several of the men in the crowd clapped and whistled.

Desirée ignored them. She seemed to be in a world of her own, insulated from the leering faces around her. One by one the veils fell as she danced to the incessant drum beat. Now she returned to retrieve the sword and, jutting out one hip, balanced it on the bare flesh above her sparkling belt. With a careful shimmy of her hips, flashes of light danced off the sword. Now she moved the sword from her hip to balance it instead on her shoulder. Holding her hands back to back over her head she launched into a series of rolling body undulations while the sword wobbled precariously but somehow maintained its perch.

"By the goddess!" Thaedra heard a woman near her exclaim. "That woman moves parts of her body I don't think I even have!"

Thaedra and others listening nearby laughed heartily when the woman's husband agreed a little too enthusiastically, thus earning himself a sharp jab from his wife's elbow.

Desirée danced on. She lifted the sword from her shoulder and held it at arm's length above her before bringing it down carefully to balance on the top of her head. The drumbeat sped up, and Desirée's zills began to play their own intricate rhythms to match. Faster and faster her hips shimmied. With hips still moving and zills still ringing, the dancer began to turn in place, gradually gaining speed. The scimitar began spinning at its own tempo. At last, when it seemed as if the sword would fly off her head at any moment, and with one final thump of the drum, Desirée's legs folded beneath her. Her hands grabbed the spinning sword and in an instant she lay on her back in the dirt, legs folded beneath her and sword held above.

Marcus placed his drum on the ground beside him and rose to his feet. Nonchalantly he strode toward the prone woman. As he reached his partner, he suddenly grabbed the sword and yanked it from her hands. In a fraction of a second the sword rested upon Desirée's neck again – but this time it was the point rather than the side being placed against her skin, and the hilt was gripped firmly in her assailant's hand. The crowd gasped. Desirée started as if to get up but then appeared to think better of it.

"You have beauty and skill, wench," Marcus said to Desirée, loudly enough for all to hear. "Have you courage, as well?" He moved the sword from her neck and offered her a hand to rise.

Silently the woman allowed herself to be drawn to her feet. Marcus drew her into an embrace, his one hand still holding the sword, and lowered his head as if to kiss her. She turned away.

114

"Reject me, shall you?" he cried out angrily. "Let us test that courage of yours then!" He gripped Desirée's shoulder and dragged her to the section of fence in the center of the tent. Pulling a length of rope from his belt, he bound her wrists to one of the planks, arms spread wide. Marcus turned his back on her, threw the scimitar to the ground, and strode a dozen paces away from his struggling prisoner.

Turning, he pulled a vicious looking dagger from his belt and raised it to throw at Desirée.

"No!" a half dozen children's voices cried out in fear, but their parents quickly hushed them. Even Thaedra felt her heart beating faster.

A split-second later, Marcus threw the knife, but not before Desirée unobtrusively stopped her struggling to allow him a clean shot. The blade sunk into the wood an inch or two from her head with a loud "thunk." He drew another from his belt. It was not long before a dozen daggers surrounded the dancer, every one of them mere inches from her appealing form.

Marcus walked back to his partner, stooping to pick up the scimitar on his way. He raised the curving blade as if to finish what the knives had only threatened – but at the last second he instead sliced through the ropes without harming the woman bound by them. Again he offered Desirée his hand.

"Ladies and gentlemen," he announced loudly to the crowd, "May I introduce to you the delightful, the daring, *De-si-rée!*"

She stepped forward smiling and curtsied to her audience as they cheered wildly.

Marcus raised his voice even further, so as to be heard above the din, and called out: "And I am Marcus, Marcus the *magnificent!*" The cheering grew louder. Still holding hands, the couple bowed in acknowledgment. Desirée leaned over to her lover and gave him a quick peck on the cheek.

The applause crested and began to die down. Abruptly the tent went dark, as if a great hand had blocked out the sun in an instant. The cheering stopped and was replaced by curious whispers from the crowd. Suspense grew.

Thaedra added her own thoughts to the hushed murmuring: "This must be the witch's doing."

Seemingly in answer, a glowing orb appeared in the center of the tent. The orb was cradled in a delicate hand hovering a half dozen feet above the dirt floor. Soon the darkness waned and daylight returned to reveal Nazera standing center stage with orb in hand. The witch seemed a tad unsteady at first but quickly regained her composure.

"That was no small trick," Thaedra muttered. "No wonder it sapped her strength." She wondered again if she was putting herself in danger by staking a claim on the witch's old friend, Falmund.

No bold pronouncement of her abilities issued from Nazera's lips; no barking or bragging filled the air. Still holding the orb above her head, she turned slowly and silently, staring intently at her audience. When she had turned full circle, she spoke in a strange, drawn-out whisper that nonetheless could be heard throughout the tent: "Do you wisshhhh, to sssseeeee, your future?"

Nazera brought the orb down to chest level and cradled it in her arms. It sat in the crook of one elbow while the other hand caressed it lovingly, as one would stroke an adored pet. She looked down to stare into it. After a moment her hand paused. Looking up, she pointed a slender finger at a young man standing in the crowd. "You, sir. Your son will grow up to be a great warrior and be known throughout the land."

"Son? I have no son!"

"Yet," replied Nazera knowingly with a nod.

The crowd chuckled and a few men standing near the future father thumped him on the back heartily. Thaedra wondered if anyone else noticed a young woman sitting nearby place her hand on her stomach and blush furiously. There was no ring on the woman's finger.

Thaedra returned her attention to Nazera, only to discover that the witch now pointed in her own direction. Thaedra felt distinctly ill at ease.

"You, sister." Nazera's eyes met Thaedra's. "You have found peace after many missteps, but you shall step falsely again and rue it for many nights thereafter."

Thaedra longed to escape her rival's gaze but the crowd hemmed her in. She felt their curious stares upon her.

After what seemed like an eternity, Nazera moved on to the subject of her next prediction. Thaedra was free to find her way out of the tent.

Out in the sunlight, Thaedra blinked and tried to clear her head. Were Nazera's words an honest prediction, a fervent hope, or a veiled threat? Thaedra rubbed her forehead trying to think and became aware of the headache building in her temple. She pushed Nazera's prognostication to the back of her mind and looked around her.

Off to her right was Hargot, and beyond him, Falmund. A fair-sized crowd had gathered outside the tent during the performance, hoping to catch the next show. In the meantime, Hargot and Falmund were keeping them entertained.

Thaedra wandered past Hargot's ring and heard the familiar "oohs" and "ahs" of the crowd as the magician showered the dirt at his feet with sparks. Beyond that knot of spectators, Thaedra could see another group bantering with Falmund.

Thaedra moved to stand at the back of the crowd watching Falmund. She was ready to wrestle with him if need be, although right now she'd rather just have a chance to talk to him about Nazera's behavior. It was a relief to Thaedra when she saw a skinny teenager duck under the rope to take up Fearless Falmund's challenge. One glance at the young man and she knew Falmund would have no trouble besting him. This meant that Thaedra could gather her wits a bit more before she might be required to join his act.

Falmund caught sight of her through the crowd and smiled for a moment before he turned his attention to his challenger. She could not help but smile back, a smile that went all the way to the depths of her soul. Nazera's dire words suddenly seemed unimportant. Standing there in the sunshine, in the middle of the fairgrounds, knowing this man cared for her, Thaedra felt like a happy child.

Thaedra thought back on that brief part of her childhood when she had actually felt as carefree as she did right now. Abruptly, she found herself wondering: "What *did* ever happen to Josnah?"

CHAPTER 12

THWARTED PLANS

Josnah stood looking at the field of spring grass unhappily. There were no signs of the trampling it must have taken when the circus had stopped there a year prior. The locals swore the group had been there, and they remembered a witch fitting Nazera's description, but looking at the field now, one would never know that it had ever been full of wagons and crowds and tents and animals. Spring rains and the early summer sun had brought forth a rich expanse of new lawn as far as the eye could see.

"Patience, Josnah," he told himself. "You have only been riding after them for two days; they have been traveling for two years." Some of the tension went out of his shoulders. "Of course it will take some time to catch up to them, but not too long," he mused aloud.

"Blast it all! I'm tired of this chase! So many years spent in search of the Coronet and nothing to show for it." Josnah sat down heavily and rested his head on his knees. His horse grazed idly nearby. His mount, at least, appreciated the thick crop of grass.

"Just which town is this?" Josnah muttered. "They all look the same after traveling so long." He thought about it awhile. "Farmington. Wasn't this Farmington?" Something else occurred to him. He lifted his head and gazed unseeingly into the distance. "Didn't Verin originally come from Farmington?" The more Josnah thought about it, the more convinced he was that he was right about both the name of the town and about Verin's connection to it.

His mind flashed back to a long-ago evening at the tavern in Cobbleton.

* * *

"Ho! Verin! Come join me!" Josnah hailed his approaching son-in-law. The elder guardsman raised his tankard in greeting as he watched Verin make his way between the tables of The Jolly Fellow to the corner one at which Josnah sat.

Josnah couldn't help but notice the two serving girls both smile and nod to Verin, and Josnah congratulated himself again on the handsome match he had made for his daughter. The younger fellow's rugged good looks were obvious even in the dim light of the tavern. Trim and muscled with a square, clean-shaven jaw and a straighter nose than most, Verin was tall enough that he prudently chose to duck his head slightly each time he passed under one of the massive beams supporting the low, smoke-darkened ceiling.

"So, my lad," Josnah asked as Verin reached the table, "how's married life agree with you?"

"Your daughter's got much to learn," he responded with a grin and a swagger, "be it about one sort of cooking or another. But she's a damn fine student!"

Verin motioned to the serving girl for a beer and sat down across from Josnah. "In truth, this marriage business takes a bit of getting used to after so many years as my own man. But having someone on hand to warm both my hearth and my bed is a real pleasure."

"Good!" Josnah spoke with satisfaction. "You get a willing wife, my daughter gets a good home, and you and I are not only partners now, but family, as well!" He leaned forward and placed his hand on Verin's arm. "Now, *partner*, shall we make plans?"

Verin delayed his answer as the waitress appeared carrying his beer. She leaned over to place his beer on the table, deliberately presenting her customer with a close-up view of her décolletage.

With an appreciative sigh – and an affectionate slap to the serving girl's departing buttocks – Verin turned back to Josnah and resumed their discussion. "There's no great rush. It's been ten years since I heard about the Coronet from my late, unlamented father, and it was twenty years before that that he actually stumbled across the damn thing." Verin took a swig of beer. "I hardly think a few more weeks will make much difference now. Besides, I'd like to enjoy my new bride a bit longer before running off on some great quest."

Josnah paused a moment before responding. When he and Verin had simply been comrades-in-arms, Josnah would have thought nothing of the man sating himself with every willing woman he could find. Now Josnah suddenly wondered if he had let his own goals blind him to Verin's shortcomings as a potential husband for Thaedra after all. Was Josnah's own daughter simply another warm body for Verin to "enjoy" whenever it suited him?

Josnah shoved any doubts aside. "Aye, I suppose you do have a point at that. It's hardly fair to separate the newlyweds so soon! In any case, do tell me again about how you came to be certain that the Raven Coronet was more than just a children's fairy tale." Josnah leaned in once more and spoke with a quiet intensity. "I want the details this time, not just some vague promise of riches and power if only I'll turn my daughter over to you."

"Fair enough," Verin replied. Bringing his head close to Josnah's and lowering his voice he began, "My old man, a guardsman like ourselves, spent time many years ago at a border outpost far off to the northeast of here. In truth, the posting had all the appeal of a rat's dick, but we both know there's no arguing with the service. So my father, and a few dozen other poor sods, manned some old fort that stood between the United Lands and a piece of wilderness called Faerwood. There the men wallowed in ale and apathy and spent their time sharing tall tales of their glorious deeds in battle and bed.

"In the nearby forest were centaurs." Verin paused in his story to ask: "You ever seen a centaur, Captain?"

Josnah nodded and replied: "They keep mostly up north but I've traveled about enough to have encountered one or two."

Verin went on: "The men would see the creatures in the distance, just peering at 'em from the edge of the woods, but the beasts kept to themselves. There seemed to be some sort o' pact that the humans would not disturb the centaurs, and the centaurs would not loose their brutish bodies and unnatural archery skills upon the men.

"That is, there was such a pact until the day that my old man caught sight of a female centaur. It had been a very lo-ong time since his last woman, and a very short time since his last ale, and here was a shapely, bare-breasted female in front of him! So what if she was half-horse? After all, he'd grown up on a farm and had...ah...let's just say he wasn't shy as a boy. In any case, fueled by beer and lust he set off after this centauress with the insane intention of ravishing her.

"The nag knew full well that this fool's puny human legs hadn't a prayer of catching her but she played a merry game of tag with him all the same. When she finally tired of the sport and vanished, he realized that he was deep in the woods and hadn't the vaguest idea how to get back to camp.

"So he yelled. And cursed. And wondered just who might be out there watching him in his misery. Then he began walking.

"Hours later, still hopelessly lost, he stumbled upon some sort of crypt. There in the midst of the woods, in the side of a leaf-covered mound of earth, was an ancient, carved, stone door. It was covered with grass and sod but as my father began to brush these away he found pictures telling a story. Lo and behold, 'twas images of the king and the wizard and the coronet from the old fairy tales – he'd no doubt about the meaning.

"He grew pretty damn excited, mind you, but it was tempered by this overwhelming sense of calm fulfillment. My father always swore it felt as if some force within the crypt was wrapping him in its mantle to keep him safe and warm. He was trying to clear the rest of the dirt from the door when an arrow struck him in the knee."

"Ouch!" interrupted Josnah. "So someone was watching?"

Verin looked irked at having his narrative broken. "Obviously. The centaurs must have known all along that my father was roaming around in their woods; they just hadn't considered him worth troubling with until then."

Josnah motioned for Verin to continue.

"The mongrel archer who'd done it came out of hiding once the poor bloke was down. Somehow, despite the danger and the pain in his leg, my father still felt peaceful and content. Always claimed he neither flinched nor cried out when the centaur lifted him up and slung him upon its own withers.

"But as the stallion carried my father away from the crypt, that feeling vanished. Now scared and suffering, my old man struggled to sit upright on the creature's back – even wrapped his arms around its human torso so as not to fall. He used to describe how the centaur's flesh twitched with irritation beneath his hold, the way a horse twitches off flies. And he'd tell how the beast's quiver of arrows jostled wretchedly against him the whole way.

"By the time they reached the edge of the woods, my father was barely conscious. The centaur just dumped him there, more dead than alive.

"Next thing my father knew, he was in the camp infirmary. It had been hours before anyone had found him and then days before he came to. He was sent back to civilization on the next supply wagon. Still, the wound festered. The military doctors did all they could but they weren't healers. After all, when was the last time *you* heard of the king paying healer's fees for a non-com? So the old man ended up lame for the rest of his life."

"Did he ever make it back to the crypt?" Josnah asked eagerly.

"Bloody hell!" Verin erupted. "No, he did *not*. I just said he was lame for good."

Reciting the tale seemed to have stirred up old resentments and put Verin's nerves on edge. The hand with which he held his tankard clenched the vessel so tightly that the knuckles whitened. "The army sent my father home disabled, where he drank, screwed my mother, and beat her and the brats she bore him until he died twenty-some years later, old and bitter and broke."

"Easy, Verin. Perhaps I didn't think before opening my mouth," Josnah spoke soothingly. He laid his hand on Verin's arm in an attempt to calm his companion but it had the opposite effect. At Josnah's touch, Verin started and half-rose from his chair. The younger man's hand went to the dagger on his belt, and he gazed fiercely at his captain.

Josnah raised an eyebrow calmly at his fellow guardsman and asked warningly, "Son?"

The murderous anger instantly left Verin's eyes, as he realized that his superior officer was not the best person at whom to direct his long-smoldering rancor. Chastened, Verin sat back down and shrugged apologetically. "Sorry. Guess telling the story made me edgy." The remaining tension seeped from his

124

face as he reiterated: "But no, the old man never made it back what with his family, his wound, and his fear of being more than just wounded the next time."

In the recesses of Josnah's mind a nagging voice demanded, "*Is Verin's temper like this at home?*" But Josnah ignored the voice and aloud responded wryly: "Aye. I myself would prefer to come home from Faerwood alive and intact. Safety 'tis a legitimate concern to be sure and one we'll have to think about carefully." Josnah stroked his charcoal-gray goatee thoughtfully. "Do you know exactly where Faerwood and this fort are? Even if we locate them, I can't imagine the crypt is going to be easy to find."

"If I thought it would be easy I would have waltzed up there and retrieved the Coronet by myself a long time ago." Verin replied scornfully. "And yeah, I have a pretty good idea where the old man was stationed. But perhaps we should both sleep on it for a few days before we start trying to figure out a course of action. As I said before, I'm not particularly anxious to escape my new bride just yet."

Josnah felt another twinge of guilt but merely shrugged and changed the subject. "Have you thought about what happens if we find the Coronet?"

"We gain riches and power and glory?" Verin suggested.

"Presumably, yes. But just how does that happen? And which of us wears it?"

"Hmm. I guess I hadn't really thought it through." Verin scowled at the overdue realization that they could not *both* wear the Coronet. Perhaps taking on a partner had been a mistake.

"We can't exactly share it," Josnah went on, his voice growing agitated. "Its power is enormous! It's not as if you and I can take turns and expect everyone's allegiance to shift back and forth between us."

"I suppose not," Verin responded. "And the person who does *not* wear the Coronet is at the mercy of the person who *does*, given that the wearer's charisma is irresistible."

125

"I want very much to rest the Coronet upon my own brow," Josnah spoke longingly.

"As do I," Verin agreed.

Josnah eyed Verin. Josnah was determined the crown would be his, regardless of the cost. Yet he preferred reason over force, and so asked, "What drives you to seek this prize?"

Verin seemed equally suspicious. "I want to live a life of luxury and ease. I'm tired of working my arse off and always counting the hours until the next payday. What other reason would there be?"

"The adoration, of course," Josnah replied.

"Well, that, too. That's certainly part of the appeal." Verin affirmed. "But it's not what drives me. Now, if I were single, and every woman in the kingdom would be throwing herself at my feet, that might be another matter!" He chuckled at the thought.

"Ah, 'tis the opposite for me," replied his father-in-law. "I hunger for adoration far more than gold. There was a time when my life was complete, when I had a wife whose love sustained me. But I have felt no peace since she died and have found no woman willing or able to fill the void – I *will* have such devotion again ere I die." The pain in Josnah's eyes was evident as he declared, "*And the Raven Coronet can give it to me.*"

Verin looked uncomfortable. He could think of no response to his captain's admission.

Josnah realized he had said too much. Abruptly he shook off his morose mood and asked more cheerfully: "Putting aside the 'who wears it' question for a moment, just how does this thing gain us riches and power without getting us beheaded for plotting treason?"

"Who could bring himself to behead the Coronet's wearer?" Verin asked incredulously. "Isn't that the point? We just need to be very careful that no one knows about our quest until one of us is actually wearing the prize!"

"True enough! Perhaps," Josnah ventured, "if *your* main goal is money and *mine* is love, then we could come up with some sort of pact in advance that would allow me to wear the crown but guarantee you would benefit handsomely at the same time."

"Perhaps," Verin agreed sullenly. He still didn't like it. No pact could stop a man from doing as he pleased once he wore the Coronet, and there would be no one to stand against the wearer to enforce such an agreement. But without a serious suggestion of his own to offer, Verin simply added sarcastically: "Or perhaps we could just draw straws?"

"Or perhaps we could cross that bridge when we come to it." Josnah proposed, hoping to put the matter to rest for the present. Retrieve it first, he thought, fight over it later.

The two men sat silently for a moment and then Josnah spoke up again. "So, do you think it's *really* there? Do you think the Coronet's *really* as powerful as the legends say?"

"I've wondered a lot about that myself," Verin replied. "When I was little I used to listen to the kids chant the old wizard's rhyme and then go home and hear my father tell about the crypt he'd found. 'Wouldn't it be grand,' I'd think, 'to wear a crown and have everyone worship me? Even my old man would have to like me!'" Verin ran his index finger around the edge of his tankard distractedly. "That old king managed to unite all those warlords a thousand years ago. Seems to me that he'd *have* to have had some sort of magical help to pull that off."

"I always assumed the Coronet was destroyed somehow," commented Josnah. "I mean, if it was still around, you'd hear about it being on display or maybe locked up with the king's other treasures. Perhaps it really does still exist locked up somewhere – just not where anyone knows about it."

"That's pretty much how I figure it," confirmed Verin. "'Tis as likely an answer as any. My father was certainly convinced of it."

"Well, that being the case," said Josnah, "it does seem worth taking a trip up north and looking into your father's story. Maybe in a week or two we can talk about it some more."

With their plans settled for the moment, Josnah found himself eager to escape the leering presence of the man to whom he'd sold his daughter. He pushed back his chair to rise and offered his hand to his son-in-law. "In the meantime," Josnah managed to smile in spite of his discomfort, "give my best to your wife."

* * *

He had left Verin sitting there, brooding over his beer. They'd made it up to Faerwood – gotten themselves stationed there for six months – but they'd had no luck finding the crypt, despite so much time crashing around in the woods together than their comrades at the fort began to suspect something. Not that they might be looking for something valuable, but that they might be lovers! After Verin learned of that particular rumor, he refused to go into the woods with Josnah at all. And when the two men arrived home from Faerwood, and Verin started taking out his frustrations on Thaedra... Well, it had all gotten pretty hopeless after that.

CHAPTER 13

CONDOLENCES

Rousing himself from his recollections, Josnah got to his feet and brushed the grass from his britches. He reached over and grasped the horse's reins.

"If this is Verin's hometown, methinks 'twould be appropriate to look up his kin and offer my condolences after all this time. Perchance they might offer Verin's poor, tired father-in-law a home-cooked meal and a bit of conversation regarding those old family tales about the Coronet. Perchance," he continued hopefully, "they might remember some clue their father mentioned that dear, departed Verin missed."

Josnah hoisted himself into the saddle and rode back toward the center of town. It didn't take him long to find someone who could direct him to the home of Verin's sister and her family. But just as he was about to rap on the wood of her door, he paused. What would he say? How would he introduce himself? Had word ever gotten back to them of Verin's death? Or, for that matter, of his marriage to Thaedra?

Right then, the door in front of him opened. It was too late to turn back now.

"Uh, hello there," Josnah stuttered to the woman before him. He guessed her to be in her mid-thirties, but her face was as lined and worn as that of a much older woman. Life had obviously not been kind to her. All the same, the family resemblance to Verin was unmistakable.

"Yes?" She looked at Josnah questioningly.

"I believe I knew your brother. His name was Verin Miller, was it not?"

"It was. And you are?"

At her use of "was" rather than "is" Josnah felt certain that this woman already knew of Verin's demise, a fact much to his own relief. It had seemed likely that someone from the guard would have informed Verin's kin, but one could never be sure of these things.

"I am Josnah Farmson. Verin was a friend of mine. In fact, he was married to my daughter."

This piece of information obviously caught the woman by surprise. It was clear from her expression that she hadn't heard that her brother left behind a widow.

"Pardon me," Josnah continued. "Verin told me he had a sister but I'm afraid that if he ever told me your name it escapes me now. You are...?"

"Forgive me. I am Kira. Uh...your daughter was his *wife*? I had never imagined Verin to be the marrying kind."

"He wasn't, at least not for a long time," Josnah explained. "When he reached thirty he seemed to decide that he had sown enough wild oats and that settling down was the thing to do. My daughter caught his eye, and he was hoping to raise a family with her. I'm afraid it was not to be."

"Tragedy seems to follow my family," Kira lamented softly. Realizing that she was keeping her guest in the street, she chided herself, "Where are my manners? Would you like to come in?"

"Thank you, 'twould be my pleasure." Josnah assayed a small bow and stepped into the house.

It took Josnah's eyes a moment to adjust from the bright sunshine outside to the dimmer light of the interior. The first floor appeared to be just one large room. To Josnah's right was an entire wall covered floor to ceiling with cabinets and shelves, excepting a sizeable gap in the middle wherein stood a large wood stove and the kitchen sink. In front and to one side of the wood stove were a kitchen table and wooden chairs; to the other side were a rocking chair and a few cushioned armchairs. In the far corner from the stove stood a large, six-harness loom and, near the loom, Josnah noticed a staircase that he assumed led up to the home's bedrooms.

The center of the room was dominated by a huge braided rag rug. Upon the rug a small boy sat happily banging a pot with a wooden spoon; Josnah guessed the child to be no more than a year old. An older boy and girl also played on the rug with their brother, and Josnah put their ages at about six and eight. A wave of jealousy swept over him at the cozy scene. How unfair that this family should have three healthy children while death had taken both his son and his grandchild ere they drew their first breaths! Even his stepdaughter was lost to him now because of his own blunders.

The thought of Thaedra and his shameful behavior toward her was too much to bear so he shoved the memories aside. The jealousy ebbed, and gentle rivulets of sadness took its place. Josnah dragged his thoughts back to the present. Kira was speaking to him.

"Would you like to sit down? Can I offer you some water?" She gestured at one of the plump chairs near the stove.

Josnah nodded gratefully and smiled at his hostess before seating himself. The smile changed to a cheerful groan when Kira's next words were drowned out by the baby's drumming. Kira gently removed the spoon from her son's hand, placed the pot on the table, and picked up the child. Settling herself in the rocking chair across from Josnah, with the baby on her lap, Kira gestured to the older boy.

"Colin, go draw our guest a cup of water."

Obediently, the boy pulled a mug out of one of the cupboards and stepped up onto the wooden box that lay on the floor in front of the kitchen sink. Solemnly, he grasped the handle of the pump and filled Josnah's mug. As her son handed the mug to Josnah, Kira spoke again.

"So, why are you here? Farmington is a fair ride from Cobbleton where Verin lived – and where I assume you are from."

"I am indeed from Cobbleton," Josnah answered, "but I no longer consider it my home. I have no family left there and have been traveling about our kingdom to see what sights there are to see."

"No family? What of your daughter, Verin's wife?"

"Stepdaughter, actually," Josnah corrected. He considered lying and simply declare Thaedra to be dead, but that would only bring more questions of how and why. Instead he explained: "After Verin's death, Thaedra and I had a falling out. I'm afraid we no longer view each other as family."

"I am sorry to hear that. It would seem that a widow would need all the support from her family that she could get," Kira said sincerely. Pausing, she went on apologetically, "Perhaps I am too bold. I don't mean to criticize."

"No, it's all right. Thaedra and I simply had different ideas about what path she should take once she had lost her husband." Steering the conversation away from Thaedra and himself, Josnah spoke. "So tell me about your family. I only heard little bits and pieces about you from Verin, and you may be the closest thing I have to kin these days."

"As I said before, my name is Kira, currently Kira Shepherd," the woman began. "I was Verin's younger sister; we had no other siblings. I have three children who you see here before you. Completing my little family is my husband, Agio, who's currently at work in the fields outside town. Like my brother, I married late in life. Alas, I find it's quite the challenge keeping up with young children at my age!"

"I can imagine!" Josnah replied with a chuckle. He remembered how, as a child, Thaedra had always brimmed with energy long after he was worn out.

"These travels of yours, I'd love to hear about them," Kira offered. "Would you like to stay for dinner? We'd be happy to supply you with a bed for the night before you resume your journey. That way you could tell us some of what you've seen out there in the great, wide, kingdom. And perhaps," she added sadly, "you might tell a grieving sister something of Verin's final years."

"Of course. I'd be honored to join you and your family for the evening," Josnah responded, "and I'll offer you what stories I'm able. But I believe your family has tales of its own to share."

"Whatever do you mean, sir?" Kira asked in surprise. "What in the world did Verin tell you?"

"I merely refer to tales your father brought back from his stationing up north, tales which Verin shared with me. I find myself wondering if there are any more pieces to those stories that Verin had forgotten." Josnah smiled pleasantly at his hostess. "You women always seem to remember the rich minutiae of a narrative while we men just pass along the dry bones!"

"Humph," she replied coolly. "What my father brought back from up north was a rotten temper and a ruined knee. I am surprised Verin told you otherwise."

"Oh, he told me about the knee and the temper all right, but Verin also told me about Faerwood and centaurs and ancient crypts. It sounded like quite the adventure and it piqued my curiosity." Josnah's voice took on an apologetic tone as he tried to placate Kira. "I understand your father was not a kind man, and I am sorry for whatever grief that that has caused you over the years." More cheerfully he added, "Still, a good story is a good story, regardless of whence it came!"

"Aye," Kira agreed more amiably, "I'll grant you that. But I'm afraid I never heard much of Father's stories. By the time I was a girl he'd stopped telling the tale of exactly how he got wounded; people had begun to think him mad and so he ceased to speak of his experiences. For that matter, I'm surprised Verin remembered much about Father's account of his time in Faerwood either."

"So you know no more of the details?" Josnah asked in disappointment.

"Me? No. On towards the end of his life, Father started telling the stories again – it hardly mattered what people thought of him by that time – but by then I was too busy with my chores and my own life to sit at his knee and listen to an old man's ravings."

"Then who *did* he tell the stories to?" Josnah persisted.

Something flickered across Kira's face, jealousy perhaps, or maybe just plain sadness. "There was a little girl in town who doted on Father." A bit resentfully Kira added, "Though I don't know why. The child's parents couldn't control her – dreamy, flighty thing that she was – and she would run off to our house when she should have been home doing her chores. Once there, she would sit at the old man's feet and listen to him babble." The sorrow came back into Kira's eyes as she finished: "Poor, lonely, enfeebled Father loved the attention; he showed this waif the sort of gentleness and affection he'd never bestowed upon his own family."

Pausing in her narrative, Kira bent to gently kiss the baby resting upon her lap. The child had dozed off and now slept peacefully in her arms. Looking up again at Josnah she mused: "They're so sweet when they're sleeping, aren't they?"

"Yes, they are," Josnah agreed, before seeking to draw the conversation back to Kira's late father and any information the dead man might have divulged: "Could you tell me what eventually happened to this girl of whom you speak?"

"She grew up, more or less," came Kira's answer, "yet she always remained a flibbertigibbet. Last I heard, she'd run off with that traveling show that came by here some time back."

"*Really*," Josnah said in surprise. "What a coincidence!" With feigned nonchalance he continued: "I had heard mention of that circus during my travels, and I was hoping to catch up to it sometime and see the show. It appears I now have one more reason to take an interest in their little caravan. By the way, what was this young woman's name?"

"Desarah," came the curt reply. "I believe I heard tell that she goes by Desirée now. Such foolishness!"

Josnah could see that his hostess had tired of the subject, and he realized that he had stirred up old hurts and jealousies. He dared not pry any further. Instead, he tried to make amends: "Forgive me for being so inquisitive. Here I promised to share stories of my travels with you, and all I've done is ask questions. Have I been dreadfully rude?" he asked with a sheepish smile.

"No sir, not dreadfully." Kira smiled back, her irritation forgotten. "Here, let me put the baby up to bed, and I can start dinner while you regale me with the sights you've seen and the legends you've heard. Agio should be home very soon. I'm sure he'll be happy to meet you. Although," she added wryly, "I suspect he'll be significantly less pleased about meeting you if he finds I have let your presence here delay his supper!" She arose from her chair slowly, careful not to wake the sleeping child she carried.

Josnah watched the woman climb the stairs with the baby. Nearby on the living room rug, Kira's children paused in their games for a moment to gaze after their mother but soon returned to whatever it was that had been keeping them busy. Josnah sat contentedly watching them. He was warm, dry, and very comfortable. The promise of a tasty meal and a family to share it with lay before him for the first time in months. On top of that, he now knew of another potential source of clues for locating the

Raven Coronet, a source other than that deceitful witch, Nazera. What a sense of humor the gods must have to have thrown multiple keys to finding the Coronet into one ragtag band of gypsies!

Josnah chuckled at the thought. He found all this very encouraging – and he had needed some encouragement. "It won't be long now," he told himself. "I shall surely find the circus soon – along with Desarah, the witch, and finally, *finally*, the Coronet!"

CHAPTER 14

SWORDPLAY

It was not easy for Thaedra to adjust to the circus' early morning schedule. After all, she'd worked for years in a business that thrived in the dark, while the circus required ample light to enjoy its acts and antics. On this morning, she felt herself woken by a cold draft sneaking under her covers.

Something brushed her flesh lightly. "*What?*" Thaedra cried out startled. She was now very much awake. Thaedra looked up to see Falmund standing over her and lifting the bedclothes with the tip of a wooden practice sword. He grinned as he admired her nakedness.

"How dare you wave those two swords at me!" Thaedra proclaimed in mock outrage.

"Two?" Falmund glanced down at his own unclothed body and realized to what she referred.

"Help, help!" Thaedra cried out teasingly. "I am about to be pierced through...*again!*"

"Nay, lass." Falmund shook his head somewhat ruefully. "'Tis time we did some practicing. We promised Faylah a sword-fight, and we need to start putting one together."

Thaedra pushed the practice sword aside, pulled up the covers, and rolled over. "Mm. Later. Need more sleep."

Now Falmund reached down and threw the covers off his lover entirely. "'*Later*' I have a show to put on, my sweet Thaedra. I fear we must both clothe ourselves and get to work staging a battle, tempting as more time in bed might be!"

Robbed of her warm cocoon, Thaedra leapt up and grabbed the wooden sword from where it dangled in Falmund's hand. A split second later, she was behind him with the weapon at his neck. "You were saying...?" she teased threateningly.

Falmund laughed. "You continue to amaze me, Woman. Sleeping beauty to conquering warrior in but an instant!"

Thaedra let the sword slide down Falmund's torso to rest across his lower abdomen. "And what shall I take as my trophy, oh Conquered One?"

"But wench," Falmund implored, "a trophy is merely a trophy. Attached to my living, breathing self, it's so much more!"

Thaedra grinned and let the sword drop. "Aye, my dearest. I can't argue with *that!*"

Chuckling, the pair managed to keep their hands off each other long enough to don some clothes. After a bite of breakfast, they picked up a couple of wooden practice swords and stepped out of the wagon onto dewy grass under a dawning sky.

"You know, Falmund," Thaedra spoke thoughtfully as the two headed arm in arm away from the wagons wherein slept their comrades, "that sleeping beauty to conquering she-warrior idea of yours might be a plot line for our act."

"Aye, it might," agreed Falmund. He mulled the idea aloud, embellishing it as he went: "A rogue comes across a sleeping maid and thinks he can have his way with her, only to find himself fighting for his life when he discovers he's bitten off more than he can chew."

"Exactly. The maid could be 'sleeping' wrapped in a cloak that hides a warrior's armor – appropriately skimpy armor, of course," Thaedra reassured her companion.

"Of course," Falmund reiterated.

"With lots of cleavage," added Thaedra nodding.

"Lots." Falmund started to nod but only managed to complete the downward half of the action before the curves in

138

question caught his attention; his eyes glued themselves upon Thaedra's bosom. The couple's steps slowed, and Thaedra turned to face him.

Thaedra raised the tip of the practice sword she carried and used it to lift the lecher's chin so she could look him in the eye. "And I would assume this act will include lots of bawdy banter, as well?"

"Absolutely. I excel at bawdy banter. Not to mention the audience loves it, if you recall our first meeting."

"I could hardly forget!" Thaedra laughed. The two walked a ways further before concluding they were sufficiently out of earshot of their still-sleeping friends.

"All right then," spoke Thaedra. "I, the 'maiden' – ha! – suddenly show up in the middle of the ring sound asleep – we can figure out just how that happens later – and demurely wrapped in a long, hooded cape."

"Then I happen along," said Falmund picking up the plot, "dressed in something appropriate to a rogue and a highwayman. Perhaps I use the tip of my sword to lift the hem of your cloak and expose a tempting expanse of bare leg above your boot top. 'Curious,' I think, 'where are the maid's long skirts that should lie beneath the lady's cloak?' Intrigued, I bend over and gently take the edge of your cloak in my hand so that I might peek beneath..."

"'Take your hands off me sir!' I demand upon awakening," Thaedra contributed.

"'Nay, lass.' I respond," continued Falmund. "I move my hand from the edge of your cloak to place it firmly and suggestively atop your hip. Then I say roguishly, 'I shall not take my hands from you, lady, for the only thing *I* intend to take from you is that one thing that I ne'er can give back again!'"

"I'll say! When it's gone, it's gone!" muttered Thaedra under her breath.

"Don't break the mood!" Falmund chided.

"Oh. Sorry," Thaedra apologized with mock sincerity and got back on topic. "So, the rogue, thinking he has an easy victim, is caught off guard when she shoves him aside and leaps up, producing a sword from the folds of her cape as she does so." Thaedra swung up her sword dramatically.

"And the battle begins!" crowed Falmund, bringing his own sword to the ready.

Thaedra began a swing at Falmund's weapon, but stopped midway when he held up his free hand. "Hold!" cautioned Falmund. "Perhaps we need to discuss this some more before we set to. Have you ever staged a sword fight for an audience before?"

"Now that you ask, well, no," Thaedra admitted. "My fights have always had purposes other than entertainment."

"Well, I have. And there are lots of little tricks. For one thing, rather than the attacker swinging at an opening and the defender blocking, the attacker deliberately swings at the spot the defender has already brought his sword up to block. Keeps someone from accidentally getting killed."

"Good idea," conceded Thaedra.

"Another thing: Put all your power and flash into the backstroke; the forward swing should only have enough force to make the metal ring when the swords collide."

"Also a good idea," Thaedra agreed again. "There's something else to keep in mind about this particular fight," she offered. "I'm fighting in a cloak with very little underneath. We can put plenty of tease into the battle, offering glimpses of this or that but keeping the audience guessing as to just how much will eventually be revealed."

"Mm. Nice touch. You're right, it should make for a very attentive audience."

"It's one of those tricks one picks up working in a brothel," Thaedra said with a little smile.

"I can imagine."

"Anyway, at some point during the fight, you could cut the ties that secure the cloak so that it becomes a liability, and I sweep it off to wrap around my arm. That opens up the whole tactic of trapping your sword in the tangled cloak to aid in defeating you."

"And, of course, I suddenly have an unobstructed view of my luscious opponent," Falmund leered, "distracting me and furthering your advantage."

"So, do I get to win?" Thaedra asked. "Or is it a draw? Or do you intend that you should win and get to rape me in front of the screaming crowd?"

"It's a thought..." Falmund began. But he never got a chance to finish pondering the idea, for Thaedra brought her sword toward his head threateningly. He parried her swing and they began practicing in earnest.

At first they fought as if it was a real contest: all improvised, nothing planned. Gradually, the two found moves that worked well for both of them, moves that were easy to remember and to time safely but seemed to have the requisite flair. These moves they added to their developing choreography. By the end of an hour, they were growing tired but they seemed to have planned out a fair bit of their act-to-be.

"Hold, woman!" Falmund panted. He staggered backward and sat down hard in the now-dry grass. "I think that's enough for today. I still need energy to fight my adoring fans later!"

Thaedra smiled and sat down next to him. "I shall be sure to stick around and step in to battle you myself if it looks like the crowd has more fight left in it than you do!"

"Ah, what a loving partner I have," said Falmund, leaning his head affectionately on her shoulder, "to offer to beat me senseless before anyone else can!"

Thaedra chuckled and reached up to pat her lover on the top of his head. "Ah, poor, tired, Fearless Falmund! By the way, we still haven't decided the ending for our act. Might I assume from your current exhaustion and surrender that my Amazonian maid will triumph over your brash and roguish self?"

"Surrender? Did I surrender?" Falmund started to his feet as if to resume the fight and then thought better of it. He was already tired and the whole day yet lay before him. He flopped back down, sprawling flat on his back in the meadow-grass. "Aye, lass. Perhaps I did. Or if I didn't before I do now. I surrender, you may take me as you will!" Grinning, he lifted his head and looked at Thaedra still sitting upright. "*Please?*"

Thaedra laughed and stretched out atop him, kissing him passionately. Their hands were just beginning to roam to places best left untouched in public when a shadow fell across them. Falmund opened his eyes to see Faylah standing over them with her hands on her hips, or rather upon her equine shoulders.

"Ahem." Faylah cleared her throat. "I thought you two were planning to work out a *fighting* act this morning!"

Thaedra rolled off Falmund and sat up. She shaded her eyes with her hand and peered up at the centauress smiling. "Aye, Faylah, we did work on the fight. I am merely enjoying the spoils of my victory!"

"So a woman shall triumph in this act? There will be those in the audience who won't be pleased." Faylah looked more bemused than concerned.

"And there are those that will," replied Falmund sitting up next to Thaedra. "Mostly the women I suspect!"

Thaedra shoved him playfully with her shoulder. Then she suggested, "Perhaps we shall take turns, come up with two different endings. That will keep the audience guessing, and once word gets out people may be curious enough about the alternate endings to pay to see the show again!"

"An excellent plan!" Faylah agreed enthusiastically. "Just make sure you both agree on the same ending in advance lest we have a real conflict in front of the customers!" she cautioned. "And now, you two, I believe it's time you came back to camp

142

and started preparing for the day's show!" The centauress reached down to offer them each a hand and used her considerable strength to bring them both to their feet. The three performers started the trek back to the main tent.

Along the way they continued to discuss the new act. "There was something else I forgot to mention," said Falmund to Thaedra, "when we're battling, it helps to add lots of groans and grunts to make things exciting."

"What about a costume?" Thaedra asked. "A cloak should be easy, but skimpy, little Amazonian armor? I'm thinking of something brass and flashy; is there something we could come up with?"

"We don't have a skilled smith in the troupe," Faylah admitted, "and I'm not sure we could afford to pay for one to create your armor for us."

"Perhaps something like your costume with black canvas and lots of studding?" suggested Thaedra.

"I think it needs to be as different as possible; brighter, flashier," Falmund offered.

"He's right," agreed Faylah. "Perhaps we could cover an entire brassiere or corset with chain mail, either of rings or of overlapping metal scales. Or perhaps use studs combined with some other sort of flashy metal design. It's really the breast area that's got to be eye-catching. A leather loin-cloth and flashy sword belt will do for below the waist, and some nice soft boots."

Falmund couldn't resist smirking. "I think the breast area is already pretty eye-catching. But it'll be competing with the miles of lovely, bare legs showing from hip to boot top! How ever shall one decide which to leer at?"

Thaedra poked him in the ribs with her elbow. It abruptly occurred to her to ask: "Do you have a problem with the world admiring your woman?"

"As long as it's me you come home to and they only admire from afar, I shall grin and bear it, or rather, let you bare it!"

Thaedra poked him a bit harder.

"Ouch," he declared.

"Hush," Thaedra chided cheerfully. "Faylah, is there someone in particular in this group in charge of costuming who might be able to help me put this together?"

"Desirée is the best at designing costumes. And she's accumulated quite a store of baubles and trimmings that she keeps in her own wagon," Faylah replied. "Maybe she can get you started before today's show, and you can work on it while the rest of us are performing." The little group had reached camp by this time and there was clearly a need to split up and get on with the day's business.

"Thank you. I'll talk to her about it." Thaedra was eager to get started on the costume, and this would give her a chance to get to know quiet, little Desirée a bit better at the same time.

"Just don't forget to keep an eye on my act so you can bail me out if I need it!" reminded Falmund.

"Forget about you?" answered Thaedra. "*Never!*"

CHAPTER 15

COSTUMES & CAMARADERIE

Thaedra left Falmund to get ready for his performance and hurried over to Desirée's cabin. When she reached the wagon, Marcus was just jumping lightly to the ground from the doorway, completely bypassing the little set of stairs.

"Good morning, Marcus!" Thaedra called out.

"Good morning, madam!" replied Marcus with a sweep of his cloak and a deep bow. "May I be of service?"

Thaedra smiled. The little man certainly prided himself on appearances. His graciousness tended to be so exaggerated as to make him seem a bit smarmy. Or perhaps it was all an act. From what little Thaedra knew of Marcus' former colleagues, their outward appearance was merely the face an assassin put on for the world. The real person lay hidden behind carefully chosen facades. It occurred to her to wonder if Marcus really was a *former* assassin or if his airs were all a cover for some sinister mission.

Inwardly she shrugged. Time would tell. Out loud she said: "Is Desirée within? I'm looking for costume advice."

"She is indeed. And I'm sure she'll be happy to offer her services, although I'm afraid her time is a bit limited at present what with today's show almost upon us."

"That's fine," Thaedra assured him. "I only want her to help me get started for now and after that I'll do anything I can to help her get ready for the performance. Perhaps this evening she and I can spend more time together on it."

"She'd like that," Marcus said with what appeared to be a sincere grin. "My delicate little flower gets lonely sometimes; another woman-friend and an interesting costume project would be most welcome."

Marcus tipped his head in farewell to Thaedra and disappeared around the corner of the main tent. Thaedra rapped on the wagon door. "Desirée? Hello? It's me, Thaedra."

"Oh, come in!" answered Desirée happily. "You can help me get into this silly costume!"

Thaedra stepped into the cabin and looked around. The space was laid out much the same as in the compartment she shared with Falmund, but a woman's touch was evident here while Thaedra's feminine presence had so far had little effect on Falmund's wagon. The most obvious difference was the gaily colored baskets that hung from the ceiling in every possible location where they would not invite a blow to the head and even a few locations where they might. Thaedra could see jewel-toned fabrics overflowing out the top of some of the hampers, and she suspected that they all similarly held costume supplies. It seemed that Marcus had gotten more than just a woman when he'd invited Desirée to join him; he'd gotten a costume workshop!

Sitting on the edge of the bed, oblivious to the baskets hanging mere inches above her, was Desirée. Her hands were twisted up behind her back trying awkwardly to button the glittering top of her costume.

"Oh, Thaedra. Can you fasten this for me? I can usually get it myself but for some reason I'm all thumbs this morning!"

"Of course," Thaedra agreed, sitting down next to the younger woman and leaning around behind her. "There you go!" she said with satisfaction. She felt a bit like a mother hen taking care of a particularly lovely little chick.

"Thank you!" Desirée sighed in relief. "Are you here for a reason, or just to save me from choosing between dislocating my arm and going topless?"

"Now, now, we can't go having the Delightful Desirée dislocating her wing...er...I mean arm, can we?" Both women giggled briefly at Thaedra's slip of the tongue.

"Wouldn't it be lovely if we *did* have wings?" asked the younger woman earnestly.

"Yes, it would." Thaedra humored the girl's flight of fancy, if only momentarily. "But right now I'd settle for armor. Skimpy, crowd-pleasing armor. Amazon princess sort of armor."

"Ooooooh. This could be fun." Desirée promptly stood up on the bed and started sticking her nose into one basket after the other while her bare toes gripped the uneven surface below so as to maintain her balance. With her face still buried in a basket of fabric, Desirée asked Thaedra: "Ave oooomph hot emee deees uswhah ooooeee?"

"Excuse me?" replied Thaedra in bewilderment.

Desirée pulled her head out of the fabric for a moment and said: "Sorry. Have you got any ideas just what you need?"

"Faylah and I figured it was really the chest area that mattered – lift, flaunt, and flash – if you know what I mean. But she didn't think we could afford real, sculpted, plate armor so we were talking about chain mail or scale mail."

"Oh! Oh, I know!" Desirée announced enthusiastically. Ducking from basket to basket she made her way across the bed and from there began to navigate the kitchen chairs stepping from one chair seat to the next. "No, not this basket," she announced, "nor this one. Oh, but this trim might be good and this bit of fabric. And this too. Where *has* that silly hamper gotten to anyway?"

Still sitting on the edge of the bed, Thaedra found herself showered with fabrics and leathers and shiny pieces of trim that Desirée pulled from the baskets and tossed to her. The younger woman finally found the basket for which she was searching and lifted the entire hamper from its hook to hand to Thaedra.

"Here," she said triumphantly. "If we clean these up and polish them, they should do the trick. We'll have to strike holes through them to attach them to your costume but they're worthless anyway."

The basket on Thaedra's lap was only a small one but it held dozens of little metal disks. Many were unfamiliar coins caked with dirt; others were plain bits of sheet metal, scraps from the forge. Thaedra looked up at Desirée as the young dancer gingerly stepped down off a chair. "Where did these all come from?" Thaedra asked.

"Oh, some we found along the road or at different camp sites. Some of them are slugs that our less generous clients bless us with rather than tossing coins we might actually be able to *spend* on something practical." Desirée smiled wryly but then said cheerfully: "I knew we'd find a use for them someday, and now here we are!"

"I don't recognize most of these coins at all," Thaedra commented as she sifted through the basket. "They seem very old."

"They are. They come from some of the squabbling little kingdoms that were eventually unified to become the United Lands. The gold coins were melted down long ago but the baser metals weren't worth the trouble. No shopkeeper nowadays will accept the coin of some long-gone realm, so they have no value. I think they're pretty little bits of history and legend – but you can't *eat* legends, can you?" Desirée reached into the basket herself to pull out a coin and admire it.

"You seem to know a lot about them," said Thaedra. "I'm impressed. You're so much younger than I but I've never left my little corner of the world before."

Desirée blushed slightly and looked pleased. "Oh, I didn't learn any of this by myself," she said modestly. "Marcus and

Nazera each knew a little bit about the coins, and they told me about them. Marcus is the one who's traveled all over, not me. And Nazera knows lots of stories about the past. She's a wonderful storyteller – if you catch her in the right mood."

"I'd noticed her storytelling skill," Thaedra admitted.

"I love listening to her," said Desirée with a dreamy sincerity, "all the tales of times and people long gone." She looked at the coin she held in her hand again. "Just think, people who've been dead for centuries used this little piece of metal; carried it in their pockets; bought their bread with it. Maybe noblemen, or kings, or maybe even the wizards from the old fairy tales. They say there was more magic in the world back then – great magic, the kind that could create the Raven Coronet." Desirée broke from her reverie. "The people from your town all know that legend, too, don't they?"

"I know the story," Thaedra answered warily. "We all learned it as children, and my late husband was particularly fascinated by it." Somehow she didn't like talking about the Coronet. It reminded her of Verin and his dashed dreams. It also reminded Thaedra of her own nightmares, those disturbing visions that had so often woven the childhood tale of the Coronet with the horrors of her marriage.

Desirée merely nodded. "I guess I must have a bit in common with your husband then, as I've always loved that story myself. I was never happier as a child than when imagining myself to be part of the Coronet's legend." She held up the coin and mused: "Perhaps there are traces of such ancient magic still locked in these coins!" Looking from the coin in her hand back to Thaedra she conceded: "Not really – not *useable* magic. Nazera would have said something. But perhaps the coins were there when great magic was being used and that would make them special."

Thaedra was touched by how entranced the girl seemed with these relics. "Are you sure you want me to use them for a costume?"

"Of course!" Desirée answered brightly. "We'll put them on display for our audience; it's better than having them hidden away from sight. And what better surface upon which to mount them than one where they'll be amply admired?" she added, mischievously dropping her eyes to Thaedra's chest.

Immediately after the thought passed Desirée's lips, she clapped her hand to her mouth, for she was sure she'd been too forward. The color rose in her cheeks.

Thaedra just laughed. "You imp! There certainly is a lot of emphasis put on bust-lines around here, isn't there?" She nodded at Desirée's own costume.

"Alas," Desirée joked, relieved that Thaedra was not angry, "I'm afraid poor *little* me can't compete with you and Faylah! Truthfully, though, our appearance is not the yardstick by which we judge each other, only how we titillate the customers. The gods gave women these orbs to use, not to hide!"

"Aye, to use nursing babies!"

"Suckling babes or suckering men, isn't it all the same?" Desirée asked sweetly.

"Gods, child!" Thaedra chuckled. "So many sides to you! Are you an innocent dreamer, a manipulative wench, or a wise old cynic?"

"Right now, I fear, what I am is late! We've talked too long, but I'd love to help you more later." Desirée bent to give Thaedra a quick, tentative hug. "Just latch the door behind you when you leave!" The younger woman grabbed her veils and hurried from the wagon, leaving Thaedra to sort through the treasures piled upon her lap.

After a time pondering the materials, Thaedra thought she had a pretty good idea of what she wanted for a costume. The coins and leathers Desirée had found would do nicely for

Thaedra's Amazon garb, but she still needed material for a cloak for the "modest maiden" opening of the act. Thaedra kicked off her boots to stand on the bed and do a bit of nosing around in the baskets just as her hostess had. Before long, she'd found enough yardage of a few different fabrics to make what she thought would be the perfect cape.

"I hope Desirée doesn't mind my helping myself to some extra things," Thaedra muttered as she climbed down and smoothed the wrinkles out of the bed's coverlet where her feet had disturbed it. She proceeded to pile her finds into the basket of coins Desirée had handed her earlier. "But in any case, right now it's time I put my costume-to-be away and checked on Falmund and his foes!" With that, Thaedra let herself out of the wagon. After a brief stop at Falmund's cabin to deposit the basket of materials, she headed for the ring where the strongman was performing.

There was quite a crowd gathered around Falmund's little arena, and it took Thaedra some jostling among the spectators before she could get a clear view of just what was happening. To her dismay, it appeared as if one of the locals had the upper hand in his bout with the wrestler. She suspected that fatigue had put Falmund at a disadvantage, and she cursed silently that they had practiced quite so enthusiastically that morning.

Thaedra took a deep breath, unbuttoned a few more buttons at the neck of her shirt, and elbowed her way through the crowd. "Where is he?" she bellowed. "Where is that loud-mouthed cur?" She ducked under the rope to grab the shoulder of Falmund's assailant and pull him off. "Get offa him, big guy! He's not worth *your* trouble! But *I* have a beef with him!"

Angry at the interruption, the man turned as if to slug Thaedra but stopped in mid-swing when he realized he faced a woman. He looked confused.

Thaedra stepped right up to him, hands on her hips. "Well? I said get out of my way! My friend over there..." she gestured vaguely at the crowd, "...just told me what she heard this swine say when he spotted me earlier! Do you know what he said? Well, *do you?*"

Thaedra stood nose to nose with the man. He shook his head and stepped back out of her way. One corner of his mouth curved up in a half-smile at the thought that this female ball of hellfire would be finishing what he'd started. The man glanced down at Falmund who was just now getting up off the ground. Shaking his head he clucked: "Tsk, tsk, buddy. I wish you luck!"

Now that Falmund was safe from his challenger, Thaedra turned her attention to the audience to plead her contrived case. "He *said*," she fumed indignantly at the top of her lungs, "Wouldn't I like to have myself a *mouthful of those!*" She threw her shoulders back to emphasize her point.

A snicker ran through the crowd but was quickly silenced with a glare from Thaedra. She spun around to face the now-standing Falmund. "I'll give you a mouthful of my fist, you piece of donkey dung! How *dare* you speak that way of a *lady!*"

Now the audience laughed outright at the contrast between Thaedra's haughty declaration and her raucous behavior. Thaedra didn't bother to feign outrage about their reaction this time. She merely stared daggers at Falmund as she tried to avoid breaking into giggles herself.

"But milady!" Falmund protested, "It was a compliment! I was merely admiring your generous assets!"

"Assets?" Thaedra shouted at him, "I'll plant you on *your* assets!" She placed her hands in the center of his chest and with one forceful shove landed him on his backside in the damp dirt of the ring.

"Oh, milady! Perhaps you shouldn't have done that..." Falmund warned her mischievously as he swung his leg at Thaedra, tripping her so that she joined him in the mud.

The fight was on. Their battle went much the way their first meeting had, to the audience's great delight. Finally, when both

Thaedra and Falmund were coated with mud and panting hard, they broke apart and began circling each other warily.

Between gasps for breath, Falmund suggested: "Perhaps you might accept my apology now, lady?"

"Perhaps I would have accepted it before, *if* you had offered it," replied Thaedra panting. "You mentioned no apology prior to this moment; you merely gave feeble excuses for your lewd comments." There was disdain in her voice.

"Oh. Well then, my *dearest* lady, let me proffer my most sincere and humble apologies now." Falmund shakily attempted a deep bow and almost fell back into the muck.

"Apology accepted then, sir," Thaedra replied pleasantly, as if they had been merely taking tea together. "Perhaps you might supply me with a towel with which to clean up a bit?"

Just then, Faylah and Desirée appeared at the entrance to the big tent to introduce the day's second show and invite the crowd inside. Relieved to finally lose the group's attention, Falmund climbed out of the ring and headed around back of the tent to get cleaned up.

Thaedra started to follow him, on the pretense of getting a towel, when she felt a hand on her shoulder. She turned to see the local who had been battling Falmund before she intervened.

"You're not from around here, are you?" he asked.

"Just passing through," she answered noncommittally.

"Are you with the circus?" he insisted.

"And if I am?"

"Then I'd feel cheated."

"Of what? And why?" Thaedra asked. "Would you have enjoyed yourself more getting bruised and battered fighting the strongman? Or was it more fun watching a shapely woman rolling in the mud making a spectacle of herself? And how have we cheated you? If you didn't like the show, don't throw any coins into the basket."

"I would have had more fun wrestling you myself rather than just watching..." he said hopefully.

Thaedra shook her head firmly. "Not available. Sorry."

The man shrugged and turned to walk away. Thaedra was gratified to see him pause and drop a coin in the basket that still stood in the corner of the ring. She set off to get cleaned up, and to see if there was anything she could do to soothe sweet Falmund's bruises.

CHAPTER 16

SEWING CIRCLE

Thaedra, Desirée, and Nazera sat on the benches in one corner of the big tent. The air was damp, given the downpour outside, and it was a bit drafty, but there was room to spread out their various sewing projects, and the three women could chat as they worked.

"So, Thaedra," spoke Nazera, as she mended a rip in one of her black skirts. "What do you think of life with our little circus?" She was resigned to the former courtesan's presence; it would not hurt to be friendly.

Thaedra fished out another coin to stitch onto her costume. "It is certainly an adventure," she replied. "But it is also a job, and I have always thought that a job was not so much about the work as it was about the people. I'm still getting to know everyone so I can't say for sure. Yet, as it stands now, I feel very fortunate to be here." Thaedra smiled warmly at the two other women.

"Oh, good!" blurted out Desirée. "I'm so glad you like it here. And I'm glad you like us! What were the people like where you were before?"

Nazera suppressed a smirk. She'd been wanting to ask the same question, since Thaedra had indirectly broached the topic, but she never could have pulled off such an inquiry with the same innocent enthusiasm as Desirée.

"They were..." Thaedra paused, "...people. Like any other. Most of the women had no other choice."

"And the men?" asked Desirée.

Thaedra looked at her curiously. Was Desirée baiting her for some reason? Or just treating a discussion of whoring as a pleasant, get-to-know-you conversation? If it had been Nazera asking, Thaedra would have been sure she was being tested. *No matter*, she thought. *I have no secrets here.*

"Well, aside from a steady procession of pigs and lechers," Thaedra replied, "there were a few regular customers who were a tad more interesting. The wizard whose Spell of Suspended Fertility kept the women barren was always good for a chuckle. Fertility wasn't the only thing he was able to suspend – he did equally well with entire bodies – and he seemed to feel that mid-air sex was far superior to the earth-bound kind. Unfortunately, he invariably lost his concentration at the very *height* of the experience, and wizard and working girl would come crashing down all akimbo."

"Oh, no!" exclaimed Desirée giggling.

Even Nazera had to chuckle.

Encouraged, Thaedra wracked her brain for other amusing stories to share. She saw no point in reciting the day-to-day unpleasantness of brothel work.

"There were others who were reasonably harmless also," she continued, "boys pretending to be men, men longing to be boys again, and men happy to be exactly who they were, but unwilling to bend to a decent woman's will in exchange for sex when a few coins could buy fulfillment equally well – probably better. But the majority of the johns were selfish oafs cheating on their wives, or louts too coarse or unappealing to find a woman who would play without pay."

"And," finished Thaedra, wrinkling her nose in distaste at the memory, "the biggest, dirtiest, and most disgusting of them all was Thorpe, the bouncer. We were part of his pay, and he took a particular liking to myself."

"Sounds dreadful," admitted Nazera with genuine sympathy. This mundane woman clearly had not had the options that the witch's skills and upbringing had offered. "Just how *did* you convince the house madam that *you* should be bouncer instead?"

"I fought him," Thaedra answered simply. "Calista, the madam, thought it was a good way both to test *me* and get rid of *him*. So, within minutes of my broaching the subject, she woke Thorpe up from his usual, afternoon nap on the porch, told him I wanted to talk to him, and got well out of the way."

Then Thaedra went on to lay out the whole scene for her audience.

* * *

Thorpe grinned sleepily and reached for Thaedra. "So, wench, can't get enough of me, can you?"

Thaedra took a step backwards, out of the man's reach. "No, Thorpe. I've had quite enough of you, thank you kindly. In fact, I've had way too much of you, and I believe it's time for one of us to go find employment elsewhere."

"Well, then," he answered pleasantly, as he laced his hands over his ample stomach, closed his eyes, and prepared to return to his nap, "that would be you, of course. The house has plenty of whores but only one bouncer."

"I intend to be the new bouncer," Thaedra stated flatly.

Thorpe opened his eyes again and snorted, but he made no move to get up. It was clear he thought her statement too absurd to even comment upon.

"Get up, Thorpe!" Thaedra demanded.

"Why?" he replied nonchalantly.

"Why? *To get your things and get out or to fight me, you damn fool!*" she answered with growing exasperation.

Thorpe lifted his bulk out of his chair and stepped toward Thaedra. "Who are you calling a damn fool?" he asked in annoyance. "I'd say you're the damn fool, little missy. Perhaps I need to remind a certain working girl of her place!"

It was time for Thaedra to put her money where her mouth was. She took another step backward, to center herself at the top of the porch stairs. As Thorpe came closer, Thaedra clenched her hand and swung it at Thorpe's jaw with all her strength.

The look of utter shock on Thorpe's face was one that would warm the cockles of Thaedra's heart for months to come. She hadn't expected her blow to do much serious damage – she knew straightforward boxing was not her forté – but the results were just as she had hoped. The big man staggered a few steps to one side from the impact, and that was just enough to send him stumbling down the steps, toppling bottomward with the increasing acceleration of a felled tree.

A small cloud of dust rose from the dry lawn as Thorpe plowed into it. Thaedra would have happily remained where she was, admiring her handiwork, but she doubted that Thorpe was done yet. She stepped down off the porch to face him.

"Why, you little bitch..." swore Thorpe, pushing himself up onto hands and knees. More warily now, he rose and eyed Thaedra.

There was no laughing in Thorpe's eyes now. Thaedra knew he meant business. She crouched slightly, ready to respond to whatever he threw at her.

With a wordless roar, Thorpe charged at the woman. Smoothly, Thaedra pulled back her right shoulder and shifted most of her weight to the left, thus leaving her right leg stretched out where her whole body had been only a split second earlier. Unable to shift the momentum of his charge, Thorpe tripped over the outstretched leg and sailed into the porch steps beyond.

Thorpe arose and spat out a tooth. "Fuck!" he exclaimed. Then he turned to leer at Thaedra with blood-spattered lips. "And I will, you know. If you thought you were sick of servicing me before..."

The bouncer let the threat trail off as he switched to a fighting style where he was certain he held the edge over Thaedra. No more angry rushes; he need only get good grip on the woman, and weight and muscle would give him an easy victory.

Thaedra watched the man sidle towards her and angled herself so as to provide him with a smaller target.

* * *

Desirée broke in to Thaedra's story: "Why didn't you just kick him in the crotch?"

Thaedra looked at the younger woman. "You continue to amaze me!" she teased. "Such a suggestion from such a sweet girl!"

"Well?" she demanded excitedly. "Why didn't you? And I'm not so sweet as all that; you'd be surprised just what I know!"

"All right then," Thaedra replied. "I didn't kick him in the groin because Calista was watching. And a bouncer who can't win a fight without damaging the cash part of the cow, so to speak, shouldn't be working at a brothel."

"Oh!" Desirée giggled. "I hadn't thought of that! Please, go on, and tell us how you *did* beat the big brute!"

* * *

Thorpe's big, hairy hand whipped out to grab Thaedra's forearm. Much to his surprise, she promptly gripped his own arm in return. Now the pair was locked together right forearm to right forearm. Thorpe moved to swing around behind his opponent and grip her in a bear hug, but before he was able to execute the maneuver, he felt a tug on his arm and a sharp pain in his ribs. Thaedra had leaned sideways away from him and brought her booted right foot up to jab him swiftly in the ribs.

Now, as he sought to pull away from the attack, she did it again, and his tug on her arm only added force to the blow. A third time she kicked him, and a fourth, until she finally released her grip and allowed him to retreat. Thorpe gingerly cradled his side – and what were probably a few cracked ribs, as well.

"I would say you misjudged me, Thorpe," Thaedra spoke. There was no gloating in her voice; she had no wish to fight further and hoped he could be made to see reason. "I hear there are plenty of houses in other towns that could use a bouncer such as yourself. Just think, a whole new stable of women to sample!" She felt a little guilty wishing him on some other group of women, but she couldn't worry about the whole world, only her little piece of it.

"The woman's got a point, Thorpe!" a man's voice called out. Thaedra glanced toward the sound and saw that a crowd had gathered on the house's front lawn to watch the fight. Not only that, but Calista's girls had all taken up spots on the porch from which to view the action. Thaedra wondered if the audience would add to Thorpe's determination to prove himself against a mere woman, or would instead hasten his exit from a losing battle.

"Yeah, Thorpe," cried another voice, "there's easier pickin's elsewhere, ones that won't break yer ribs."

"Thorpe," she pleaded, "I'll be happy to give you a few coins for a healer, and I'm guessing Calista has some severance pay for you..." Thaedra momentarily let her attention stray from Thorpe to where the madam stood watching.

The blow that caught Thaedra in the back knocked her off her feet and slammed her face against the porch railing. She felt the familiar, sickening crack of her nose breaking and heard the girls on the porch gasp.

Giving Thaedra no time to recover, Thorpe wrapped his arms around the injured woman and lifted her up in a bear hug. Her feet dangling, he swung her away from the porch and took a

160

step or two toward the crowd, still carrying his burden. "Now who's got the upper hand?" he whispered to her, droplets of spit landing in her ear.

The effort of lifting her was costing Thorpe and his broken ribs a great deal, and Thaedra knew it. When the man lowered her to the ground, she refused to retake her own weight, instead continuing down into a half-squat with her feet well spread. Bewildered, Thorpe tried to pull her back to standing, but as he did so she reached down between her legs to grasp his ankle and yank. His tugging at Thaedra amplified the woman's own efforts and Thorpe abruptly found himself upended. This time it was Thorpe's head that slammed into the edge of the porch floor. He lay still and didn't move.

Thaedra mopped at her bloody nose with her shirttail. "Id he breeding?" she muttered with some difficulty.

"Not with us anymore, thank the goddess – and thank Thaedra!" laughed Artella. "Yes, Thaedra, honey, he's *breathing*. Don't worry, you've only knocked him cold."

The girls all clambered down the steps to congratulate their new bouncer. Again a man called out from the crowd, but this time Thaedra knew the voice immediately.

"Why don't you girls take your friend inside and help her clean up?" suggested one of Thaedra's regulars, pushing his way through the onlookers. "I'll make sure our buddy here doesn't cause any trouble once he wakes up, and I'll see that he goes on his way peacefully." He reached over to Thaedra and patted her on the back. "Nice job, woman! But alas, does this mean the regular brothel services are no longer available from ye?"

Thaedra just smiled gratefully without answering and let the girls steer her up the stairs and into the house.

CHAPTER 17

NAZERA'S ACCEPTANCE

"It seems Falmund may have chosen wisely, after all," ventured Nazera when Thaedra had finished her tale. "A fighter, a story-teller, and a woman..." She had been about to say "who knows how to market her assets," but realized that that wasn't going to come out as the compliment she intended. "...with a sense of humor," Nazera concluded. "A worthy addition to a circus troupe."

It was true that the witch was the only woman in the troupe who did not dress to titillate – due to both personal preference and professional mystique – but Nazera knew that the earthy sensuality of her troupe-mates served their coffers well. Still, she sometimes found it difficult not to be condescending, or jealous, or both.

"You and Falmund make a good couple," Nazera declared generously to Thaedra. Although it was spoken in friendship, there was something backhanded about the approval, as if Nazera had consented to loan poor Thaedra a cherished garment.

"Why, thank you, Nazera," Thaedra replied in surprise. Quietly, she muttered: "I think." Speaking up again, the newcomer joked wryly: "But perhaps he didn't choose that well after all. I've been doing so much talking that I've hardly gotten a dozen coins sewn on my costume!" Thaedra held up the partially finished top and shook it to jingle the few, dangling, bits of metal.

"Then it's Nazera's turn!" exclaimed Desirée. "Nazera has wonderful stories!"

"What about yourself?" asked Thaedra.

"Oh, me?" replied Desirée. "I'm a listener not a storyteller. My tales are all just dreams that dance in my head, or the legends and lives that I've soaked up listening to others speak. But Nazera? Nazera is a witch from one of the oldest towns in the kingdom, and I'm sure *she* could tell us all sorts of magical tales if she chose!" Desirée's eyes sparkled with a strange excitement.

Thaedra and Nazera looked at each other, each clearly wondering what the other thought of their flighty companion's demeanor.

"What sort of story are you looking for?" Nazera asked guardedly.

"Well, I know you have a raven tattoo," the girl replied with barely contained eagerness. "Do you have any stories about the Raven Coronet?"

Nazera saw Thaedra frown and glance from one woman to the other. She wondered why her new comrade should be uncomfortable with mention of the Coronet.

Still, in spite of Thaedra's reaction, Nazera sifted her memories for an appropriate legend to share. When she finally spoke, it was with the intense, conspiratorial tone that she so often used in her act to weave a spell around her listeners.

"Magic-workers do indeed go back many generations in my family. And yes, magic-workers tend to pass along tales of long ago, much in the same way they pass along the wisdom of their trade. Whether those tales are true is anyone's guess, but among them are a few of the Raven Coronet."

There was suddenly a voice inside Nazera's head gnawing at her consciousness: "*The tales are true; do not deny them. You are kin to Aza the Great! You are the last heir to the power that created the Raven Coronet! You need only answer my call and all will fall on their knees before you."*

Visibly shaken, Nazera lost her focus. "And... and..."

"And what?" demanded Desirée, jumping to her feet and letting her sewing fall from her lap into the mud. Her usually quiet voice bordered on hysteria.

Thaedra scooped up the fallen fabric and put herself between Desirée and the witch. "Here, Desirée. You dropped this."

Desirée looked confused and then a bit embarrassed. She took the chiffon from Thaedra's outstretched hand and sat down meekly. Thaedra returned to her own spot on one of the benches. For a few minutes, everyone focused on their sewing, and all that could be heard in the awkward silence was the drumming of rain on canvas.

"Ahem," Nazera cleared her throat. "I'm sorry. I lost my train of thought. I was going to tell you a story about the Coronet." This time, she made no effort to put on the bard's mantle, and she explained in her normal speaking voice: "My mother had a few stories that she had heard from her grandfather about the Coronet. My favorite was the one about the squirrels."

"The squirrels?" asked Thaedra, relief in her voice that whatever had sparked the upset was past.

"Squirrels," repeated Nazera. "Think about it for a minute. The Coronet made everyone adore the king. *Everyone.* True, the effect was strongest on humans, but it affected other creatures too."

"So the castle was overrun by a sea of chattering, squabbling squirrels?" Thaedra smiled.

"Perhaps it was. But that's not what the story tells. The story talks about their tributes."

165

"Tributes?" spoke up Desirée. She appeared to have returned to her usual, cheerful self.

"Oh yes. Acorns," Nazera explained cheerily. "They brought acorns and buried them everywhere. Great-Grandpa used to say that nowhere in the kingdom were there as many oaks as at the old ruins at Ravenkeep!"

"Ha! Not quite the tale I was expecting," laughed Thaedra.

"Nor, I," giggled Desirée. With a hint of disappointment, she asked, "Have you no other tales of the Coronet to share?"

"Not today. Maybe some other time," Nazera dissembled. Before Desirée could protest, the witch was on her feet and gathering her things. "It seems my mending is done. I'm feeling rather tired; I think I'll join Hargot in our wagon for a nap before dinner." She turned to Thaedra. "I've enjoyed getting to know you a little better. We'll have to do this again." With a nod to Desirée, she left the tent and stepped out into the rain.

Nazera flicked her fingers over her head, and the raindrops parted to run down in rivulets a few inches to either side of her, leaving the witch and her burden perfectly dry. Behind her, back in the tent, she could hear Thaedra trying to convince Desirée to focus on helping her with her costume rather than musing about the Coronet.

Tears threatened, and Nazera blinked them back angrily. "Everything is fine," she muttered. But it didn't help. Much as she had to admit that Thaedra might be good for both Falmund and the circus, she couldn't give up wanting him to want *her* instead.

"*I want you,*" whispered a voice inside her mind.

"Well, I don't want *you!*" she snarled aloud into the whipping wind. Reaching her cabin, she ran up the steps and burst into the cozy enclave. "Hargot!"

"Yes, my love?" he looked up at her from his book. Her abrupt entrance might have startled him, but not enough for him to leave the comfort of their bed.

166

Without answering, she was upon him, kissing his neck and running her fingers through his hair. "Want me," she begged, too soft for him to hear. "Someone other than that damnable crown must want me."

Having moved the book out of the way of his wife's assault, he still held it in midair with one hand as he asked a tad peevishly, "Can I at least finish this page?" But he felt the dampness on Nazera's face where she burrowed against his neck, and so he set the book aside.

"Well, my mercurial darling," he said, wrapping his arms around her, "I can't imagine what has set you off this time, but I do believe you have come up with an excellent way to spend a rainy afternoon. Much better than a book, I am sure!"

By the time Nazera got her nap, her ego was well satisfied – for now, anyway – that even without any witchery, she was perfectly capable of making at least one man desire her.

CHAPTER 18

NEW ACT

The timing of the rain in Skylark had been much the same as the weather's timing in Cobbleton. When the rain ended in the dawning hours of the morning, it was agreed to move on.

Again the troupe-mates struck the tent and packed the wagons. When finished, they grouped together to double-check their preparations before heading out.

"Are we ready to go?" Nazera asked the others. There were nods of agreement.

Rather than answer the witch himself, Falmund turned to his consort and inquired: "Are *you* ready to travel on with us, Thaedra? Or have you had enough of our little gypsy band and cannot bear another minute of our company?"

"Let me just say," Thaedra answered thoughtfully, "that this life has its ups and downs... especially when you put the pair of us in a muddy ring together!"

A few of the group chuckled, including Falmund. But then he persisted: "Seriously, though, do you think you'll tire of it – and of me?"

"Oh, Falmund," she teased, patting his cheek, "are you worried? You needn't be. In truth, I find that the more I have of you, the more I want." Thaedra looked around and directed the rest of the answer to the entire group. "As for circus work, I'd say it's a job, much like many other jobs. It takes hard work and

169

skill, and it isn't all peaches and cream, but it's interesting and keeps one fed. It is a serious improvement from whoring or wifehood, at least the wifehood I experienced."

"Perhaps some day you'll get to experience a different type of marriage," offered Hargot, putting his arm affectionately around Nazera.

The witch turned to smile at her husband and whisper in his ear: "Nice to know you appreciate me."

"Perhaps," Thaedra agreed with Hargot. "Marriage, like most jobs, is best when shared with people who are kind and accepting of you. Which, as I was telling your wife yesterday, is the real joy of this job. I've only been with the troupe for a week, yet I feel less like an outsider than I have since I was a little girl. I feel as if I can be my own unique self at last," she concluded with a grin.

"Who would try to change a goddess such as yourself?" exclaimed Falmund with genuine astonishment.

"Fools and imbeciles!" pronounced Thaedra cheerfully, to the amusement of her listeners. "For, if I am a goddess, who but fools and imbeciles would use a goddess as I have been used?"

"Thou art a strong and shapely goddess," Falmund assured her with an admiring smile and a kiss on the cheek. "And merciful," he went on with overdone awe, "to have not smote all such fools from the face of the earth long ago!"

"No, I just smote the one," Thaedra muttered sadly, leaning her head on her paramour's shoulder. "In truth, Falmund, there are times when I feel less like the strong and determined survivor I've been since Verin's death, and more like some wounded bird now that I'm with you."

"Then I shall heal your wings and teach you to fly again!" answered Falmund with his usual, over-the-top enthusiasm.

"Ahem," interrupted Nazera. "A lovely sentiment, but perhaps you two should continue your discussion along the way – without an audience. It's time we were off."

"Absolutely," replied Thaedra sheepishly. "Forgive my rambling."

A short time later, the group had left Skylark well behind them.

* * *

Two weeks and three towns later, Falmund and Thaedra's "Amazon and Rogue" routine was added to the middle of the troupe's lineup. It was only a few weeks after that that Faylah reluctantly broached the subject of reordering the acts one more time.

"One of my responsibilities," explained the four-hooved ringmaster to the assembled troupe, "is to make the most out of the assortment of acts we have and to arrange them in the order that makes the most sense. Right now, as Nazera pointed out weeks ago, with our 'maid' coming right before our dancing 'ingénue' we have two 'Threatened Female' acts back to back. On top of that, Falmund and Thaedra's act reaches such a crescendo that the acts that follow it have a hard time competing."

"What are you proposing?" asked Nazera suspiciously. She had seen this coming, but she still didn't like it.

"I think that 'The Amazon and the Rogue' needs to be the finale.

"Oh, Nazera," Desirée gushed, "I'm *so* sorry!"

Everyone else held their breath. Thaedra looked particularly uncomfortable.

Nazera could feel that familiar, indignant anger rising, but she fought it down. With some effort, she said coolly, "You may have a point. It's hard to compete with that amount of skin."

Thaedra flushed, but she looked more relieved than anything else. "If you've got it, flaunt it!" she joked awkwardly.

"Oh, I've got my own strengths..." replied the witch nonchalantly. To herself she thought, "You just better hope I don't ever use them."

With Nazera's apparent acceptance of the change, the group relaxed and switched to small talk. Thaedra and Falmund became the show's grand finale the following day.

* * *

Around the same time that Nazera lost her plum spot in the lineup, a particularly interested spectator began appearing in the audience. Josnah had finally caught up to the troupe and now he began to nose about, being careful to remain as inconspicuous as possible.

"Thaedra!" he had exclaimed in astonishment the first time he had caught his daughter's act – before ducking quickly behind another spectator. He did not want her to spot him and call him out in front all her troupe-mates, turning them against him before he could learn what they knew of the Coronet.

For weeks he followed the circus, eavesdropping when he could, occasionally catching the show, but always staying out of sight. Once or twice, the dancing girl almost bumped into him, for she seemed to be as fond of lurking in the shadows and listening to the others as was he. But she'd never met him before and had no reason to take note or to remember, so he went undetected.

At night, he would find a cheap inn in town or, if funds were low, would camp in the woods a safe ways away from the performers.

"I remember this place," Josnah spoke to the glowing coals before him one evening. He stirred the embers of his campfire, and the flames jumped up anew. "Verin and I camped around here somewhere on our way to Faerwood."

Dark shadows wove in and out of the trees around him, and Josnah recalled all the hours spent wandering among the great trunks of that ancient forest, fruitlessly searching. Not far away, Windweaver paused in his grazing and snorted as if he, too, remembered being here before.

"The fates are toying with us, Windweaver. How else can one fathom the unlikely chance that all roads have led me to this one little group of players?" He closed his eyes and tried to grasp how the broken shards of both his dreams and his family had washed up in this spot.

"Damn it, Verin!" Josnah exclaimed, opening his eyes again. "Why did you have to treat her so?" But no ghost spoke up from the darkness to answer his question.

"You drove her from me," Josnah ranted to the empty night. "Even after you were dead and buried, she would not forgive me for making her your wife. And I lost track of her...

"And then that fool Goodwin, that sleazy little weasel of a guardsman, couldn't just quietly let me know that my widowed daughter had taken desperate measures to make a living. No, he had to brag to me in front of all my men about how much he'd enjoyed Calista's new *whore*..." Josnah spat the word angrily.

Josnah recalled Goodwin's words that day in the bunkroom.

"Just thought I'd mention how nice it was to *have* your daughter last evening," Goodwin had boasted. The non-com had just returned from an entire night at Madam Calista's, and there was no mistaking his meaning.

Josnah's hands were around the other man's neck before he even realized what he was doing. "You're crazy," Josnah growled. "Thaedra's no whore!"

The other guardsmen quickly pulled their captain off.

Goodwin rubbed his neck. "Don't blame me that your daughter's a slut!" He couldn't resist adding with feeling: "Gods, *what* a slut!" Josnah struggled against the arms that held him back. Goodwin went on: "If you don't believe me, why don't you go visit Calista's and see just how crazy I am."

There was no answer Josnah could give except to go. He shook off the hands that held him. The roomful of soldiers was silent for now but he knew there'd be plenty of talk and laughter at his expense once he left.

As Josnah strode over to the stables, he felt as if all eyes were upon him. Who else knew? Much as it tore him up to admit it, he couldn't imagine Goodwin making up such a tale.

The guard on duty at the stable nodded to Josnah and offered a casual salute as the captain entered. Josnah looked at him intently. Was the salute *too* casual? Did this man know? Had *he* lain with Thaedra, also? Josnah turned away and silently cursed himself – for his imagination, for his ill-made alliance with Verin, and for his wretched daughter. Quickly, he saddled his horse and headed out of the yard toward the town's infamous brothel.

When he reached Calista's he looped Windweaver's reins about the porch railing and took the steps two at a time to the front door. It was mid-morning now, and even Josnah knew that such an hour would find most of the women asleep after having plied their trade through much of the night. He didn't care. In fact, he took perverse pleasure in disturbing the slumber of the house's licentious occupants. He pounded on the door.

Thorpe yanked open the door and rumbled at Josnah. "Yes?" He had the look of a bear whose hibernation had been disturbed.

"Is Thaedra here?" Josnah demanded.

One corner of Thorpe's mouth twitched into a twisted half smile thinking of his time with the new girl, but he was admitting nothing to this intruder. "And if she is?"

"I want to see her."

"You'll have to talk to Calista about that. No one sees anyone without talking to the madam. Wait here." With that,

174

Thorpe shut the door firmly in Josnah's face and left Josnah on the porch to stew.

Ten minutes later, Josnah's anger had reached the boiling point. Just as he was about to pound on the door once more, it opened to reveal Calista in her dressing gown.

"May I help you, Captain?" she purred soothingly. He might never before have patronized her establishment, but Calista obviously made it a point to know every man in town who held a position of power.

"I will see my daughter Thaedra. *Now.*"

Calista merely raised one eyebrow and said calmly: "Of course. Right this way, please." She gestured for Josnah to enter and then closed the door behind him. Waving Thorpe away, she led Josnah through the elaborate parlor where the girls greeted the guests each evening and up the stairs to Thaedra's bedroom.

"Thaedra?" Calista knocked gently and put her ear to the door. Hearing Thaedra's voice respond, Calista added, "There's someone here to see you." Without giving Thaedra a chance to answer this time, Calista opened the door wide and stepped aside to let Josnah enter.

Thaedra lay in a large canopied bed. Calista clearly saw fit to outfit the second-floor bedrooms elegantly, probably more for the customers' benefit than that of the girls. Thaedra's eyes were yet closed, and her response to Calista's knock must have been only the briefest of awakenings, for now her face had the relaxed, childish innocence of deep slumber. The waves of chestnut hair that Josnah so remembered gracing both his bride and his young stepdaughter spread across Thaedra's pillow. Gazing upon her, hot anger warred with a sense of tragic, overwhelming defeat in Josnah's heart. A hard lump formed in his throat, and none of the words that he had planned to speak were able to pass his lips.

Even in her sleep, Thaedra sensed people in her room and sat up with a start. The sheet fell to expose her nakedness, and

Josnah stared in shock at the womanly attributes his little girl now displayed.

"Josnah?" Thaedra exclaimed in horror, yanking the sheet back up to cover herself.

"Hello, Thaedra," he said sadly. Anger crept back into his voice. "What do you think you're doing here?"

Thaedra looked at Calista, as if hoping for some help, but Calista averted her eyes. "I'm making a living," his stepdaughter replied defiantly.

"This is *not* making a living. This is a filthy occupation no decent woman would pursue. You could have come home; you could have come to me for help."

"Why? So you could trade me off to another of your buddies? No decent woman would have married Verin if she'd known what he expected of her! I am what he made me."

"I know what else he made you – I figured out that it was you who did it," said Josnah, letting the unspoken label "murderess" hang in the tense air between them. There was an implied threat of exposure underlying his words. "Come home to me. We can start over in another town. I had planned to move on anyway. I sold the house weeks ago; today was to be my last day in Cobbleton."

Josnah could see Thaedra's resolve waver momentarily, but her bitterness returned to crush Josnah's dreams of resurrecting their little family. "I am what I am," Thaedra declared with a cold, pragmatic edge. "But at least I am my own boss now. I'll not come with you."

Rejected again by this woman, this *whore*, Josnah's anger knew no bounds. "Your own boss, are you?" he said through clenched teeth. "I think not."

Calista had watched wordlessly through the exchange. Cynical and experienced, she showed no surprise when Josnah pulled some coins from his purse. Taking the money from him, she looked over at Thaedra, sorrow washing briefly across her face.

Then the brothel mistress turned to Josnah and spoke in a voice devoid of emotion. "If you hurt my employee, I *will* have Thorpe show you out, captain of the guard or not." With that, she stepped out and closed the door softly behind her.

Thaedra started to get out of bed but Josnah strode across the room and pushed her back upon it. "I paid for you," he said coldly. "Remember, this is how a whore makes her living. If that's what you want to be, then that's how I'll treat you." A part of Josnah still hoped he could make his stepdaughter see the truth, see how horrible it was to sell herself to any man with a few coins. But there was no question that, in his wrath, he also wanted to see her pay for her insolence. He would show her who was *really* in control.

There was fury in Thaedra's expression as she looked up at him, but even more frightening was the cold, hard look of resignation that lay in the set of her jaw. Her stepfather threw back the covers and gazed at her naked form. Power and lust washed over Josnah, and he couldn't tell if he loved or loathed the woman before him. Without preamble, he unbuttoned his trousers and climbed atop Thaedra.

She lay silent and unmoving and waited for him to finish.

"Thaney," Josnah murmured, forgetting himself in the heat of his lust.

Sickened at his use of her mother's name, Thaedra closed her eyes and turned her head away.

Josnah lay spent upon her for only a minute. As his ardor ebbed, the overwhelming realization of what he had done flooded in on him, and he was filled with self-hatred. Arising hastily, he adjusted his clothes. He could not look at his stepdaughter, could not lift his head at all for fear he'd see his debauched reflection in the mirrors scattered about the room. Instead, he kept his eyes glued to the floor. Josnah reached inside his blouse and pulled out the purse he still carried. He hadn't the heart to stand there and split the money evenly between them, as had been his original intent when he'd first made plans to leave town, so now he simply dropped a handful of gold pieces on the dresser. It would not erase his shame, but it might ease Thaedra's future.

Without a word, Josnah left the room and left the house. He had ridden out of town that same day without a goodbye to anyone.

* * *

"I shall have to face her again sometime," he told himself. "If I am to gain answers from the witch and the dancing girl, I will have to reveal my presence to Thaedra, too.

"But there is no great rush," he went on with a yawn. "The group seems to be headed north, which takes it in the general direction of Faerwood anyway, so I can bide my time and still be getting closer and closer to my quarry. I shall gather what information I may for awhile longer by simply keeping my eyes and ears open.

"And when I at last have the Coronet, the past won't matter, for Thaedra will love me again just as when she was a child."

Nodding to himself, Josnah tossed another log on the fire and bedded down next to the circle of flames for the night.

CHAPTER 19

A PROPOSAL

The summer was passing, and the little caravan did indeed intend to reach the corner of the United Lands nearest Faerwood before the season ended. Unaware of Josnah and his plans, the group simply sought to give Faylah a chance to spend time with her own kind for a few days.

From there the company would head southward for warmer climes and the more populated areas. In the cities there might be an indoor venue or two where they could perform during the long, dreary winter. Other than that, winter was a time to settle the wagons on the edge of some hospitable town and spend as much time as possible indoors resting, visiting, or planning new acts.

In the meantime, while the weather held, they would do their best to keep the crowds and the coins coming.

Unbeknownst to Thaedra, Falmund began to plan a surprise for his partner, a surprise he intended to spring on her during the course of a regular performance. On the particular day in question, the troupe was yet a few towns away from Faerwood, and autumn still but a whisper in the air.

Thaedra stood in Falmund's wagon getting dressed for the day's show. She put the top of her Amazon costume on backward at her waist, so as to more easily fasten the clasp securely, and then twisted it around to its proper position. Reaching purposefully into each cup, she hoisted her breasts in and upwards to display ample cleavage above the rows of coins and scrap metal disks that jangled from the bra. The move reminded Thaedra of Calista, and she mused happily about just how much she *didn't* miss her previous life. Going on with her preparations, Thaedra strapped a sheath containing an exotic-looking dagger to her upper arm and latched metal gauntlets about her wrists.

Below the waist she wore a leather loin-cloth that looped between her legs and over a cord tied about her hips to hang down to mid-thigh both front and back. While it covered what needed covering, it left a large swath of tanned feminine flesh completely bare from ribs to thigh and on down both shapely, muscular legs. Bare, that is, except for where it was broken by the heavy, leather, studded sword-belt that Thaedra wore slung over the loincloth. The sword that the belt's sheath bore had the edges and point dulled, but the metal had been polished until it sparkled brightly.

On her feet were a pair of soft suede boots; on her head a simple metal circlet shone atop masses of curly brown locks. Earlier that day Nazera had, to Thaedra's surprise, generously offered to trim her fellow performer's hair. The witch had then used one of her herbal brews to make Thaedra's shoulder length mane glisten. The swordswoman paused to examine her appearance in the mirror and marveled at how sensuous she felt now that her sexuality had finally become a gift rather than a curse.

Pulling her gaze away from the magnificent image in the mirror, she flung a black, ankle-length cape over herself. Thaedra drew up the hood and knotted the two sets of ties, one at the neck and one at the bust, sets that she had just replaced for the umpteenth time. Taking care not to knock over anything in the confined space, given the sword at her waist, she left the cabin and headed for the tent.

Thaedra arrived at the rear entrance to the tent midway through Nazera's act. When the witch had finished with her

180

prognostications, she used her magic to drop the tent into darkness just as she had at the opening of her performance. In the unnatural gloom, Thaedra slipped into the tent and settled herself in the center of the ring as if sleeping, being careful to see that she was properly covered with the cape.

The darkness faded, and daylight returned to the scene. Falmund made his entrance and began ambling about the ring of spectators. He wore a dashing, broad-brimmed hat with a large, red, ostrich feather tucked in the band; on his hands were leather gloves with gauntlet-like cuffs at the wrists. His black cloak flashed a scarlet lining as he moved, and silver buckles graced his leather boots. Beneath the cloak a plain, white blouse was open to the waist of his breeches displaying a deep V of hairy, muscular chest.

Thaedra had no idea if anyone would actually dress as Falmund was dressed. *She'd* certainly never seen a man in such an outfit, but they'd used materials the troupe had had on hand to suggest the role of traveler, rogue, and braggart that Falmund sought to portray. He flirted unabashedly with his audience, and each time he bowed to kiss a woman's hand, his sword angled backwards to lift the hem of his cloak.

Thaedra could sense the crowd's impatience as they began to wonder just when this rogue would realize that there was a vulnerable female reclining in the center of the ring. At last, he took note of her.

"Aha! What have we here?" Falmund announced, spotting Thaedra's inert form. He paced a circle about her, examining his find from all sides. Then Falmund gazed searchingly about the tent as if to locate anyone who looked inclined to interfere with whatever he might have planned for his victim. Satisfied that there were no such busybodies present, he drew his sword and carefully lifted the hem of Thaedra's cape to expose bare leg above her boot tops.

The crowd leaned forward, vying for a better view.

Falmund dragged the cloak further up Thaedra's leg until it was obvious that the woman wore less than the average citizen. Now he dropped to one knee and lay a gloved hand on the exposed thigh.

"Sirrah..." Thaedra's husky voice said firmly, a note of warning clearly present, "...take your hand from my person."

"Nay, lady," Falmund replied with a nasty leer as he slid his hand further up Thaedra's leg, "What I'll take from your person is that which I may never return."

A few of the women in the audience gasped while several men chuckled. Over the rustling of the crowd could be heard one or two children being shushed as they asked their parents what item the man with the fancy hat might be talking about.

Abruptly, Thaedra rolled out from under Falmund's hand and in a split second was on her feet, sword drawn. Falmund leapt up and drew his sword also.

The fight began. As they battled, the two mocked each other, prompting the intended snickers from the audience. The drama increased with each flash of the swords, each ring of metal upon metal, the participants grunting and straining. As Thaedra spun this way and that, there were glimpses aplenty of bare flesh and shining mail beneath her cape to tease the onlookers.

At last Falmund sliced through the cloak's ties, and Thaedra whipped the fabric from her shoulders to wrap around her free arm. With her bosom heaving and her rippling muscles glistening with sweat – and a generous coating of mineral oil – she was an impressive figure. While most of the men watching would have chosen the meek and pretty girl Thaedra had once been over the scarred warrior they now saw in the center of the ring, there was no doubting that this scantily clad Amazon commanded their undivided and enthusiastic attention at present.

THE RAVEN CORONET

To the women, Thaedra was a shocking creature – one to scorn, or admire, or envy, or some combination of the three. But she was definitely spellbinding.

To Falmund, this apparition before him was better than any woman he could have created in his own imagination. The ether crackled with the electricity that flowed between them.

Abruptly, Falmund shifted from their usual choreography. Rather than swing his sword at Thaedra's legs as she was expecting, he lunged for her sword-hand with his free one. Grabbing her wrist, he turned it so that, to avoid injury, she was forced to drop her sword and let him draw her arm up behind her back. Surprised as she was at his actions, she trusted him enough to go along with whatever he was planning.

Falmund pressed himself to her back and brought his sword up against his lover's neck. In a voice that carried clearly about the tent, he spoke: "Now, wench, wilt thou marry me?"

At his words, Thaedra was truly startled. She whispered to him: "This has to be the oddest proposal ever. But if you would offer it thusly, I shall answer as befits the occasion." Then she raised up her voice, so that all might hear: "Art thou serious? Is this how thou wouldst woo a maid?" Thaedra spat disdainfully at the ground. "Pshaw, I'd not marry a man so desperate as you, so desperate as to take a woman by force! Use your sword if you will. Better you take my head than my body!"

Now it was Falmund's turn to be confused. The folly of his little public proposal of marriage began to dawn on him. What had seemed a unique and fitting idea to seal their relationship, much in the same way as it had begun, now seemed the height of stupidity. Where did the act end and her true answer begin? "But woman," he pleaded, "'Tis only thy wondrous self that makes me desperate!" Falmund no longer knew whether he spoke for her or for the audience, nor did he care. Distracted, he loosed his grip on her wrist.

Thaedra saw her chance and took it. Yanking her arm free, she used both hands to grasp his forearm, the forearm that was holding his sword to her throat, and pulled hard. Falmund dropped the sword just in time to fly over her head and land with a jarring thump upon his back. In seconds, Thaedra had retrieved her own sword and put the tip to his throat.

"Now, sirrah," she challenged him for all to hear, "wouldst thou take a woman to wive who was thy equal in all things?" The crowd waited silently, watching the drama play out.

"Oh yes, love," Falmund spoke loudly and with feeling. "Yes, I would."

"Well then, shall we?" Thaedra sheathed her sword with a grin and offered Falmund her hand. There were no games this time, and he rose to his feet easily with her help.

Falmund placed his arm around her shoulders. "Is now acceptable?"

"Aye," she nodded enthusiastically. "If it's worth doing, it's worth doing now." Thaedra, herself, was surprised at just how certain she was that it was indeed worth doing.

"You've no family you want present?" he queried further.

Thaedra thought of Josnah and replied curtly: "No. None."

"That being the case..." Falmund looked from his new fiancée to the audience and called out: "Is there a clergyman in the house who might join us in marriage? Would you ladies and gentlemen like to be guests at our wedding?"

The crowd cheered. Several members of the audience began pointing and gesturing to a small, nervous looking man in a black robe who seemed to be edging toward the exit. Unable to slip away unnoticed, the minister stepped forward reluctantly into the ring.

"But the marriage banns have not been posted! How do I know you both are free and eligible for marriage?" he protested unhappily.

184

"Why, you have my word, sir!" Falmund answered slapping the man on the back. "Is that not enough?"

The minister looked at the size of the man who'd just slapped his back *and* at the size of the sword the man's intended was wearing and muttered ruefully, "I guess it had better be." He went on more loudly, "Do you wish the whole ceremony? Or perhaps just the vows?" he asked hopefully. He clearly felt that the quicker he was done with this, the better.

"The vows alone will be fine. The shorter the wedding, the longer the party, " Falmund paused to leer unmistakably at Thaedra. "And the faster I reach my marriage bed!" Here the crowd applauded and stomped their feet enthusiastically.

Thaedra muttered wryly, "At least this time it's not just the *groom* looking forward to the wedding night."

"Ahem." The minister cleared his throat. "Shall we begin?" Thaedra and Falmund brushed themselves off and tried to look serious.

Falmund turned to smile at Thaedra. He couldn't resist glancing down at the brass and spangles of her revealing Amazon costume and commenting with zeal: "Nice wedding gown!"

"Amen!" called out a man in the crowd. His words were followed by a smattering of applause.

Thaedra smiled sweetly and punched Falmund gently upon the nose.

The minister cleared his throat one more time and spoke loudly to Falmund: "Repeat after me: I, Falmund, take thee, Thaedra, to be my wedded wife..."

"I, Falmund, take thee, Thaedra, to be my wedded wife..." Falmund grinned from ear to ear as he spoke the words.

"...To haven and to holden, for fairer for fouler, for better for worse..." The minister paused and waited for the groom to repeat his words before he continued: "...for richer for poorer, in sickness and in health..."

Falmund repeated each phrase dutifully, beaming all the while.

"...From this time forward, 'til death us depart, if temple and town will so ordain, and so to thee I plight my troth." Once Falmund had spoken these final vows, the minister turned to Thaedra and began anew.

Thaedra repeated as she was told for the first phrases.

Then the reverend recited, as he had hundreds of times to hundreds of other women: "...in sickness and in health, to be bonlich and buxom in bed and at board..."

"Never again!" Thaedra burst out, her eyes flashing as she spoke. Her hand rested reflexively on her sword hilt. "I'll pledge meekness and obedience to no man!"

The little man's jaw dropped, but Thaedra merely shouldered him aside and turned to face Falmund herself. She took her lover's hands in hers, and her voice rang clearly through the tent. "I, Thaedra, take thee, Falmund, to be my husband, my love, my consort, my friend – and my equal. With my body I thee worship, upon thee all my worldly goods I bestow, for richer for poorer, for fairer for fouler, in sickness and in health, from this time forward until death us depart. So to thee I plight my troth." She looked into Falmund's eyes longingly, hopeful that this last declaration of independence would not be one step too far.

Falmund dropped Thaedra's hands and clasped her in an embrace so enthusiastic that it threatened to crush her.

A man standing in the crowd called to Falmund: "That's not an offer I'd take! A wife who thinks she's your equal? Ha!" The woman sitting on the bench directly in front of the heckler brought her elbow back and up with a particularly well-aimed jab, and her husband promptly found himself doubling over to the sound of laughter from the surrounding audience.

Falmund looked back at Thaedra and said: "I'd not have you as anything *but* an equal." He looked at the minister and raised his eyebrows. "Well, is that it?"

"Uh, I'm guessing this was all too spur of the moment to want to include exchanging rings or wedding gifts?" The man's voice quavered a bit. He had found having the bride usurp her vows to be somewhat unnerving. Of course, he found this whole impromptu wedding unnerving.

Falmund and Thaedra looked from the clergyman to each other and nodded sheepishly. "So, then," the reverend spoke with obvious relief that his task was virtually complete, "I now pronounce you man... uh, husband and wife!" The man prudently chose symmetry over the usual implication of ownership.

Falmund gathered Thaedra into his arms once again and gave her a kiss that she felt to her very soul. When the pair at last looked up, they found themselves surrounded by friends and well-wishers. Falmund struggled to see over the heads of the crowd, evidently looking for someone.

"Aha, there he is!" Falmund breathed a sigh of relief. Thaedra caught a glimpse of someone waving at them from the entrance to the tent but then the figure was gone. She looked at her new husband questioningly.

"Right this way, my love." Falmund used the arm he held around Thaedra's waist to propel her gently toward the open tent flap. "I believe my old buddy has come through for us. After all, what's a wedding without a party?"

Thaedra looked at him and spoke firmly, "One would hope that a wedding is the beginning of a happy marriage, with or without a party."

"Of course it is, woman. Or, at least, of course ours will be." He used his free hand to take her chin and plant a kiss on her nose. "Nonetheless, wouldn't you agree that our marriage is worth celebrating?"

"On that, you'll get no argument from me!" Thaedra answered happily.

"Well then, here you are!" Falmund gestured broadly as the newlyweds stepped out of the tent into the fading afternoon light.

In front of the couple was a blazing fire over which a pig was roasting on a spit. To one side, stood a wagon with kegs of ale, and beyond that was a groaning board spread with fruits, cheeses, and breads, and supported by two sawhorses. A fiddler struck up a lively tune at the couple's appearance. Next to the fiddler stood a musician playing a three-hole pipe with one hand while simultaneously drumming upon a ribbon-bedecked tabor with the other.

"By the goddess!" Thaedra exclaimed in surprise. "How did you manage all this? And besides, what if I'd said 'No' or 'Not now'?" she added teasingly.

"Oh, I ran into an old friend of Hargot's and mine in town yesterday, one who used to be a barkeep in Belton before relocating northwards. We worked it all out with him," Falmund replied. "Had you said 'Not now' it would have been an engagement celebration. As for the possibility of a 'No' answer, how could you possibly refuse such a wonder of manhood as my humble self?"

"Humble?" Thaedra snorted. "'The wonder of manhood' part I shan't quibble about." She spoke fondly, with a hint of pride in her voice that Falmund was hers. "But I draw the line at humble!" she taunted cheerfully.

Falmund bowed his head and spoke softly. "Before my gods and before my lady, I am indeed humble." The moment passed, and Falmund returned to his usual boisterous self. He lifted his head and looked about him at the scene. "The barkeep did do rather a nice job of it, didn't he?"

"Rather!" replied Thaedra. She felt the press of the crowd against her back and realized they were blocking the tent's exit.

188

"Shall we go partake?" she spoke to Falmund. The newlyweds waded forward into the crowd together.

The party continued long into the night. The fact that most of the crowd had never met the bridal couple before that day did not seem to discourage them in the least from partying boisterously and from offering their hearty congratulations whenever they spied Thaedra and her consort.

As the most recent celebrant to congratulate them staggered away from the couple, Falmund leaned toward his wife and spoke quietly: "If I am slapped on the back one more time I believe I shall be bruised beyond all hope!"

"Perhaps it is time we retired, and I can tend to those bruises." Thaedra rested her cheek on his shoulder and ran one finger lightly down his back before bringing her hand to rest on his buttocks.

"Perhaps you are right," Falmund replied eagerly. "Oh, blast! Here comes Nazera! I haven't seen her all evening. I suppose we must stay for one more round of good wishes."

Much as Nazera was probably the last person she wanted to speak to, Thaedra could not imagine anything dimming her happiness. "Come, husband, a few more minutes wait won't kill us. I think, perhaps, that the woman is to be pitied, for her marriage will never equal ours. So let us be polite."

Nazera picked her way through the crowd and came up to the pair. "There you are! It's such a madhouse around here that I thought you'd escaped without my having had a chance to offer my congratulations!" The witch extended her hand to shake Falmund's. Without letting go of the groom, she proceeded to reach for the bride's hand and clasped hers, as well.

"You two are so lucky to have each other," the woman continued. "You don't seem to fight the way Hargot and I do."

"Well, no," Falmund interjected, "we fight with swords instead."

"Oh, you know what I mean!" Nazera replied brightly. "And, of course Hargot is no Falmund!"

Falmund looked uncomfortable. Thaedra just wished Nazera would drop Falmund's hand and leave. She considered forcibly removing the offending hand.

A moment later Nazera did drop their hands and turn to go – but not before saying firmly: "I want what you two have."

Falmund looked at the departing witch and then at his wife. "That was rather odd, but odd is normal for Nazera, I suppose. Should we be flattered or offended?"

"Flattered, I guess." Suddenly it didn't matter. Nothing much seemed to matter. She looked at her husband and spoke dully: "I find myself very, very tired. Can we leave now?"

"Of course," he replied. He took his arm from about her waist and led the way to their cabin. They climbed the little ladder and closed the door behind them. Exhausted, the couple stripped and fell into bed. Dutifully, they consummated their marriage.

Just before drifting off to sleep, Thaedra muttered into her pillow: "I'm just tired, so very tired. Tomorrow everything will be fine." But despite her attempts to reassure herself, a tear ran down her cheek. And it was not from happiness.

CHAPTER 20

DOLDRUMS

Thaedra awoke the next morning feeling much better rested – yet the world seemed a more somber place than it had a day earlier. Could simply saying a few words in front of a cleric serve to make her feel like a plodding ox yoked to its mate? Must marriage always kill love?

"Nonsense," she whispered with a smile. Thaedra rolled over to snuggle with her new husband, but it felt awkward and contrived. She found herself overly conscious of her arm trapped between them. And oblivious to all the delightful places that their bodies normally touched and melded.

Thaedra tried to shift to a more agreeable position, but each new one seemed worse than the last. Despite her squirming, there was no response to her embrace from Falmund. Unable to tell if this was due to slumber or to indifference, Thaedra gave up her efforts to get comfortable. Instead she simply shrugged and crawled out of bed.

The new bride glanced at her golden Amazon bra where it lay on the floor and snorted in amusement. "I do know how to dress for a wedding, don't I?" she chided. Thaedra thought back to her first wedding; she remembered sitting swathed in her finest gown with orange blossoms in her hair, all innocence and curiosity. There had been no innocence this time, and the only curiosity had been in Falmund's peculiar and unexpected proposal. But there had been warmth and joy of such depth that she had felt her very soul smile. This morning she felt as numb and confused as she had that first morning as a bride; it was not a pleasant feeling. Thaedra strove to banish the sensation and to hold the joy of yesterday in her heart.

Picking up the discarded piece of minuscule armor and putting it aside, Thaedra wondered if any of last night's feast was still available to serve as breakfast. She pulled on some comfortable clothing and stepped out of the wagon into the autumn sunshine.

"Good morning, Thaedra!" Faylah greeted her. "Leaving your bridal bed so soon?" the centauress asked with a rich, mellifluous chuckle.

Thaedra offered her a half-smile and replied mischievously: "I seem to have worn out my husband; he's still sleeping. But as for myself, I find that I am famished. Perhaps some of last night's feast remains?"

"Desirée had the good sense to wrap the meat well in canvas and oilskin and anchor it in the brook to keep it chilled," Faylah replied. "She and Marcus just went down to retrieve it. The rest we wrapped and tucked away in the supply wagon after you newlyweds went off to bed. I can't imagine that anything would have spoiled during the cool of night."

"It sounds as if breakfast will be a hearty meal!" exclaimed Thaedra.

"Aye," agreed Faylah. "Should you go waken Falmund?"

"I'll leave him be a few minutes longer. Will Nazera and Hargot be joining us for breakfast?" Thaedra had little interest in seeing the witch this morning, or most mornings for that matter, but she liked Hargot and pitied him his trials as Nazera's husband. She had no desire to deprive the poor man of a sumptuous breakfast.

Faylah grinned with amusement. "It appears that the celebratory mood of the wedding has rubbed off on them. Judging by the sounds I heard when I passed their wagon, I'd say that Hargot currently considers Nazera his beloved rather than his bane."

For some reason this thought irked Thaedra. But aloud, she said "All right then, I'll leave them be. All the more food for the rest of us!" She turned to go wake Falmund and nearly bumped into him already dressed and coming down the cabin steps behind her.

Together, Falmund, Thaedra, and Faylah retrieved their breakfast from the storage wagon, plus a blanket on which to picnic. Spreading it in a convenient patch of morning sunlight, they had just settled down to eat when Marcus and Desirée arrived bearing the rest of the leftovers from the brook. The group set to enthusiastically and managed to consume a large portion of the food in short order.

Nazera and Hargot arrived just as the others were finishing. The pair appeared breathless and smiling with none of the pouting looks or outright antagonism so frequent between them. As witch and wizard helped themselves to the remaining food, the earlier risers set about readying themselves for the day's show.

Thaedra hurried to keep up with Falmund as he strode back to their wagon.

"Are you mad about something?" Thaedra asked, wondering why they were not strolling happily hand in hand this morning as they usually did.

Falmund's steps slowed, and he looked at his new bride in surprise. "No, I'm not angry. I thought perhaps you were, the way you sneaked off this morning."

"I didn't want to disturb you. You seemed to be sleeping contentedly, and my stomach was rumbling so loudly I was afraid I'd wake you!" Thaedra tried joking in an effort to lighten the awkwardness they both clearly felt.

Falmund drew her to him in a hug, but the strange, uncomfortable feeling was still there. The hug felt all knees and elbows and angles rather than the heartfelt embrace they had shared a thousand times before. Had she never met Falmund, the stiffness would have felt normal, much like every time Verin had held her. But she *had* met him, and she was all too aware that the lovely sensation that normally made his arms feel like home was somehow missing.

"Are you sorry you married me?" Thaedra asked him, looking up into his eyes.

He averted his eyes from her gaze. "No, of course not! After all, it was my idea." But Thaedra had seen the uncertainty in his eyes before he turned away.

"I think it's going to take awhile to get used to the idea of being husband and wife," Thaedra said ruefully. "Perhaps we've both spent too many years watching others make a mess of marriage for us to be completely comfortable stepping into these roles ourselves."

Falmund looked relieved to know his wife shared his sense of unease. "I do believe you may be right," he said with a nod. He managed to reclaim some of his enthusiasm. "But we, of course, shall master our chosen roles and carry them off with the greatest of élan!" He swept out one arm in a grand gesture.

Thaedra felt somewhat reassured – but she couldn't help notice that they still traversed the rest of the distance to their cabin without any further physical contact.

The show that day was a smashing success. Nazera practically glowed, and her performance showed an intensity that seemed to surprise even the witch herself. Hargot's fireworks sparkled and danced as never before. Desirée, Faylah, Marcus, and even the animals seemed to give their best performance. But to Thaedra and Falmund, everything felt flat. Nonetheless, the crowd was predisposed to love the pair of combatants after participating in yesterday's wedding celebration, and in their eyes the newlyweds could do no wrong.

The bridal couple had agreed that on this day they'd use the ending where Falmund's ruffian was victorious over Thaedra's Amazon maiden. Thaedra had, after all, gained the upper hand at the end of yesterday's strange swordfight so it only seemed fair. This annoyed Thaedra no end – though she couldn't say why – and she had to suppress the urge to either fight to win in earnest or to throw the bout so badly that it made Falmund look like a bully.

When the performance was over, and the couple had stood together sufficiently long to receive the crowd's accolades and good wishes, Thaedra staggered out of the tent alone while Falmund stayed inside to chat with the crowd. Exhausted, Thaedra let herself sag against the storage wagon. A sad lethargy engulfed her, and she wished to sleep more than anything.

A member of the audience slipped out the performer's exit after her and followed the forlorn woman.

"Hello, Thaedra," he said with the self-satisfied tone of a man who's found someone who sought to escape him. It was a smirking tone, one that brought to mind images of a little boy sticking his tongue out and chanting "Nyah, nyah, nyah!"

"Josnah?" Thaedra exclaimed in surprise. She strove to come up with some polite pleasantry but failed. "Damn," she muttered quietly. "Not today. I don't need this today."

"Is that how you greet your long, lost stepfather?"

"As I recall," Thaedra answered, her voice dripping sarcasm, "you weren't exactly acting fatherly last time I saw you."

Wincing at the memory, Josnah returned the barb, "I see you've gone from one highly respectable occupation to another – or have you kept both jobs? A few horizontal tricks and thrusts to go with the vertical ones perhaps?" He leered at her in a way no man should look at his daughter, all the while hating himself for doing it.

Thaedra just glared at him. It wasn't worth the trouble to take a swing at him, or even deny his rude accusations. She was too tired.

Josnah retreated. This wasn't what he wanted; he hadn't intended to argue. "Look, Thaedra, I'm sorry. That was uncalled for. And I'm sorry about what happened before. I wanted to make you see what a bad choice you'd made, how awful it would be, and, and..." he wanted to let her know how appalled he had been at his own actions but he couldn't bring himself to admit it out loud. "And it got out of hand," he finished lamely.

"Hah!" Thaedra snorted. She could think of a million things she wanted to say – to *scream* at her stepfather – but she hadn't the energy. She didn't seem to have the energy for anything just now.

Josnah sought to change the subject and salvage the reunion. "The show was quite impressive. You've really learned to handle a sword well, for a woman."

"For a woman?" she spat at him. "If I weren't so damn exhausted, I'd show you just how well I can handle a sword, and I dare say you wouldn't be giving me such condescending garbage by the time I was done!"

"Condescending?" Josnah was truly bewildered. "Because I don't think a woman should wield a sword? It just isn't the way of the world, Thaedra!"

"It's the way of *my* world, and your world pays a pretty penny to see it!"

"I... I..." Josnah stuttered. He could think of no response. Instead, he tried again to make amends. "Can we call a truce?"

Thaedra, too, was sick of the verbal sparring. "Truce," she agreed with relief. After a moment's pause she asked: "What are you doing here, anyway?" She wondered if he was still seeking the fool Coronet, but she had no desire to bring up the subject herself.

196

Neither did Josnah. He simply stuck to the same cover story he'd used before: "I've been roaming about the kingdom and along the way I heard mention of a particularly entertaining, traveling circus – although I certainly never imagined you were part of it! It sounded like a show worth seeing so I've been keeping my eyes open for an opportunity.

Abruptly, Josnah shifted gears. "By the way, did you know that Desarah, uh, Desirée, hails from Verin's hometown? I was passing though there awhile back and got a chance to chat with Verin's sister. According to her, Desirée was quite close to their father." The corner of Josnah's mouth twitched in that same knowing smirk as he dropped this little bit of news in his stepdaughter's lap.

Thaedra refused to give him the satisfaction of seeing her surprise. She merely commented nonchalantly: "Small world, isn't it?" Deep down, Thaedra suddenly had the sense that Desirée was somehow tainted by this association with Verin's father. After all, the sins of the son had been born of the sins of the father. What mark might have the father left on young, impressionable Desirée? It occurred to Thaedra to wonder just how little Desarah had come to be close to Old Man Miller in the first place. Still, Thaedra was disinclined to ask Josnah for details. Indeed, she was disinclined to ask Josnah for *anything*, *ever*.

Unaware of his daughter's thoughts, Josnah simply responded to her remark. "Aye, a small world it is indeed! Imagine my surprise when I found my own daughter was traveling with this gypsy circus, as well!"

"I can certainly imagine!" Even Thaedra had to smile at the thought. She was hardly the little girl he'd raised anymore; she didn't even bear much resemblance to the woman her stepfather had last seen at Calista's. Tanned and muscled and scantily clad in jingling coins and leather sarong, Thaedra did make quite a sight these days; her eye-catching appearance happened to be an integral part of how she made her living. Just what *did* Josnah think of his little stepdaughter now?

"So," she inquired of her stepfather, "do you think me some sort of unnatural freak now that you've found me?"

"Freak?" he responded, somewhat taken aback. "Nay, Thaedra. For all that's happened, you are still my daughter. Granted, I would have chosen differently for you, but you are a handsome and resourceful woman, with that I cannot argue." Josnah was surprised to find that he genuinely meant what he said, despite the girl's wildly unconventional path.

Thaedra was still wary of the man, but she was pleased. She held out her hand in a gesture of peace, and he grasped it in a firm handshake. "So now that you've seen our little show, what next? Will you continue traveling about or are you planning to settle quietly in some corner of the United Lands?"

"I thought I might travel along with you for a bit, if you don't mind."

"It's a free road," Thaedra said carefully. She wasn't sure just how she felt about this possibility. It made her decidedly uncomfortable.

"Perhaps you might introduce me to your companions?" Josnah inquired.

"Oh." Thaedra imagined herself dragging Josnah through the mob of townspeople that still milled about as she tried to introduce him to everyone. Her head ached at the thought. "Not now," she protested, "but come back tonight when the crowd has left and our little group gathers around the fire for dinner. You can meet the other troupe members then."

Josnah nodded in agreement.

Thaedra looked at him uneasily and wondered if she was expected to give him a hug goodbye. Josnah made no move toward her but neither did he walk away. She realized that she had no intention of ever letting her stepfather put his arms around her again. In fact, her skin crawled at the thought. Still, she hoped there could be peace between them. Shrugging, she said casually: "Goodbye, then. See you tonight." Without waiting for a response, Thaedra turned and left.

As she walked away she could feel Josnah's eyes following her. She ignored his stare and distractedly watched her own boots scuff through the dust. Thaedra's head felt as if it would explode. She had started the day as a confused newlywed, one who suddenly felt a wall between herself and her beloved. Now she must absorb the knowledge that her estranged stepfather planned to travel with the group and that little Desirée was somehow connected to her late husband's family, a family that had lost one of their own by Thaedra's hand. Thaedra felt everything slipping away from her. The dynamics of the group were changing by the minute, and she had no idea how she would regain the warmth and security that she had so cherished these past months.

As she passed the corner of the main tent, she spotted Hargot and Nazera standing in the shadows, their arms wrapped about each other and their lips locked together.

"What, by all the gods, has come over them anyway?" Thaedra muttered. "The witch normally spends more time trying to get under poor Hargot's skin than under his robes!" Her comment went unnoticed by the pair, for they seemed oblivious to the world around them.

Sighing heavily at this additional bit of salt in her wounds, Thaedra headed back to her wagon to lose herself in the welcoming arms of Morpheus until dinner.

CHAPTER 21

INTRODUCTIONS

T he nap did nothing to lessen Thaedra's headache; the throbbing resumed with her return to consciousness. She lay in bed and dreaded dinner but knew she could not avoid Josnah forever.

Falmund had also returned to the wagon after the day's final show and had stripped off his boots and britches before slipping into bed beside his sleeping wife. Now that Thaedra was awake, his gentle snoring seemed to vibrate in tandem with the ache in her head. With the growing pain came a growing irritation at her husband. Thaedra bit her lip and pushed back the angry words that seemed ready to fly off her tongue. What was *wrong* with her? Her headache was not *his* fault! She rolled on her side to stare at Falmund in the fading light and tried to remember how much she had loved him so recently. Could it really be only yesterday that his love had been the greatest gift she had ever known?

Thaedra watched as Falmund stirred in his sleep and waited for him to awaken. She needed to talk to him. About the two of them. About Josnah. About everything. But he only snorted a few times before returning to his rhythmic breathing. Thaedra shifted about in bed, making no effort to avoid jostling the sleeping man, in fact, just the opposite. With one last jab of his wife's elbow, Falmund finally awoke, but in a mood as foul as Thaedra's.

"Hullo," he said dully. No smile, no kiss on the nose for his sweetheart.

At his indifference, all the words that Thaedra had longed to speak turned to bits of stone in her throat; they tumbled down to lie heavily in the pit of her stomach. Frustrated and anxious, Thaedra threw back the covers and scooted down her side of the bed to crawl out at the foot, forgoing her usual giggling, grope-filled exit route across Falmund. She stood and lit the lamp as Falmund himself rolled out of bed.

"Do you suppose Desirée needs any help with dinner?" asked Thaedra, more to break the silence than anything else.

Falmund shrugged. "She could probably use some, I suppose."

"Then I think I shall go offer. Are you coming?"

"You go ahead, I'll be along shortly." Falmund stepped over to his wife and brushed his lips against her cheek in the merest of kisses. Thaedra was all too happy to leave the tense air of their home; she was out the door and down the steps before Falmund could see the glistening in her eyes.

Desirée seemed to be handling dinner just fine. Thaedra set about slicing the loaves of fresh bread one of the townspeople had bartered for admission to the afternoon's show. It wasn't long before the group was gathered around the fire, relaxing and devouring the meal with a minimum of idle chatter. Thaedra kept glancing nervously into the darkness beyond the firelight until she finally spied Josnah approaching on Windweaver.

Thaedra nodded to her stepfather as he dismounted at the edge of their little circle. "Hello, Josnah."

Josnah returned the greeting. "Good evening, Thaedra."

All eyes turned to the newcomer – and then questioningly toward Thaedra. All but Nazera's. The witch continued to stare at Josnah as she scowled in recognition.

"People," Thaedra announced without bothering to rise, "this is my stepfather, Josnah Farmson. He caught up with our little group this afternoon and was eager to make everyone's acquaintance. Given the usual show-time chaos, I suggested he come back when things were quieter."

Before anyone could comment, Thaedra began the introductions. "Josnah, the centauress to your right is Faylah."

"Welcome, Josnah," Faylah spoke in her deep, honeyed tones. It's a pleasure working with your daughter. She's a fine woman – for a human, that is," she added teasingly.

Thaedra gave a small smile and went on: "Josnah, I believe you know Desirée, or rather of her."

Desirée looked confused. "I don't recall..." Her voice drifted off uncertainly.

"Desirée," Thaedra said, leaning over to place her hand over the other woman's, "it seems we have a connection of which we were unaware. Josnah tells me you were close to the Miller family in Farmington."

"The Millers?" she asked in bewilderment. "What do you know of the Miller family?"

For some reason, Thaedra thought she heard a touch of fear in the younger woman's voice. Dismissing it as nothing, Thaedra replied to Desirée's query, "I know little of the family in Farmington, but I was married to their son.

Here Desirée gasped in surprise.

Thaedra ignored the curious stares surrounding her and kept going. "Josnah has been traveling for some time. That's how we lost touch." Thaedra saw no need to elaborate on why they didn't even *try* to keep in touch. "He decided to visit his deceased son-in-law's family, and they mentioned a local girl who'd run off with the circus. Josnah had already heard rumors of a traveling circus and this piqued his curiosity even more. So he's been trying to catch up with us for awhile now – little knowing that he'd find his own lost daughter here, also!"

Nazera interrupted. "A lovely story, Thaedra, but I believe there's more to it than that." She glared at Josnah suspiciously.

"We've met before, Josnah and I, and I think perhaps he has sought me out again."

"There's truth to your words, Nazera," admitted Josnah, "but the explanation I gave Thaedra when I saw her this afternoon is true, too. I swear, finding myself with so many reasons to pursue your group was quite the surprise, to me as much as anyone!"

A quiet laughter ran through the group at the coincidence.

"So, my beloved," spoke up Hargot as he took Nazera's hand in both of his own, "why should Thaedra's stepfather seek you out?"

"I shall explain it all after the introductions are finished." Nazera obviously felt very charitable as she basked in her husband's devotion. She looked up at Josnah. "Perhaps I shall even explain it all to *your* satisfaction."

"Well then, let me speed things up," said Hargot. "I am Hargot, a humble wizard, and Nazera's husband."

"And I am Marcus, former assassin, current knife-thrower extraordinaire, and consort to Desirée," Marcus added helpfully.

As Thaedra listened, she was reminded that all her southern-born comrades went by a single name only. Desarah had joined the group well north of the others and had dropped her last name when she became Desirée. Thaedra had never offered her own surname to any of them; her membership in the Miller clan was something long gone and buried. But it felt odd to be offering only one name up for each of them to Josnah's two. She wondered if her marriage to Falmund had legally erased the "Miller" from her name.

Thaedra's musings were broken when Falmund arose to shake Josnah's hand. "I am Falmund, sir, your new son-in-law."

Josnah raised his eyebrows and feigned surprise at the revelation, although he was already well aware of the previous day's events. "Thaedra! I had no idea you'd remarried," he lied. "And you didn't invite me to the wedding? Shame on you!"

Pleased that Falmund had pulled himself out of his doldrums long enough to greet her father properly, Thaedra defended herself with the cheerful admission, "I'm afraid I couldn't invite you because I didn't know myself that I was getting married!"

There were chuckles and nods all around her. Falmund stepped back to stand proudly next to his seated wife; he placed his hand affectionately upon her shoulder. For an instant, Thaedra could almost taste the sweet glow of the wedding again, just as one can remember the true depth of a dream in that split second between sleeping and waking. Then Falmund withdrew to his former seat some feet away, and she was lost once more.

The introductions complete, it was Nazera's turn to speak. Everyone had finished eating and set their bowls aside, shifting their positions to find a comfortable one for the tale they knew was coming. Even Faylah folded her equine legs beneath her and settled upon the ground. Josnah took a spot on the grass between Faylah and his daughter.

Nazera straightened her shoulders and her pale, fluid hands gestured gracefully toward Josnah. "As I said before, Josnah sought me out previously, back before we left Belton. He had come to speak to me of fairy tales, of the Raven Coronet."

Thaedra felt her heart sink but the rest of the group all seemed entranced.

"He sought me out because another seer had told him that only I could help him in his quest to locate the Coronet, a legend that he believed to be fact. His information was correct, for I am the sole living descendent of the wizard, Aza, who created the Coronet a thousand years ago. Our family's fortunes may have fallen, our magic may not be what it was, but there are certain tales and tutoring that have been passed down faithfully."

There was a rustle of amazement among the troupe. Nazera obviously relished the stir she was causing as she loosed secrets long repressed. She went on: "For various and compelling reasons, which I shall explain momentarily, I chose not to help

205

him. Instead I sent him off to the archives at the center of the United Lands to search for clues on his own. I had hoped that eventually he would give up his obsession. Even if he didn't, I expected to be long gone should he return to seek me out in Belton again. Clearly, I was mistaken in thinking I could avoid him so easily.

"Since subterfuge failed to work, let me offer fact instead. The legend of the Raven Coronet does indeed contain kernels of truth. But it has been cleaned up and simplified to promote the glory of Dargason's Unification and to offer happy tales of wonder for little children."

"So," asked Falmund attentively, "just what is the truth of the story?"

In response to Falmund's question, Nazera seemed to slip even deeper into her storytelling persona. The very air about her shimmered with eagerness – it begged to reverberate with this tale told aloud, a tale that had been no more than a hushed whisper for forty generations.

"A thousand years ago, good King Dargason ruled that corner of our world where Belton still stands. His home was Raven Keep – now fallen to ruins past the outskirts of that city – and his friend and advisor was my ancestor, Aza, the wizard. As long as anyone of Dargason's time could remember, the little kingdoms of the human world had squabbled and fought, merged and split asunder, time and time again. It was Dargason's dearest wish to put an end to this bloodshed, and so he sought Aza's advice."

Now Nazera's voice deepened into the rich bass of a man of stature. The little group around the fire realized that they were hearing the words of a king long dead. "Aza, my wise, old friend," Nazera's altered voice rang out, "isn't there something we can do to stop the killing? Can't the population be left to raise their families without fearing some new atrocity on their doorstep? Think what mankind could achieve if it were freed from all these petty wars!"

The response that issued from the witch's lips came in a voice that was neither hers nor the king's. "Ah, Dargason, I too despair at all the suffering," came the raspy tones of an elderly Aza. "The obvious thing to do would be to raise a massive army of your own and conquer the world so as to rule it justly and peacefully."

Nazera's voice fell again to that of the legendary king. "But the carnage! I have no desire to instigate such slaughter, even for a goal so worthy as eventual peace. Have you no magicks that might ease a unification?"

Aza's voice replied thoughtfully: "There might be a way. I could create a crown of charisma, a talisman that would make all men love you and yearn to please you."

Dargason's sonorous bass responded with enthusiasm: "Aye, man, that sounds like just the thing, since what would please me most is peace!"

The witch's voice became her own again: "So Aza gave the matter study and thought and used his powers to create the Raven Coronet. It was ravens who served as familiars to all the magic-wielding members of Aza's clan, and he drew his magic from the creatures." Nazera looked around at her audience. "And the nursery rhyme you all chanted as children? Those are the actual words he spoke to weave the crown."

She held out one hand, palm up in invitation, and then drew it to her as if drawing words from her listeners.

Desirée was the first to begin: "*Come to me brethren, my life's breath on wing...*"

The others joined in, all but Nazera: "*Masters of air and sky, whose praises I sing.*" The leaves began to whisper along in the darkness, and a breeze came up to churn sparks into the air. The voices around the fire grew firmer: "*Feathers of velvet night, wisdom of old, black bird of family mine, of futures foretold.*"

207

The speakers' faces looked uneasy, as if they had no choice but to continue: "*Give me a token each, from under your wing, that I may great magic work, in service of our king.*"

Nazera dropped her hand and the voices stopped. Before anyone could be sure of what had just happened – or protest – the witch continued her story.

"It is after the spell was cast and the Coronet placed upon Dargason's brow that the old tales stray from the truth. The Coronet did indeed bring adoration to the wearer, though the effect of the Coronet was not instantaneous. The talisman's magic first affected the people of Belton; from there it churned torturously across the land. Within days, there was nothing that anyone anywhere wanted more than to please the famous King Dargason at Raven Keep. Anyone anywhere *except* Aza and his family, that is. They alone remained untouched by the spell, protected by their blood from the raven magic.

"The first indication of trouble came from travelers arriving at the Keep. These travelers described how farmers had left crops to rot in the fields as whole families abandoned their homes in order to move closer to Raven Keep and their beloved king. Livestock grazed untended and unkempt; the sicker animals lay where they fell, the healthy wandered at will. In response to these reports, the king sent out messengers to coax the farmers back to their lands and the shepherds back to their flocks."

Nazera's tone dropped again to become Dargason's. "Tell my subjects that it is my will to bring peace and prosperity to our land – but for that we need food!"

Returning to her own voice, Nazera went on: "Dargason's message traveled throughout the lands, and the farmers returned to their homes as bidden. These tillers of the soil now saw their work as a sacred mission for their king.

"But that crisis had only been a taste of what was to come. Pleasing the wearer of the Coronet was an irresistible desire; it was all that people thought about. Relationships between husband and wife, between mother and child, between brother and sister became unimportant by comparison. Families frayed. And everyone wracked their brains to come up with the one thing that would be most likely to make the king take notice of him or of her, the thing that would most please their lord.

"One would think that announcing his desire for peace and prosperity would have been clear enough, but, humans being humans, they each saw the way to the king's heart through the prism of their own desires and experiences."

Nazera's words seemed to burrow into the souls of her listeners, and they dredged up different memories for each of them. Thaedra's thoughts drifted back to how she had wanted desperately to please Verin but had ended up murdering him. For Josnah, they brought back the image of how he had been so determined to save his daughter from prostituting herself that he had betrayed the filial bond. For each listener the experience was unique – but for each it brought a sense of foreboding as to where Nazera's story was leading.

"Dargason and Aza were standing atop the tower at Raven Keep when they spotted a group of supplicants on the road below." Nazera paused to let her listeners create the image in their minds. When she resumed it was in the creaking tones of the elderly wizard. "Something is wrong, my lord. I see trouble coming."

Then it was Dargason's voice speaking: "I see nothing but a delegation approaching; the leader on horseback and his men bearing poles."

Aza's response came in the weary, aged tones of one who's seen too much for too long: "Look more closely at the poles, your majesty. I fear the populace has decided to win your love by eliminating those subjects they have deemed unworthy."

Horror dripped from Nazera's voice as the pitch dropped one more time to that of King Dargason. "What say you? Oh, gods, there are heads, severed heads atop the poles! Men's heads...and *women's...and even children's!*"

Nazera's listeners shifted uncomfortably. They could all picture the gruesome sight that the king had beheld from his vantage point atop the tower. Hargot grasped his wife's hand in concern. At Hargot's touch, the mood was broken, and Nazera became simply Nazera again. She shook off the spell that had engulfed her.

"So you see," she told her audience, "natural love is unpredictable enough, but magically induced love is worse still. That's why the magic guilds still frown on love spells, even all these eons later." Suddenly nervous, Nazera fingered a little leather pouch that hung at her neck next to her ever-present pentagram. A shadow flickered across the witch's face. But then it was gone again, and Nazera tilted her head to rest her cheek tenderly on Hargot's shoulder.

"But what of the Coronet?" insisted Josnah.

"And just how *did* the kingdom end up united?" broke in Marcus.

Nazera lifted her head again and finished the story, this time without any theatrics. "When Dargason saw what the Coronet had wrought, he tore the wreath from his head and handed it to Aza. 'Destroy it,' he told the wizard. But Aza himself wasn't quite sure how to destroy the thing, and the destruction of a talisman of such power cannot be taken lightly. The wizard *had* included something in the spell about the Coronet's obliteration being linked to the demise of its wearer – but he had no desire to put the crown on some innocent and kill them just to be rid of the Raven Coronet. Besides, Aza had a craftsman's pride in his creation, despite its flaws, and was reluctant to demolish it at all.

"So he hid it away, as far from civilization as possible. He sealed the Coronet in a crypt in the middle of a distant forest that lay at the very edge of the lands of man. Somehow, probably by appealing to their honor, the wizard managed to extract a pledge from the local centaurs that they would guard the crypt and keep the Coronet safe for all time.

"It was, admittedly, rather selfish and short-sighted of him," Nazera added, "but being a worker of magic doesn't automatically mean being infallible."

Thaedra snorted at the idea that Nazera might somehow be less fallible than the rest of them. The witch's first reaction was to glower; her second was to relax and crack a knowing little smile. Thaedra couldn't be sure exactly what was behind Nazera's smug look, but the swordswoman was quite sure it would be very satisfying to slap it from her. Thaedra reluctantly tucked her hands safely under her thighs where they couldn't *accidentally* collide with Nazera's face. A few days earlier, Thaedra probably would have twined her hands in Falmund's to keep them in check, but the invisible wall between them this evening made that seem almost as inadvisable as striking the witch.

Thaedra turned her thoughts back to what Nazera had been telling them. "So the crown lies in a crypt somewhere within Faerwood with centaurs guarding it," said Thaedra, finishing the witch's story. She noticed Faylah looking discomforted, but dismissed it as the unpleasant memories of a fellow outcast.

Nazera confirmed Thaedra's statement slowly, as if trying to determine how her rival had come by such knowledge. "Yes – it does. But how...?"

"...do I know it's in Faerwood?" Thaedra interrupted. "Josnah and my late husband searched for it there. It seems Verin's father had long ago had a chance encounter with the Coronet before being badly wounded by a centaur's arrow." Thaedra was pleased to see that there were yet a few things she could tell the witch about her precious Coronet.

Several people now turned to stare at Josnah, the man who had come so close to realizing a fairy tale. Josnah nodded in confirmation before explaining, "We had no luck though. Those

211

woods are deep and dark and the threat of suddenly being shot by a centaur hung over us every minute we were within the forest."

"Perhaps I should have sought harder to dissuade you when you first questioned me," said Nazera. "I had no idea you had come so close to finding the Coronet."

"You would not have managed to discourage me at our prior meeting," said Josnah flatly, "nor have you at this one. I am still determined to find the Coronet, and I believe it can be used wisely and beneficially."

"You are wrong," said Nazera with equal firmness. "It is dangerous and should have been destroyed long ago. In truth, it never should have been created in the first place."

"Speaking of which," asked Marcus again, "if the Coronet was useless in bringing about peace, just how *did* King Dargason manage it?"

"The old fashioned way, the way he had hoped to avoid," answered Nazera. "He sent emissaries to each of the other warlords and requested their cooperation. A few of them saw the logic in his arguments but most of them just scoffed. So Dargason went to war against the uncooperative ones. And one after another he succeeded in conquering each faction. It took him many, many years and wiped out most of a generation of young men, but in the end the king won. Once victorious, he strengthened his hold on the land by appealing to the war-weary masses to support him in his quest for peace. Through all this, he was aided and counseled by Aza, and then later, after Aza's death, by the wizard's daughter.

"Eventually, the capital city was moved from its corner in Belton to the center of the unified kingdom. The new capital was christened Azenburg in honor of Dargason's beloved wizard and advisor. My family, however, chose to remain in their ancestral home in Belton and only sent a representative to the capitol when it was required for the good of the kingdom. It has been a hundred years since we were called to Azenburg for anything. Magic plays only a minor role in government these days, a role easily filled by more convenient, local magic-workers."

"An interesting bit of history," responded Marcus, "but not nearly as grand and mysterious as the idea of some great enchanted crown bringing the people together. I can see why Dargason and your family distorted the legends to make the unification seem more the will of the gods than simply of one determined mortal."

Thaedra found herself much more concerned with her stepfather's intentions than with the accuracy of old legends. "What will you do now, Josnah?" she asked.

He shrugged. "I haven't really any plans now that Nazera has spoken her piece. If no one minds, I may tag along with your troupe for a bit. It would be nice to spend some time with my daughter and get to know her traveling companions."

This response was not what Thaedra wanted to hear. She was sure Josnah had not given up on the Coronet, not after all these years, not when he still believed the evil could be kept in check. Even as a teenager, she had realized that her stepfather was constantly seeking some simple way to gain instant happiness and snuff out the darkness in his soul. He now believed that the Coronet was the answer; she was certain that he would never let it be. She suspected that Josnah had hopes of wearing down Nazera and eventually winning the witch's cooperation.

Even if Josnah's goal was as he said, simply to spend time with his stepdaughter, it was not a goal Thaedra shared.

"Well I, for one, *do* mind," she replied.

Falmund turned to look at his wife. "Why would you mind?" he asked in annoyance. "Whatever disagreements you two may have had in the past, surely he's entitled to try to make amends."

213

Thaedra's unease grew stronger. She winced at the thought that Josnah was somehow winning over a second husband to side against her. Again she was an outcast in her own marriage.

At her lack of response, Falmund continued: "Besides, we welcomed you to our little band of misfits, how can you refuse your own family the same courtesy?"

Thaedra wondered whether Falmund's words came from the heart, or were just an attempt control a wife he suddenly saw as headstrong. It was the kind of little power game Nazera and Hargot had played constantly until recently. But regardless of Falmund's motives, his words cut deeply. Thaedra couldn't bear the thought of risking her standing with the group, or of incurring her new husband's displeasure, simply because Josnah's presence made her uncomfortable. She acquiesced.

"Fine, then. He's welcome to come along." Hard as she tried to be nonchalant, a trace of bitterness showed through. Yet she would manage to handle the situation somehow. And, she promised herself, she would keep her guard up and her eyes open.

CHAPTER 22

TRICKERY

So Josnah camped out near the embers of the fire that evening after the others retired.

The following morning Thaedra stepped from her wagon to see Josnah already receiving instructions from Faylah on how to take down the big tent in preparation for moving on. He seemed eager to help and smiled warmly when he spotted his stepdaughter.

"Good morning, Thaedra!"

"Good morning, Josnah," Thaedra replied much less jovially. She doubted she could ever bring herself to call him "Father" again. "Still planning to travel with us?" she asked, hoping for the miracle of a negative reply.

"Aye, that I am. But I intend to be a boon, not a burden to your little troupe!" He gestured from the mallet in his hand to the tent and grinned at Thaedra.

She just nodded curtly and walked away.

* * *

In the days that followed, Josnah proved true to his word. It had always seemed as if the troupe could use an extra person who wasn't actually performing; someone to collect the money, to keep track of the props, to send Marlon in on cue, and to help water the rings. Now, here was Josnah, cheerfully and efficiently handling all these chores. Everyone seemed grateful for his presence, everyone but Thaedra.

She still didn't trust him. Part of her wanted to believe that Josnah's happiness was due to suddenly finding himself with a family and a day-to-day purpose after years of wandering. But Thaedra couldn't allow herself to be that gullible. She knew the troupe was currently making its way from town to town along the northern edge of the United Lands; they would soon be close to Faerwood and the cursed Raven Coronet. Thaedra was convinced that their proximity to the Coronet was the source of Josnah's enthusiasm, not some simple sense of camaraderie.

There was a friendship blooming between Josnah and Falmund that added to Thaedra's anxiety. The pair joked and laughed together like the former guardsmen they were. By contrast, it seemed as if Thaedra could no longer do anything right in her husband's eyes; their staged battles for the crowd were beginning to stray from the choreographed routine to become nastier at each performance.

One evening in bed, after Josnah had been with the troupe for some days, Thaedra tried again to talk to her husband about her concerns.

"Falmund?"

"Yes?"

"You and Josnah seem to be quite chummy."

"So?"

"So..." Thaedra replied hesitantly, "I don't trust him."

"Look, Thaedra, I'm sorry you don't trust the guy, really I am, but I like him. And I don't see as you have a right to dictate my friends."

"I know that," Thaedra replied, irritation obvious in her voice. "If I had a right to dictate your friends, I would have dictated Nazera right out of here a long time ago!"

"Nazera is totally smitten with Hargot these days; she barely gives me a second glance. Frankly, you could learn something from her about how to treat your husband."

Thaedra struggled to stifle the rage she felt at being compared with another woman, particularly *that* woman, and tried to drag the conversation back to Josnah. "I guess I should be glad you like my stepfather; he is the only family I've got left, *but...*"

"But what? What is it you've got against him that you can't let got of?"

Thaedra took a deep breath. "When I was first working at Calista's, he came to see me – and he paid to rape me."

Falmund looked shocked, but only for a moment. Then he defended his friend. "You can't rape a whore, Thaedra. I guess that's something else he and I have in common, we both know what a good lay you are!"

Thaedra was speechless at his response. Falmund took her silence to mean the discussion was finished, and he rolled over and pulled up the covers to get some sleep.

The discussion *wasn't* finished. She couldn't *let* it be finished. This was all wrong and she needed to tell him that; he mustn't go to sleep. She needed to have him on her side the way he used to be. She needed him to talk to her, to respect her, to soothe her fears and quiet her anger. But she couldn't let him know the depth of her fury; that would put him on the defensive. And she couldn't command him to go on talking to her; he'd just be sullen at being deprived of sleep.

No, she would get his attention the way she could always get a man's attention. Thaedra's hand reached out and ran gently down her husband's body; shoulder to back to hip to buttocks to thigh. Her breath was warm in his ear, and her lips brushed the nape of his neck. Her breasts pressed against his back. Falmund responded as she had known he would.

But they still didn't talk – and she was still mad – yet she knew of no acceptable way to stop what she had started. All her life it had been drummed into her that it was a woman's duty to satisfy the man she aroused. To draw back and beg understanding was unthinkable.

In the midst of their lovemaking, she felt a sickening familiarity; Falmund could have been any other john. Thaedra knew it was the buried anger making her feel numb and indifferent – and she suddenly realized how very angry she must have been all those other times with all those other men. How could she not have seen it before? How could she have thought she loved Verin when there was so much anger eating her up? Falmund had been the first man to show her what sex was like free of resentment – for a few, short, glorious months the anger had been gone.

Now it was back. But why?

Falmund finished and rolled off of her; Thaedra could soon hear him snoring peacefully. The former courtesan was left to silently ponder this new revelation. What was happening here? It was as unthinkable now to return to the cold, dutiful sex of the past as it had been unimaginable then that one could experience lovemaking as the melding of mind and heart and body that she had known so briefly with Falmund. Thaedra couldn't understand what had gone wrong. They had made magic together, not the magic of Hargot or Nazera, but their own private magic, a deeper magic. Hargot's magic was an empty parlor trick, and the witch's was all insidious incantations and contrived talismans.

"Contrived talismans..." Thaedra whispered aloud. "That's it!" On the far side of the bed, Falmund snorted in his sleep and flopped onto his back. Pieces of the puzzle started to fall together in Thaedra's mind. Nazera's words at the wedding festivities came back to Thaedra: "*I want what you have...*" Thaedra remembered the witch's nervousness when speaking of the perils

218

of love spells and the little leather pouch Nazera wore at her neck.

Thaedra slipped quietly out from under the blankets and quickly pulled on breeches, blouse, and boots. If Falmund heard her moving about, he apparently didn't think it worth rousing himself enough to inquire as to what she was doing. Thaedra grabbed her jacket from the hook by the door.

Moments later, Thaedra stood outside their wagon willing her eyes to see through the darkness and searching for Faylah's distinctive silhouette. There was enough moonlight beyond her own wagon's pitch-black shadow to pick out two other wagons, and she could see the mules tethered nearby, their warm breath visible in the chilly night air. Gazing further, Thaedra caught sight of the gleam of moonlight off a white flank and spiraled horn, and she realized Crystal was cantering in a playful zigzag across the nearby open field toward a solitary figure. There Faylah stood unmoving, her fondness for the unicorn showing clearly on her face in the dim light.

Thaedra wondered once again about the relationship between the two four-legged females. Were they lovers? Were Crystal's happy dashes from side to side a courting dance? Embarrassed, Thaedra turned away from the scene, for she was reluctant to intrude on whatever it was that the two had together. Retreating into the shadow of her wagon, she pondered her next move.

"Out so late, Thaedra?" Thaedra looked up to see Faylah standing before her. Crystal was next to the centauress but kept a bit more distance; white withers pressed against spotted flank.

"I'm sorry, Faylah. I had planned to ask you something but I didn't want to disturb the two of you." Thaedra gestured toward Crystal. "It can wait."

"No need to wait, friend. What did you want to ask? More concerns about Josnah?" Centauress offered human an understanding smile.

219

"Not this time; this time it's something else. Faylah, I know very little of the mechanics of witchcraft but I have reason to believe that a spell has been cast using a talisman, a spell I would very much like to break." Thaedra spoke calmly but there was pleading desperation in her eyes.

"I think that your suspicions have the ring of truth," answered the centauress. "Such a spell would explain a great deal about the rather surprising changes around here these past weeks." She nodded thoughtfully. "So, what is your question? I am no witch myself, but I know a bit about witchcraft."

"Can I just destroy the talisman to break the spell? Burn it, perhaps? Or will destroying the charm destroy that which is trapped within it?" Thaedra asked.

"Burning the fetish will free that which is trapped, not destroy it, and the spell will be broken." Faylah answered firmly.

"You're sure?"

"There exist spells where there might be some risk," Faylah explained, "but love spells, and I believe that is what we are talking about, are readily broken by destroying the charm that made them, and all goes back to as it was."

Faylah smiled reassuringly at the woman and then added: "I trust you are only planning to burn the fetish and not the witch who wears it?"

Thaedra scowled, and her lips formed a tight line. She spoke: "The thought had occurred to me. But no, simply having things return to the way they were will be reward enough for me – and punishment enough for her." The grimace gave way to a wry smile. She thought of her anger at Falmund and her struggles to find common ground with him these past days, and she almost felt sorry for Nazera – *almost*.

Faylah chuckled. "Do you have a plan to tackle this witch?"

"I am a trained fighter," Thaedra puffed out her chest with a playful show of bravado, "and I have the element of surprise on my side – and a certain righteousness to my cause!" After a bit of thought, she went on a little less assuredly: "This all assumes I can find their wagon in whatever secluded little spot the enchanted lovers have parked it this time!"

"It's in a grove just beyond that stand of trees." Faylah gestured toward the edge of the field helpfully. "I wish you luck."

"I'm off, then! Better sooner than later!" And away Thaedra strode on her mission. She did, however, make one brief detour to knock at the door of Marcus and Desirée's wagon. After apologizing for disturbing the couple, she obtained the loan of one of Marcus' nastier daggers to aid in her little, late-night hunt, for she did not wish to return to her wagon for a weapon and risk questions from Falmund.

Thaedra's footsteps slowed as she neared the stand of trees Faylah had pointed out; she placed her feet more carefully so as to avoid broadcasting her approach. Through the trees, she could see the missing wagon, and she crept up to it in silence. Stealthily, she peered in the window, the lower edge being level with her chin.

The vision that greeted her eyes made Thaedra's throat tighten. It should have been Falmund and herself making love with such passion, not Hargot and Nazera! Another woman might have turned away, ashamed to watch the lovers, but Thaedra's ire and her years in the sex trade kept her from caring. Through the glass pane, Thaedra could see Nazera kneeling over Hargot's sweat-soaked body; light and shadows from flames within the stove's slotted belly danced across the witch's pale, naked flesh. Her upper back bore the tattoo of a large, black raven, the wings arched across her shoulder blades. Between Nazera's own rhythmic motion and the fire's flickering light, the bird assumed a life of its own. Any second, it seemed, the creature would rise from her skin and take to the sky. Hargot reached up to caress his wife's face; Nazera tipped her head and brought up her shoulder to squeeze his hand in acknowledgment.

Aside from the raven, the only ornament interrupting Nazera's flawless expanse of bare skin was a cord around her neck, a cord from which hung the witch's customary pentagram and a little leather pouch. It was this pouch that particularly interested Thaedra. The swordswoman clutched her borrowed dagger more tightly and considered how best to make an entrance.

Focusing her attention on the window itself, instead of the figures beyond it, Thaedra realized that the window was much the same as those on her own wagon. Four panes of glass in a wooden frame, it was hinged at the top so that it could swing out and up and be latched to the edge of the roof with hook and eye. In the cramped confines of the wagon, it made sense for the window to swing out rather than in, and swinging it up in such a fashion kept any passersby from striking their heads on the protruding window.

Thaedra grasped the sash's wooden edge and gently attempted to pull the window open. It refused to budge. Hoping against hope that the window would be secured with a simple hook rather than a barrel bolt, she slipped the blade of her dagger between sash and frame and slid it carefully along the sill.

"Aha," Thaedra whispered under her breath as she felt the knife catch on something and then push it aside. She suspected the lovers were too involved to have noticed anything, but she crouched out of sight for a few minutes before risking another glimpse inside. As she waited, Thaedra looked about her for something to give her a boost to the window. Nothing caught her eye that would do the trick. She hoped that the strength and agility built up by her sword fighting would be enough.

"It's now or never," Thaedra muttered in a voice inaudible to anyone but herself. Placing her left foot atop the large, spoked wheel that rested to one side of the window, she tucked Marcus' dagger into her other boot before grasping the window frame with both hands and hoisting herself up until her waist was even with the sill. Awkwardly, she supported herself on her left foot and one arm while she drew the window toward her with her free hand until she could get her upper body through the gap.

Nazera and Hargot were oblivious to her intrusion, wrapped up in each other as they were, but Thaedra knew that she must act fast. She drew up her free leg and swung it through the opening as her other foot pulled free of its perch on the wheel. In seconds, she was inside the wagon. Whipping the dagger from her boot, she leapt forward to straddle Hargot's legs, thus placing herself directly behind Nazera. Thaedra brought the knife up to the witch's throat.

The witch froze unmoving, and Hargot paused in mid-moan to stare up in utter bewilderment at the two women straddling his body. A lecherous smile began to spread across his face.

"Why, Thaedra, darlin', tired of your husband so soon? Come to join my sweet Nazera and myself?" Hargot's voice was hoarse with lust, and with a deep thirst born of his exertions.

Without bothering to answer, Thaedra slipped the tip of her blade under the necklace Nazera wore. As it sliced through the cord, Thaedra grabbed the little pouch and dumped the contents on the bed by her knee. There lay a tiny, carved, wooden heart bound to a jet-black raven's feather by several stands of hair. Thaedra recognized the chestnut strands from her own head and the darker ones as being Falmund's. She scooped up the talisman and clambered off the bed to yank open the stove and throw in the cursed item.

"No!" cried Nazera in desperation, making a futile lunge for the charm. But it was too late.

"Yes!" Thaedra crowed with glee. It was time to beat a hasty retreat while things were still confused. She jumped for the door and was out of the wagon in a flash, leaving the door wide open to the night air. The first flush of success began to grow into a feeling of warmth that permeated Thaedra's very soul. She knew the spell had been broken.

Behind her, she could hear Hargot's voice rising in anger; no hint of lust remained as his head cleared: "Why you blasted bitch! You put another of your stupid love spells on me, didn't you?"

Thaedra didn't wait around to hear more. Instead, she set off as fast as she could for her own cabin – and the warm and loving husband she knew would be hers once more.

CHAPTER 23

VENGEANCE

Nazera sat curled forlornly in her cramped cabin's lone armchair, her thoughts a jumble of rage and humiliation. She had thrown on a robe after Thaedra's disastrous visit but hadn't even bothered to tie it. Hargot, however, had gotten completely dressed, grabbed a blanket, and stormed out of their home.

"Damn," she muttered to the empty room. "That damn rotten bitch, *Thaedra.*" The name came out as an evil snarl. Nazera knew that she was being unfair, knew that this mess was of her own making, but the knowledge only made her angrier and more defiant.

"I had it all – the warmth, the peace, the passion – and that bitch ruined it. Now it's gone. *Hargot's* gone." The witch choked back a sob when she thought how much she had loved her husband just hours ago – how much she could love him again – if only he were here. But he wasn't. And it was *Thaedra's* fault.

For those few weeks of stolen harmony, the unceasing itch of the Coronet's pull had paled beside the power of Nazera's amplified bond with Hargot. With the abrupt ending of the spell, that blessed sense of contentment had been ripped from her. But Nazera had felt what love could be like – now she *knew.* She could never bear to go on as if nothing had changed, to live once more with her soul constantly buffeted by warring emotions.

"'Twould have been better to have never experienced such fulfillment, to have never seen what *could* be only to return to what *is*," Nazera whispered as tears ran down her face. "But I *have* known this bliss – and I *will* know it again."

She struggled to hold onto the deep connection she had had so recently with Hargot. Perhaps, she reassured herself, she might love her husband joyfully once more without magical aid.

"I just need to *remember* how it felt," Nazera insisted aloud. "We were so *good* together, so *right!* If only I can stay true to that knowledge!" Nodding thoughtfully to herself she continued: "I shall strive to wrap myself in happy memories so that all of Hargot's minor sins may roll off me as rain rolls off oilskin. Surely a witch and a wizard can achieve a rich and lasting love without stealing it!

Yet, for all her promises and proclamations, the tighter Nazera clung to her memories of rapture, the more they slipped through her fingers. In their place crowded anger and hatred and despair. The distraught woman tried desperately to drive away the leering images of Thaedra that haunted her – but her efforts were in vain. She could still hear the sound of Thaedra's gloating laughter, of how it had pealed through the night as the talisman burned, and Hargot's adoration turned to disdain.

"*Thaedra...*" Nazera mouthed again in silent fury.

There was a knock at the door.

"Hargot?" the witch cried out jumping up eagerly, her pulse racing.

"No, it's me, Josnah," came the reply. "I heard yelling and saw your husband storm by. I became concerned."

"Oh," Nazera's heart sank again, though she could still feel its nervous pounding in her breast. "No, it's nothing," she replied dejectedly. "Just go away."

In her disappointment, Nazera's mournful thoughts flooded back, darker than ever. The blackness within Nazera rapidly expanded, a blackness that extinguished every spark left in Nazera's soul as it took on form and shape all its own. Soon, where there had been joy before, there was only a hungry chasm of longing and despair. With each second that passed the chasm grew bigger – and the witch's footing at its rim more precarious. Thoughts of giving up and simply stepping off into oblivion began to gnaw at Nazera's brain.

Even as some force urged that she surrender to these shadows, a tiny ray of light pierced Nazera's inner gloom. Soothing thoughts issued from this pinprick of radiance, sweet promises that she might yet return to love's grace.

Some part of Nazera knew that both her dark hunger and this offer of salvation were the work of the Raven Coronet. Deep down, the witch understood that the ever-waiting artifact was using her confusion and unhappiness to manipulate her mind.

She knew also that she was duty-bound to resist its influence; she could hear her mother's voice warning her anxiously, cautioning Nazera now as she had all through the witch's childhood.

"But Mama's gone," Nazera said sullenly. "Poor little Neesa did her best, tried so hard for so long, always kept the Coronet at arm's length." There was a sarcastic edge to the witch's voice. "But what did it get her? Not Mama's love anymore! Or Papa's – Papa's dead, too.

"*And Hargot!* Even Hargot has abandoned me. Falmund's got his damned *whore* back, and I have nothing! Everyone I cared about, everyone who cared about me, *they're all gone.*"

"*I care*," the Raven Coronet told her.

Everything that was good in the witch screamed: "*Deny the Coronet!*"

But Nazera's anger at Thaedra and her need for solace were greater than her willpower. Softly, in a voice filled with shame, the witch replied to the artifact's call: "You were always with me, weren't you? *You're all I have now.*"

Reluctantly at first, and then more willingly, the tortured woman surrendered herself to the tiny, insistent firefly of false hope that the Coronet had set flickering in her mind. In a few brief moments of weakness, a lifetime of denying the Coronet's pull gave way under the strain of Nazera's anguish.

Victorious at last, the Coronet put forward a plan to its new ally, a plan that would serve them both.

Mere moments after dismissing Josnah, Nazera called out to him again through the closed door, "Wait, Josnah, hold a minute. I need to talk to you." Her magic-enhanced voice had no trouble reaching the retreating figure.

What better way for Nazera to have vengeance on Thaedra than to make the woman grovel before a stepfather she detested? Nazera had never delved into what was behind the tension between Josnah and his stepdaughter – but she could think of no better way to humiliate the arrogant whore than to have stepdaughter ache for stepfather the way Nazera now ached for Hargot. The fact that this vindictive scenario was incestuous and twisted made it all the more appealing to the obsessed witch, steeped as she was in the corruption on the long-imprisoned Coronet.

A wicked smile played about Nazera's lips at the thought of her proud, self-assured rival crawling before the man she loathed. Equal parts bitter and bewitched now, Nazera whispered vehemently to the empty room: "Everyone around here thinks I'm a simple carnival trickster, but *I'll* show them. I carry the blood of legend in my veins! Aza's legacy is *my* birthright – and I'll be denied it *no longer*. Soon those mere mortals shall know what *real* power is and *just who wields it!*"

The darkness in the witch's mind had become the walls of a tunnel – and at the tunnel's end lay the euphoria of the Coronet's embrace and the bright light of Thaedra's comeuppance. All the woes that the ancient crown would cause mankind became as nothing to Nazera. The goal in front of her was all that mattered. She would see Josnah claim the damned Coronet and humiliate his slut of a daughter.

Long minutes had passed since her cry for Josnah to wait. Now his hesitant knock came again at the door.

"Nazera?" Josnah's voice called uncertainly through the door. "I thought I heard you cry out for me. Are you all right?"

Roused from her thoughts, the witch drew her robe about her and threw open the door. Without preamble she spoke: "Josnah, do you still want to find the Raven Coronet?"

Josnah was caught off guard. He had hoped to console the witch in the midst of her marital problems and thus win a measure of her trust – but this sudden turnaround was more than he had dared to imagine. "Yes," he answered suspiciously, "I am still interested in the Coronet."

"Then help me hitch the mules to my wagon, and we'll go get it. We're practically at Faerwood now anyway."

"Why the change of heart?" Josnah asked, hardly believing his good fortune. "What about all those reasons you gave why the Coronet should never be found?"

"I've given it some more thought. None of that matters anymore." Under her breath she spoke, too soft for even Josnah to hear: "Nothing matters anymore, nothing but freeing the Coronet and making Thaedra pay."

CHAPTER 24

MISSING!

Only a hint of the approaching dawn was peeking through the cabin windows when Thaedra opened her eyes. Her head rested on Falmund's shoulder, and his arm was curled about her protectively. A wave of happiness washed over her as she burrowed her face into her husband's neck, an action that prompted a fond squeeze from the encircling arm. Thaedra drank deeply of her blissful contentment. Although, in truth, she knew she could never get enough to completely quench her desire for more. It felt as if she could melt right into the man who lay next to her, and still she would want to be closer to him; such was the strength of the bond between them.

Thaedra tilted her head to see if Falmund was awake. "Husband?" she whispered gently. For the first time in her life, the word was magic on her tongue.

Falmund kissed his wife affectionately on the nose and searched her eyes for the woman he had rediscovered the previous night. Relieved to find that Thaedra was yet Thaedra, and that he still loved this woman in a way he'd never thought possible before meeting her, he chuckled happily and hugged her to him.

Their joyful reunion was interrupted by the sound of Hargot's voice calling to them: "Falmund! Thaedra! She's gone!"

The words were accompanied by an anxious pounding on the door.

Falmund rolled out of bed and pulled on his britches. "Hold a moment, Hargot! I'm coming." He yanked open the door, and Hargot stepped in breathlessly. Thaedra sat up in bed and covered herself with the blankets.

The movement caught Hargot's attention, and he flushed in embarrassment. "About last night..." he began.

"It's all right, Hargot," Thaedra assured him. "I gather you didn't know what Nazera had done."

"I had no idea, I swear. I just knew that suddenly we weren't constantly annoyed at each other and always vying for the upper hand. I found myself dwelling on everything that had ever drawn me to Nazera. And all the things that normally would have gotten under my skin were unimportant. Gods, I simply couldn't get enough of that woman!"

Falmund and Thaedra looked at each other with knowing smiles.

Hargot continued: "But I *am* sorry, truly. Although..." He hesitated as he gave the matter some thought. "...if Nazera's spell simply exchanged your type of love for our own, then I might also add that I am terribly, *terribly* envious of the two of you!"

Falmund grinned outright at this remark. More seriously he asked their guest: "What was so urgent that you were pounding on our door this early? You said something about 'she's gone'?"

Hargot abruptly recalled why he was there. "Nazera's gone. I was so appalled and outraged at what my wife had done that I left the cabin after our little argument last night, left and spent the night in the supply wagon. After some sleep, I thought that maybe I should try to talk things out with her. But when I went looking for her I found that our wagon was gone and Nazera with it." Ominously he added: "I didn't see Josnah sleeping in his usual spot by the fire either."

"The Coronet!" exclaimed Thaedra with dismay.

"My thought, as well," admitted Hargot.

"Would Nazera really take him to the Coronet when she knows how dangerous its reappearance could be?" asked Falmund.

"I'm afraid that if my wife felt wronged badly enough she'd do anything for revenge, at least until she calmed down enough to stop and think. And there's something else – I don't believe Nazera has ever been this close to the Coronet's resting place before. Remember, she told us that Aza hid the thing in a *far-off* place; my own training in enchantments suggests that this was to weaken the bond between his blood and his creation. In the course of traveling so far north, we may have unwittingly strengthened the Coronet's influence over Nazera's behavior."

Before Falmund could reply to Hargot's assessment, there was another burst of frantic pounding at the door. "She's gone!" came Marcus's voice.

This time Hargot, standing nearest the entrance, opened the door and told the agitated assassin, "Yes, we all know already that Nazera's gone."

"Not Nazera...*Desirée!*"

"*What?*" came three voices in unison.

"She slipped out during the night," Marcus said pushing his way into the wagon. "I heard her get up but I assumed she was merely heeding nature's call so I went back to sleep. But this morning she was gone!" The assassin's usual, smooth veneer seemed to have vanished as completely as had his lover. Gradually, Hargot's earlier words managed to penetrate the man's distracted brain, and Marcus asked in bewilderment: "You say Nazera's gone, too? Do you think she's taken my Desirée for some reason?"

"The theory is," spoke Thaedra firmly and patiently from the bed, still wearing nothing but a blanket in the increasingly crowded cabin, "that Nazera has gone off with my stepfather to find the Raven Coronet. I have no idea what happened to Desirée. Perhaps she followed them."

Thaedra wondered if the senior Miller's friendship with little Desarah had included sharing an old soldier's stories of stumbling across the Coronet. If Josnah knew such to be the case, he hadn't told Thaedra. The more Thaedra thought about it, the more certain she became that Verin's father had indeed told his tales to the girl – and that dreamy, doe-eyed Desirée had now gone in pursuit of the Coronet herself.

Reluctant to believe Thaedra's theory regarding the missing troupe members, Marcus protested: "But Nazera told Josnah that she'd never help him, that the Coronet was too dangerous!"

"Well, yes," admitted Hargot, "but...uh...let's just say she's furious at the world right now, for reasons I won't go into, and my dear wife doesn't always think when she's angry."

Just then Faylah appeared at the open cabin door and everyone began talking at once trying to tell her what had happened. The centauress held up her hand for silence before saying in her usual, calm voice: "I know, I know. Nazera, Desirée, and Josnah have disappeared. I heard much of your conversation as I approached and, even if I hadn't, I already knew something was amiss. Crystal has also left us." It was impossible for Faylah to fit into the wagon comfortably to join the discussion, so she spoke from where she stood at the foot of the steps.

"This is bad," said Falmund quietly. *He* might have his woman back but everyone else seemed to have lost theirs. And – on top of all the concerns about the Raven Coronet – if one believed the old superstitions about unicorns bringing luck, then Crystal's departure was a decidedly bad omen.

The crowded wagon grew silent, the air heavy with dread. Hargot stared at his feet, Marcus glanced anxiously about the cabin, and Falmund looked worriedly at his wife who still sat cocooned on the bed; all were frozen with concern and indecision.

"Enough!" exclaimed Thaedra, throwing back the covers and standing up. "We have to *do* something." Given all the men who had seen her naked in the past, it seemed foolish to continue this passive charade of modesty when action was what was required. Either her stature, her words, or her nudity caught the group's attention and spurred them back to life.

After a quick grin at his shapely wife, now standing with her hands on her hips beside him, Falmund spoke: "Does anyone know just how far it is to Faerwood from here? And have we any idea how much of a head start Josnah and Nazera, and possibly Desirée, have on us?"

"They can't have left more than four or five hours ago," offered Hargot, dragging his gaze from Thaedra's attributes to look Falmund in the eye. "It was the middle of the night when I last saw Nazera, and it's only just past dawn now. As for Faerwood, I'm afraid I can't help you there."

"I can," stated Faylah. "Faerwood is the home of my people and where I spent my childhood. I, like all of my kind, know of the crypt and the Coronet. I can take you there."

Though startled by Faylah's admission that the Coronet's location was known to the entire centaur race, Thaedra asked simply, "How far is it? Can we catch them in time?"

"Nazera and Josnah appear to have gone by wagon rather than riding double on Josnah's horse," replied Faylah. "By wagon it will take them seven or eight hours and then they must enter the woods on foot."

"Can you go ahead and warn the other centaurs to stop them?" asked Thaedra.

"I can, but I can't see that warning my kin would make a difference. The occupants of the forest are sure to be watching and will know when Nazera and Josnah near the crypt. The question is whether Nazera's magic will be potent enough to repel the tomb's guardians."

"Isn't there anything we can do?" asked Hargot.

"I, for one, certainly intend to at least *try* to stop them!" exclaimed Thaedra.

"Has anyone any idea how Desirée fits into all this?" broke in Marcus.

"We have to assume she's gone after them, probably riding Crystal," replied Thaedra, "although I can't say whether it's to stop Nazera and Josnah or to grab the Coronet for herself."

"She wouldn't do that!" protested Marcus. "She must be trying to stop them!"

"Believe what you will. We need to go after them now!" said Faylah. "Marcus, you're small enough that I can carry you, and you're skilled with knives if it comes to that. I think you and I should go ahead of the others and see what we can do. Falmund, Hargot, and Thaedra can follow in this wagon."

Falmund nodded in agreement. "We'll have to just leave the tent and the other wagons behind and hope no one steals anything. If things work out, we'll come back for them. If not, they'll be the least of our worries."

"If Falmund and Hargot will go fetch the mules, it'll give me a chance to put some clothes on," Thaedra suggested. "Faylah and Marcus can get their things and be on their way. The rest of us will follow.

There was a flurry of activity and the crowded wagon emptied out. In short order Thaedra was dressed, and the mules were in position.

"Faylah!" Thaedra called out just as centauress and assassin were about to take their leave. "Make sure you mark the way for us! It'll do us no good to get lost in Faerwood!"

"That I will!" assured Faylah. "The road here will take you to the next town and on through to the old outpost that lies at the edge of the forest. From there Marcus and I will be sure to notch the trees so you may find your way after us. Good luck to you! May the gods watch over us all!"

With that, the centauress turned and started down the road at an easy canter, Marcus clinging tightly to her back.

Moments later, Thaedra slapped the now-hitched mule team with the reins and clucked at the beasts to move. As usual, Marlon made a few unhappy noises at his fate but started plodding along obediently.

"Hargot," spoke Thaedra impatiently to the man who sat beside her, "I hate to suggest it, but we might get a bit of extra speed out of the mules were an occasional spark to land on their rump. Not to be cruel, but…"

"I quite understand," he assured her. "Desperate measures for desperate times and all that." He sent a single spark from his fingertip to sting Marlon's rump.

"Oh! Ouch! My goodness!" exclaimed the mule indignantly. But he picked up his pace, and his non-verbal partner did the same.

Falmund had chosen to ride inside the cabin instead of up on the driver's bench with Hargot and Thaedra. He had said something about preparing their swords, just in case they should need them. Thaedra knew that before she and Falmund had begun performing with the weapons, they had purposely dulled the edges. The couple had only worried about keeping up the shine of the blade for effect. Now Thaedra heard the sound of whetstone on steel coming from within the wagon.

Thaedra again urged the mules forward. As the wagon lurched along the rutted road, she contemplated with horror the thought of sinking the newly edged weapons into one of their troupe-mates. She prayed that there might yet be a chance of dissuading the treasure seekers with reason rather than with steel – and that it would not already be too late by the time Thaedra and her allies finally reached the missing trio.

237

CHAPTER 25

DESARAH

Desirée clung to Crystal's back and buried her face in the unicorn's flowing mane. The young woman's legs were tired from gripping the animal's sides through the long ride, but her delicate fingers twined the mane tightly and still she held fast.

The rider lifted her head clear of the whipping mane and told her galloping steed: "They all thought it was a fairy tale. They all thought it wasn't real – everyone but Pappy Miller; *he* knew. Pappy used to tell me how he found it, found the great Raven Coronet, but he lost it again. It made him so sad to lose it." Years dropped from her voice as she spoke; she sounded more and more like a child of three or four and less and less like a grown woman. "I wanted to find the crown for poor, old, Pappy Miller. I wanted to find his smile again, and then maybe he wouldn't hit Goodie Miller." Desirée clucked sadly as she remembered the Millers. "I liked Goodie Miller," she declared, "even with her stooped shoulders and tired face. She always patted my head and gave me cookies. But she was *so* scared of Pappy!"

The childlike voice became sulkily indignant as it rambled. "Mama and Papa thought I was stupid, I know they did. 'Can't you pay attention child?' Mama would ask. And Papa was always scolding me: 'What *were* you thinking? Have you no brains at all?' But I had brains! They were just busy – busy thinking about important things like castles and kings and magic and enchanted crowns!" Desirée came out of her trance enough to pat Crystal's neck appreciatively while adding, "And unicorns. Oh, how I dreamed of unicorns as a child! Who would ever have imagined I'd actually ride one?" She grinned happily and buried her face in the creature's mane once more.

Crystal snorted in acknowledgment and kept onward. Desirée was right to marvel at her current method of transportation. There were few unicorns left in the world, and even fewer humans who would ever sit astride one. But Desirée's tiny frame kept her from being too great a burden for the delicate creature, and her tenuous grip on reality – rather than any long-gone claim to virginity – made her one of the chosen few that legend said might ride the beasts.

Desirée picked up her head and resumed her soliloquy. "And with all my dreaming I could see what my parents could not! When I ran off with the circus they thought it was nonsense, thought I was just a silly girl in love. But it was not just my darling Marcus that I followed. I saw the raven wing on Nazera's shoulder and I knew that she must be filled with raven magic. That tattoo of hers was a sign from the gods that I should go with the troupe.

"Then tonight I heard Nazera tell Josnah that we were near the Coronet and that it was time to go find it. I had heard Thaedra at our door earlier, and then the row between Nazera and Hargot, so I had slipped out to take one of my little strolls and see what the fuss was about." She giggled happily. "I must indeed have the luck of the unicorn to pick such a perfect moment to eavesdrop!" Again she patted the unicorn's neck fondly. "And who but you, dear Crystal, could help me find the way and get me there well before Josnah and Nazera? I shall have the Coronet long ere they reach the crypt!

"Now everyone will see how smart I was to figure it all out," Desirée bragged. "Once I wear the Coronet, I'll be the princess that everyone loves. Won't Mama and Papa be proud of their little girl then? And Pappy Miller – he'll be so happy when everyone knows that there really is a Raven Coronet and that he *wasn't* lying!" The knowledge that Old Man Miller and his wife were long since dead and buried seemed to have vanished from Desirée's mind completely. "And I'll see that sweet Goodie Miller never has to be afraid or tired anymore. She'll have people to do all her work for her, and she'll have lots to smile about. Once I have the Raven Coronet and am rich and powerful I shall see that everyone who was ever kind to me is well cared for."

Desirée fell silent then – as if she realized that she was forgetting something important. Chewing her lip nervously, she struggled to surface from her confusion. But it was to no avail.

All this time Desirée's magical companion kept cantering on untiringly. They had followed the highway for much of their journey, but now Crystal balked as they approached one last bit of civilization, and unicorn and rider turned from the main road. There was no danger of them getting lost; the unicorn was drawn unerringly to the powerful magic of the Coronet by its own enchanted instincts.

At long last Faerwood loomed in front of them, its huge trees blocking out the lightening sky. Crystal slowed to a trot as she picked her way carefully between the trunks. Even so, it was not long before Desirée had to dismount or risk being cracked on the head by an errant tree branch. Barely a trace of the pre-dawn light succeeded in making its way to the forest floor, and Desirée could see little of the surrounding landscape, yet Crystal's silver-white coat shone despite the gloom. Desirée focused on the comforting sight of the unicorn rather than letting her thoughts stray to whatever evils might lurk in the shadows.

Autumn leaves crunched under Desirée's feet. The young woman shivered, fear and excitement amplifying the effect of the chill dawn air.

"Hurry, Crystal!" she whispered nervously. "We'll find the treasure and get out of these nasty woods and be free to do whatever we please!"

The urge to either dash forward recklessly or to run away home was tempered by Desirée's fear of the dark, treacherous landscape – and the certainty that she would be lost without her magical guide. Even Crystal twitched her tail anxiously as she pressed forward. The unicorn's hooves negotiated fallen limbs and other obstacles soundlessly, while her ears pricked up as if straining to hear the siren call of the Coronet.

It was another hour before they finally reached the crypt. During that time, the morning had at last found its way through the forest canopy, and the resulting shafts of sunlight held glittering specks of dust dancing within them. Up ahead, unicorn and human could see a particularly broad beam of light pierce the foliage to illuminate an earthen mound that tree and bush had left untouched. Freshly fallen leaves covered the entire bare space ankle-deep, and even where the land sloped sharply the leaves yet clung to downed twigs and climbing vines to form a solid shroud over this patch of earth. But, when a gust of wind came from nowhere to set the leaves a-twirling in glowing, golden circlets, Desirée caught sight of a door set into the side of the hill.

"Oh Crystal! There's magic all around us! Just look at it – just *feel* it! And the door, the door to the crypt, I can see it now! It's here – the crypt is here!" An odd mix of contentment and excitement bubbled up within the girl.

The unicorn moved forward into the clearing, but promptly came to a stop again at the overgrown door of the crypt. Unhappily, she pawed the ground. The animal had been drawn to the Coronet's magic but had no means to unlock the tomb.

Desirée knelt in front of the door and began to push aside the vines and earth that covered it. Her dainty fingers were soon caked with dirt but still they slid along the cool surface of the ancient, carved stone trying to brush away the dust of eons. So engrossed was Desirée in her work that she took no note when Crystal's ears suddenly pricked up and the unicorn shied nervously away from the crypt to vanish into the surrounding trees.

Nor was Desirée aware of the young centaur who'd been trailing them since they entered Faerwood. Now he stood just beyond the gap in the trees and watched the female human unhappily. She was young and beautiful and fragile and reminded him of the wood nymphs that had still dwelled in the Faerwood of his childhood, wood nymphs that had all died or moved on since that time. Yet he knew his duty; it was a responsibility shared by all the members of his race and sealed by a thousand-year-old vow.

The centaur pulled an arrow from the quiver he wore and cocked it upon his bow. The goal was not to kill, but to wound. Killing was an evil only done out of absolute necessity; wounding would suffice. The wounded human would serve as a warning to others against entering Faerwood. And any rantings from her about the crypt would be dismissed as hallucinations. The Raven Coronet – and humanity – would be safe for awhile longer.

He raised his bow and pulled taut the bowstring. But just as he let the arrow fly, he felt Crystal's horn pierce his elbow, thus sending the missile astray. The centaur cried out in agony. At his tormented shriek, Crystal reared back in a frantic attempt to pull free of her victim's wound. With a gruesome tearing of centaur flesh, the unicorn's horn came clear. Crystal raced for her companion – only to find Desirée face down in the leaves, the wayward bolt projecting from her back.

With teeth clenched in pain, the centaur cradled his mangled arm and watched the frantic unicorn nuzzle her fallen friend. The arrow that had been intended for Desirée's shoulder had been sent just far enough off-course to lodge instead in the woman's heart.

Quietly, he cursed at this outcome. "By my hide and hooves! 'Twas not my intention!" He could see Crystal gripping the arrow's shaft with her teeth and tugging gingerly in a desperate attempt to withdraw the dart.

"Hold there!" the centaur called to her as he stepped forward. Crystal released the shaft and lowered her horn threateningly in his direction. He tried to make the creature understand. "It was an accident. I did not aim to kill. If you want the arrow removed, let me do it. 'Tis a task more suited to hands than teeth."

Crystal raised her horn in wary acquiescence. Cautiously, the centaur approached Desirée's corpse; he had no desire to invite another attack, for his arm already pained him fiercely. Without taking his eyes from Crystal's horn, the centaur reached forward with his good arm and wrapped his fingers about the fatal bolt. One swift yank, and it was out.

The centaur stepped back, bloody arrow in hand, and observed Crystal's next actions with fascination. Delicately, the unicorn used her horn to tear Desirée's blouse away from the wound. Then she gently placed the tip of her horn to the bare skin of the human. A healing radiance poured from the unicorn's horn and swept across the woman's flesh like the whitecaps of a tiny ocean wave washing across the sand, a wave that withdraws again to leave the surface clean and unmarked. The centaur could not help but mutter in amazement: "I had heard of their healing powers but never had I imagined that they could cure such a wound!"

Yet something was still wrong. Desirée's flesh now whole but the woman lay as unmoving as before. Crystal nuzzled the inert form and looked up woefully at the centaur. He shook his head helplessly, for he could see what had happened. The unicorn might be able to heal the flesh, but she could not restart the heart. Even a creature with such magic as Crystal possessed could not reclaim a soul from death.

244

The centaur felt a heavy weight in his chest as he gazed at the mournful scene. There was nothing he could do here. It was time for him to tend to his own injury, and he certainly could not expect the unicorn to heal it under the circumstances.

The stallion turned and moved off sorrowfully in search of a centaur elder capable of helping him. He would send someone else back to guard the crypt in his place – and to deal with the corpse and the unicorn.

CHAPTER 26

RAVEN MAGIC

Nazera could feel it; she could feel the magic of the Raven Coronet flowing through her. It burned in her veins and made her head spin. The Coronet's voice was inside her thoughts soothing her, praising her, promising her relief from all her hungers. The pull was a thousand times stronger than what she had known all her life in Belton. It was obvious to her now why Aza had hidden the Coronet as far from his blood kin as possible.

"Just how much wizardry did Aza himself possess?" Nazera wondered under her breath. "And how much of it did he and his raven familiars pour into the Coronet?" She could not help but marvel at the magic that crackled in the very air around her.

The witch felt her powers grow with each stride of the mules and realized that it was the troupe's increasing nearness to Faerwood that had made her daily performances more and more impressive these past weeks, not just her own growing expertise or some fleeting burst of marital bliss. Now, as she and Josnah neared Faerwood, it was a small enough thing for the witch to toss out a thread of this legendary magic to speed their journey. With a mere flick of Nazera's fingers, the mules broke into an easy gallop, a stride far too smooth and too fast for any common beast of burden to manage on their own.

"There's Faerwood," came Josnah's voice from beside her.

Nazera merely nodded at the blatantly obvious remark. The ancient forest had been a dark line on the horizon for some time, one that had widened and taken on more specific features as they approached it. The morning sun shone brightly upon the towering expanse of trees, and a person could hardly have doubted that this was indeed the legendary forest the pair had traveled so far to reach.

The road ahead, such as it was, curved to the right to end at the old fortress, but Nazera had other ideas. With the Coronet singing in her brain, she clucked to the mules eagerly, and the enchanted beasts veered left into the meadow to head straight for the timberline. In the blink of an eye, they had reached the trees and the witch was reining in the animals.

Nazera spoke impatiently: "We'll have to go on foot from here."

"Are you sure you can find the way?" asked Josnah as he helped Nazera down from the wagon. "I have already spent far too many days searching these woods fruitlessly."

His response was a haughty glare from the witch.

Chastened, Josnah fell silent and went to his horse. Poor Windweaver stood to the rear of the wagon, panting and flecked with sweat. They had tied the animal's lead rope to the hitch for the journey, and when Nazera had enchanted the mules he'd been left to keep up as best he could. Patting the tired beast sympathetically, Josnah pulled a longsword from the horse's pack and hung it upon his belt. He glanced toward the fort in the distance and wondered if anyone there had noticed the travelers. He doubted it, given the watchmen's usual level of apathy.

Even a delay so brief as this one caused Nazera to fidget anxiously. When Josnah was at last ready, the pair strode purposefully through the outermost line of trees and into Faerwood itself. As they entered the forest, Josnah peered into the darkness around them trying his best to watch for danger. But he was soon forced to abandon any attempts at caution to focus solely on keeping up with the determined witch.

For her own part, Nazera moved through the forest with an unerring sense of direction as she obeyed the summons of the Coronet. Every nerve and synapse sought to trace the magic that boiled within her blood to its source. Overhead, the leaves had begun their annual display of autumn reds and oranges. Late morning sunlight shone through the latticework above to dapple the skin of the humans with gold and crimson.

The pair hurried along for what seemed to Josnah to be both hours and mere seconds. Time had no meaning to the man as he focused on nothing but following Nazera. He had no idea from which direction they had come, or in which direction they traveled.

At last, the witch's steps slowed, and she came to a halt. Over her shoulder Josnah caught a glimpse of something white moving about ahead of them.

"Crystal," Nazera muttered in surprise. More cautiously, she began moving forward again until she finally emerged into the ancient forest clearing within which stood the crypt. As she stepped from the dim crush of the trees, her eyes fell upon the form at Crystal's feet.

"Desirée..." the witch murmured with dismay. A stab of guilt managed to penetrate Nazera's Coronet-induced fog.

"What?" exclaimed Josnah, craning his neck to see past his guide. "How did she and Crystal get here? And what happened to her?" He pushed by Nazera and moved cautiously past the nervous unicorn to reach the prone figure. "She's dead," he said solemnly after searching for a pulse under the girl's rapidly cooling skin.

The former guardsman took a deep breath and worked to regain his composure. He was no stranger to death, but never before had he seen it take such a young woman in such strange circumstances. Nor had he ever before felt somehow responsible for the death of an innocent. "What do you suppose killed her?"

he asked his companion. "There's blood upon what remains of her blouse, but no mark upon her flesh."

Nazera shook her head; for a brief moment the witch felt tears of shame welling in her own eyes. She had no answer for Josnah, but she was sure that if she'd just left the Coronet alone, Desirée would still be alive.

"Are we in danger as well, do you think?" continued Josnah, drawing his sword. He looked about anxiously and saw with a start that he at last stood by the elusive crypt that he had sought for so long. Nonetheless, he knew he must focus on their safety before he focused on their prize.

Nazera lifted her gaze from Desirée to stare in surprise at Josnah. Her mind might be muddied by the insistent pull of the Coronet, but she knew immediately that the mortal was right – *and* exactly what to do about any threat to their well-being. It was not just ancient magic that had grown stronger within Nazera over these past hours, but ancient wisdom also. The old enchantments and the knowledge of how to use them swelled in the witch's breast with every breath she drew.

"Of course; how stupid of me!" Nazera replied, chiding herself for her carelessness. With a sweep of her hand Nazera formed a spell of protection about the pair, a spell that she had had no knowledge of mere hours ago.

It was but an instant later that an arrow whizzed through the air toward Josnah. He raised his sword to deflect the missile but the arrow never reached the blade. Instead, it skidded off sideways several inches short of impact. Nazera smiled with satisfaction to see her spell work so well. Beside her, Josnah strained to see from whence the arrow had come.

"There!" he cried out. Josnah pointed toward the edge of the clearing. "There he is!" The man could just make out a worried centaur beyond some trees, empty bow in hand. Wary of the centaur but satisfied that they were safe for the moment, Josnah turned back to the witch. "Is there nothing you can do for Desirée?"

"There is no magic to resurrect the dead, at least none that would bring her back as she was. There is nothing we can do for her now but offer her a decent burial – *after* we get the Coronet." The witch's voice quivered with urgency as the opiate of the Coronet clouded her reasoning once more.

Nazera stepped close to Josnah and took his hand in both of her own, gripping it so tightly that his fingers tingled. She stared into his eyes with an expression that showed the depth of both her wonder and her fear.

As she gazed at him, a new understanding of Josnah's part in all this bubbled up in Nazera's brain. He was no longer just some treasure seeker she was humoring, or some tool for vengeance on Thaedra. He was the Coronet's chosen; he was the great King Dargason incarnate. It had never been meant for Nazera herself to wear the Coronet; she knew that. No, it would rest upon the man before her.

And so she admitted to Josnah what she had kept secret from all but family. "It's calling to me," she whispered fiercely. "It's called to me all my days – but now, now, it sings, it shrieks, it tears at me! With each step towards this tomb, the Raven Coronet's voice in my head has grown a hundred times louder. I *must* set it free. It has been trapped for so long. The Coronet *demands* release. It begs me to set it on thy brow."

A strange mix of dread and fervent anticipation filled Josnah despite the calming warmth emanating from the crypt. He pulled loose his hand from Nazera's grasp and bent to lift Desirée's corpse from where it rested at the base of the stone door. The sooner he set their fallen comrade aside, the sooner Nazera could see to their mutual goal. Laying the dead girl down gently at the edge of the clearing, he returned to stand guard at Nazera's shoulder. Eagerly, he gestured to the witch to unlock the Coronet's tomb.

Nazera took up where Desirée had left off, continuing to clear the debris from the stone that yet separated her from the Raven Coronet. Her fingers lovingly caressed the timeworn pictographs carved into the door's surface – the rough granite felt as if the finest silk to her bewitched touch. Nazera could not resist pausing briefly to press her ear to the cold stone, as if in this fashion she might hear the Coronet's sweet, calm, whispered wooing of earlier rather than the deafening cacophony of terse commands now swirling in her head.

Moment after moment slipped by as the descendent of Aza worked at her task. And all the while unicorn and centaur each paced anxiously a safe distance away, unable to interfere.

CHAPTER 27

ANCIENT RHYMES

Faylah stepped into the dappled shade of Faerwood and paused for Marcus to slip off her back. The normally auburn fur of her withers was a matted chocolate brown and bore white speckles of sweat. Her long hair stuck to the back of her human neck despite fall's nip in the air.

"Home," she whispered in hushed reverence. The cool, green familiarity of the forest did much to ease the aches and exhaustion she felt from their long, desperate journey. She moved forward with Marcus at her side.

Marcus looked at her curiously. "I thought your kind had rejected you. Is coming back to their lands really such a pleasure?"

"Home is still home. It is the home of my youth, before I was cast out." She shrugged as she spoke, but her honeyed voice was nonetheless laden with emotion.

"And what will the others think of your return to their precious Faerwood? Marcus stopped momentarily to leave a mark upon a tree with one of his daggers for the others to follow.

"In truth, they'll be distressed," she admitted, still moving onward into the woods, "but not for the reasons you might think."

"For what reason then?" asked the assassin as he hurried to catch up again.

"I suppose there's no point in secrets anymore," she conceded. "I was, as I said all along, a misfit among my people.

My appearance made the other centaurs uncomfortable, and their discomfort in turn made me unhappy. But the wiser of the herd knew perfectly well that, whatever prank of the gods might be behind my unusual features, it did not make me evil. I had proved myself to be honest and intelligent through all the years of my childhood. Thus, when it was decided that I would part ways with the others and set off on my own, I was asked by the elders to keep an eye out for anyone who might endanger the Raven Coronet that we were all sworn to protect.

"When I ran into your little troupe that evening," Faylah continued, "perhaps I might have joined you anyway. But when I saw the raven tattoo on Nazera's shoulder and heard that she was a witch from the ancient city of Belton, I was convinced that she must be a descendent of Aza's and a link to the Coronet. Having learned that much, there was no question that I should join you." Faylah finished her explanation, "The centaurs of Faerwood will know that if I'm am returning now, it is only because something is seriously wrong."

"If you were a spy all along," said Marcus, "couldn't you have stopped this mess before it got this far?" Even as he spoke, the assassin wasn't sure which irked him more; that Faylah had not been entirely honest about her reasons for joining the troupe, or that, having joined the troupe, she had not managed to fulfill her mission and save them all from disaster.

"Short of killing Josnah or Nazera in cold blood," Faylah replied, "I'm not sure what could have been done. Nazera claimed she would never agree to help Josnah since she knew how disastrous the reappearance of the Coronet would be. I had no way of knowing that some little intrigue of romance and revenge could change her all-too-human mind in a matter of minutes." The centauress shook her head regretfully. "And I'm still not sure how Desirée fits in, although I gather from Thaedra that there's some sort of connection between Thaedra's first husband and our young dancer – *and* that Thaedra's late husband was obsessed with the Raven Coronet. He seems to have passed his obsession on to his father-in-law, Josnah. Perhaps one man or the other somehow infected Desirée with these insidious desires, as well."

"Oh my poor, misguided Desirée," murmured Marcus, agitatedly leaving a particularly deep mark on one hapless tree. "I hope she's all right."

The pair traveled on in worried silence after that. Every so often Marcus would cut a mark into a tree as they passed, or Faylah would stop to examine a broken branch and try to estimate how far behind Nazera and Josnah they were. They had entered the woods at the spot where they found Nazera's abandoned wagon, so they knew that they followed the same path the witch and her companion had taken.

"We can't be far behind them," mused the centauress. "I'm sure we made better time by hoof than they by wagon, and I doubt they're gaining any on us now weaving through these trees.

They hurried on until a rich, bass voice sounded softly nearby. "Hello, Sister."

Faylah stopped and turned to look toward the sound. "Hello, Brother. How goes it?"

A centaur stallion stepped into sight. From his appearance, Marcus doubted that the two were genuinely siblings and suspected that this was simply a traditional greeting.

"Not well, Faylah," he replied. "One centaur has been wounded and one human has died already. The other humans use magic to repel our arrows as they seek to open the crypt. I fear they will succeed, and all will be lost for humankind."

"And what of centaur-kind?" interrupted Marcus. "The crown does not affect you, as well?"

"It does not," he explained, shifting his attention from Faylah to Marcus. "At least not as deeply; it only makes us reluctant to do the wearer harm. But with the protection magic

255

the witch wields, and all of humanity soon at the wearer's beck and call, that will be more than enough to render us helpless to save you humans from one another."

Marcus abruptly realized that the centaur had spoken of at least three humans at the crypt and one of them was dead. "The dead human," he asked urgently, "*is it a man or a woman?*"

"A woman," came the reply. "Young and pretty. It was an accident – a lunge by the unicorn sent the guard's arrow astray."

Marcus' hand gripped the dagger he carried more tightly. For a moment, it seemed as if the assassin would turn his knife upon this four-legged bearer of bad tidings. Faylah moved to put her bulk between the two males, although she knew that the skilled and wiry performer would have no trouble getting past her should he choose.

Seeing his path blocked by a creature he considered his friend, Marcus relaxed his grip on the knife. Still, his distress was so great that the throaty, anguished sound that issued from his lips when he next spoke sounded barely human. "*Which way?*" he demanded.

The centaur looked to Faylah for advice; she simply nodded her ascent to Marcus' wishes. Without another word, the centaur turned and led them toward the crypt. Now it was Faylah bringing up the rear and using her own dagger to mark the trail.

As they closed in on their destination, Faylah spotted a familiar white flash of mane through the trees, and seconds later Crystal stood at her side.

"There, there, Crystal," said Faylah soothingly, running her hand down the fidgeting unicorn's neck. "You didn't know what would happen. You could only follow your magical nature." Pulling away reluctantly, the centauress went on: "But I must go now, must go and see what can yet be done."

The unicorn hung back unhappily while Faylah moved forward to join Marcus and the centaur. The three stepped into the little clearing, and Marcus' gaze fell immediately upon his lover's body. He took no notice of Josnah and Nazera as he leapt forward to cradle Desirée's corpse in his arms. Her sightless eyes looked up at him; his own eyes filled with tears.

"Oh, gods... Desirée..." he choked, gently closing her eyes with the palm of his hand. He lowered her carefully back down and was suddenly on his feet, a dagger in each hand.

"You couldn't let it be..." he growled at Josnah. He took a step toward the older man threateningly. "My Desirée would still be alive if you had not filled her head with the hope that the blasted Coronet was real."

"She knew it was real the same way I knew," protested Josnah, "from the stories Old Man Miller told of how he stumbled upon this crypt decades ago."

'But Nazera would have kept her secrets to herself were it not for you, and Desirée would have forgotten her wild dreams," Marcus insisted as he took another step forward.

"Marcus," Faylah interrupted, "killing Josnah will not bring Desirée back, even were Josnah not under Nazera's protection at present. Take poor Desirée out of here and leave Nazera and Josnah to the rest of us." Faylah spoke in part out of sympathy, but pragmatism also influenced the centauress. It hardly seemed prudent to have a trained assassin in the vicinity should Josnah gain the Coronet and enthrall those around him. It would only make the situation far more dangerous.

Marcus started to protest but changed his mind. The fight seemed to have gone out of him. He sheathed his knives and carefully lifted the girl's corpse. The rest of the group was silent until the little man and his mournful burden were out of sight among the trees.

Faylah turned her attention to Nazera who still knelt before the stone door. "Nazera, we have been friends a long time; *listen* to me. Will you not stop while there is yet time? It was the will of your ancestors that Aza's creation be locked away for all time. Would you defy the bloodline that bore you?"

Nazera turned her head away from the crypt to look at Faylah. The centauress could see the hint of madness in her eyes and knew at once that the witch was overwhelmed by the forces emanating from the entombed Coronet. Nazera replied to Faylah's entreaties with desperation in her voice: "I can't abandon it. It's *calling* to me."

Faylah moved as if to stop Nazera by force, but was blocked by the invisible wall the witch had thrown up around Josnah and herself. Faylah and her four-legged companions stood by helplessly, their sense of dread mounting, as Nazera turned back to the door, intent on removing any overgrowth that might yet hinder access to the crypt.

All too soon thereafter, Nazera was finally satisfied that the door was clear enough. Rising, she stood back and extended her hands toward the ancient entrance. Her palms were angled together and upwards. Her fingers were bent back at an impossible angle. Her arms offered an embrace of such power, such longing, that the limbs themselves appeared stretched and distorted.

Softly, she began chanting.

"Feathers of velvet night,
Wisdom of old,
Wove here this ancient crown,
Its legend oft told.

Her voice gained in strength. Her tongue wrapped itself around every word and made love to it. Now there seemed to be two voices coming from her lips, now ten, now a hundred, until the voices of a thousand of her kind overlaid her own to sing the rhyme in unison.

The words wove their magic there in the midst of the forest trees.

Free now this magic great,

258

THE RAVEN CORONET

This crypt open wide,
That legend might grace the brow
Of this man at my side.

Centaur, unicorn, and human all stared at the witch as if they were frozen in place. But as her final words reverberated through the trees, and the last notes of the song were replaced by a creaking from the very earth upon which they stood, the onlookers found their attention drawn from the enchantress to the door of the crypt itself. All present knew that a millennium had passed since the tomb's interior had known the light of day. It seemed impossible that anything could open it now. Yet finally, with a cloud of dust, and an immense groan that rumbled and pealed through earth and air to set the listeners' teeth on edge, the door swung open.

CHAPTER 28

FREED

By the time Falmund's wagon reached Faerwood, the mules were on the verge of collapse; even Marlon had no breath left with which to bemoan his poor treatment. Other than one brief stop, during which Falmund had traded places with Hargot, it had been a desperate and hushed journey. Thaedra and Falmund had spelled each other as driver and had taken comfort in each other's presence, but they had spoken very little. Hour after hour had passed with no sound but the rumbling of wagon wheels, the jingling of bit and buckles, and the creaking "whoop" of the mules' labored breathing. Now Falmund turned to rap his knuckles against the little window behind the driver's seat.

"Hargot! We're there! I can see your wagon just ahead!" Falmund called to the man riding inside.

Thaedra brought the wagon to a stop next to Nazera's. She yanked forward on the brake pole to clamp the wheels in place, and then looped the reins loosely about the handle to keep them from being trampled beneath the mules' hooves. Hurriedly, she jumped from the wagon.

"Ouch," she exclaimed, as joints stiff from the long drive absorbed the impact of her leap.

"Are you all right, love?" Falmund inquired, climbing down a bit more cautiously himself.

"Aye, Falmund. Merely a tad less nimble than I thought," she replied wryly.

Just then Hargot emerged from the wagon. Thaedra and Falmund stared at him.

"Hargot?" Thaedra began uncertainly. "You look – different." Instead of being a reflection of her own disheveled state, Hargot looked energized and self-assured.

"It's the Coronet, isn't it?" asked Falmund.

Hargot nodded. "Primeval magic is thick here. Even a magic wielder with so small a gift as mine is affected by it. The Raven Coronet knows freedom is at hand, and it is flexing its power."

"Do you think we're too late?" Thaedra asked anxiously.

"No, there's yet a chance," Hargot replied. "But we must move quickly!"

"You two," Falmund directed, "fetch water for the mules and for Josnah's horse here before they collapse of thirst, then we'll be off. I'll get the swords and scout ahead for the trail Faylah and Marcus promised us."

Hargot opened his mouth as if to argue but apparently thought better of it. He and Thaedra did as they were told, drawing water from the large barrels strapped to the side of each wagon. Just as they finished, they heard Falmund's voice from within the forest.

"Here's the trail! They were good as their word and marked it well."

Leaving the water buckets for the animals, the two humans hastened into Faerwood after their friend. Behind them, Marlon recovered his voice just in time for the trio to catch his hoarse moans fading into the distance: "Ah me. I shall never be the same after such a cruel run..."

Thaedra felt a twinge of guilt for having driven the mules so hard but it had been necessary. As she and Hargot caught up to Falmund, Hargot pushed past the strongman and took the lead.

"We don't need the trail," Hargot declared firmly as he strode deeper into the woods. "Even *I* have enough knowledge of magic to find the Coronet now."

THE RAVEN CORONET

Falmund and Thaedra looked at each other unhappily. Neither the obvious strength of the Raven Coronet's magic nor its growing effect upon their companion bode well for their mission. Without a word, Falmund handed Thaedra a sheath and one of the newly sharpened swords that he carried. Quickly, the pair strapped on their weapons and followed the wizard.

Ahead, Hargot moved so rapidly through the trees that even the two trained fighters had trouble keeping up, especially since the swords now hanging from Falmund's and Thaedra's belts were in constant danger of catching on fallen branches. More than once, Thaedra or Falmund had to pause to free their weapon before racing desperately after Hargot.

Skillfully, the wizard threaded his way around such obstacles. Yet his vision seemed focused not on their immediate surroundings but rather on some point far ahead of them. And so it was Falmund who first caught sight of Marcus approaching them.

"Ho! Marcus!" the strongman called out. "What news of Nazera and the rest?" Then he saw Marcus's burden and his voice fell. "Oh gods, I'm sorry." Marcus' expression and Desirée's pallor told Falmund all he needed to know.

Marcus said nothing in reply but simply continued to place one foot in front of the other, as if that was all that his mind could manage at present. Hargot stepped wordlessly from the path to allow Marcus passage. The wizard glanced agitatedly in the direction from which Marcus had come but nonetheless waited while Falmund pumped the man for information.

"Marcus," Falmund pleaded, "you must tell me what's going on."

The bereaved assassin paused to look at Falmund dazedly. "Desirée..." he began and his eyes fell to the corpse in his arms, "...Desirée was killed by a centaur trying to protect the crypt." He looked back up at Falmund. "They say it was an accident. It must have been an accident, mustn't it? Who would have chosen to harm my sweet little flower?"

"Marcus," Falmund stood blocking the man's path, "what of Nazera? What of Faylah? *What is going on?*" There was an edge of desperation in his voice.

The assassin shrugged and jerked his head over his shoulder. "They're back there, alive, last time I saw them – but not my poor Desirée. No, not my poor, poor Desirée." Marcus fell into anguished silence again. He took a step toward Falmund as if to continue on his mournful trek right through the man before him.

Convinced that any further questioning of Marcus was a waste of valuable time, Falmund and Thaedra took Hargot's cue and stepped aside to allow the assassin to pass. Each of the three in turn placed a comforting hand upon the grieving man's shoulder.

Thaedra felt a tear sliding down her cheek and wiped it away angrily. She would not succumb to despair or sorrow; no, she would grit her teeth and steel herself for whatever was to come. Under her breath Thaedra muttered: "What hasn't killed me has made me stronger. And I swear by all the gods that I'll allow no magic talisman to destroy all that I've won!"

As Marcus moved out of sight behind them, the trio redoubled their efforts to reach the crypt as soon as possible.

Soon they heard Nazera's voice carrying through the trees. But it was different. It was base and alto and soprano layered one atop the other. The words shimmered and danced in the air around them. All three immediately recognized the rhythms and rhymes of the chant as being those from the old children's legend – but these words were different.

"...This crypt open wide,
That legend might grace the brow
Of the man at my side."

THE RAVEN CORONET

From somewhere in front of them, Faylah's voice rang out over the witch's: "Nazera! *Stop!*"

Hargot ran ahead of his comrades and burst into the clearing. Desperately, Nazera's husband added his own entreaties to Faylah's. "*Nazera! I love you! I forgive you! Just let the Coronet be!*"

But it was too late. Hargot was flung back when he collided with Nazera's protection spell in his frantic rush to stop his wife. Falmund and Thaedra themselves stepped from the trees just in time to see Hargot land hard at their feet. At that same moment, the great stone door ground open.

Grey smoke rose in the shaft of sunlight that fell upon the crypt – and the earth *breathed*. Air and dust that had lain untouched in the dark for a thousand years now flowed out of the tomb with an enormous, mournful sigh.

Nazera did not hesitate. She ducked through the doorway and very shortly emerged again bearing an elaborately carved, obsidian box. Its sides bore pictographs similar to those seen on the door to the crypt. Turning to Josnah, Nazera placed the box reverently into his hands and dropped to one knee.

Entranced, Josnah looked first at the box he held and then at the woman kneeling before him. "Rise, oh daughter of Aza!" he commanded in a voice so deep and formal that it surprised even himself.

Nazera rose. "My lord," she spoke solemnly, "I give you the Raven Coronet." She carefully opened the jet-black box in Josnah's hands and removed the crown from its velvet-lined case.

Without taking his eyes from the circlet Nazera held, Josnah bent to one side to place the empty container upon the ground by his feet before drawing himself upright once more.

A gasp echoed through the clearing as each person present saw ancient legend become real. There, in Nazera's hands, was the silvery wreath of fairy tales, the wreath that Verin and then Josnah had sought for so long. The onlookers were transfixed.

265

Rays of sunlight gleamed off the Coronet's tiny, iridescent feathers and each feather's color fluctuated ceaselessly. It was impossible to tell from one moment to the next if the crown was silver, or black, or a muted reflection of every color that ever was.

Slowly, deliberately, Nazera lifted the Raven Coronet high – before setting it firmly upon Josnah's head.

CHAPTER 29

FEALTY

As Nazera stepped back again from her newly crowned king, she sensed something had changed. Until that moment, the Raven Coronet's power had been felt only by those who already knew the ways of magic, its call heard only by she whose blood was one with the blood of its creator. Now things were different.

"*Nazera!*" Hargot hissed at his wife. "Nazera, get back! It doesn't need you anymore." He gestured desperately for her to come to him, as if fearing for her safety.

"Nazera," he repeated, extending his hand. "Please come with me. I still love..."

He stopped mid-sentence and looked confused. His lips moved, and he seemed at first to be trying to form the word "you," but no sound issued forth. When he tried again, his lips mouthed "Josnah" instead.

Even as Hargot fell silent, his entreaties at last penetrated Nazera's consciousness. The witch looked from Josnah to her besieged husband, and the fog began to clear from her eyes. She had done what the Coronet commanded. The pleading, cajoling, insistent voice in Nazera's head was finally quiet.

A dim awareness seeped to the surface of Nazera's conscious mind, an awareness that the Coronet's silence meant that it was satisfied. And if the Coronet were satisfied, then that meant that the enslavement of all humankind was at hand, that only Josnah with the crown upon his head and herself with the blood of Aza in her veins would remain untouched.

"Josnah and I..." she muttered, "...only Josnah and I." She looked dazedly at the man in front of her and watched him drink in the contentment and power emanating from the artifact.

"He wears his great Raven Coronet at last," Nazera observed barely whispering, "and see how he savors it." Josnah's expression appeared somehow familiar – and then Nazera understood. "An addiction...it is an addiction to him." The witch shook her head. "I was wrong; he is as much in its thrall as anyone."

The newly awakened witch looked around her at her friends, all of them in various stages of struggle against the enchantment she had loosed. Again, her eyes settled on Josnah and the Coronet. "No, 'tis only I – I alone in all the world am free to follow or to forget that wretched crown." Nazera briefly considered strolling away from the scene before her, away from Faerwood, totally unfettered by the demands of the Coronet for the first time in her life.

But she could not. For what would become of her comrades? Nazera tore her eyes away from Josnah and looked more closely at the humans and centaurs that stood about her wrapped up in their inner conflicts.

"How...how did it come to this?" Nazera asked aloud. But no one answered. The witch looked from one to the next. "Hargot?" she queried. "Falmund? Faylah?" Her friends were far too busy resisting the Coronet's spell to respond. And Josnah? Josnah merely stood there dumbly offering his recent ally a triumphant grin.

Nazera went on sifting numbly through her own thoughts. Until a short time ago, she had been aware of little except the need to reach the crypt and liberate the Coronet. Gradually, she put together what had happened and tried to remember why,

why she had chosen this path after so many years of fighting the temptation.

"Thaedra..." the witch muttered. Memories and emotions began to emerge from the gray confusion in Nazera's head. A smile tugged at the corners of the witch's mouth when the image of the swordswoman crawling before Josnah sprang again to mind.

But as understanding continued to return, it was harder to smile now, harder to shut out the sense that Thaedra was guiltless and Nazera herself was to blame for everything.

"Ah well," the witch murmured with nonchalant maliciousness, "what's done is done. I'll enjoy Thaedra's comeuppance for a bit and then correct the situation before it goes too far."

Nazera's disoriented brain still did not grasp the seriousness of the group's predicament, of all *humanity's* predicament. Soon enough, the old tales of horror from her childhood would come back to her, but right now she was too recently freed from the lovely promises of the deceptive crown.

As Nazera struggled to drive away the last wisps of her previous trance, one by one her comrades began slipping into the hypnotic trap from which she had just escaped.

It was Falmund who was first to succumb to the wave of magic that had begun radiating outward from Josnah. Without Hargot's wizardry, Thaedra's hatred, or a centaur's resistance, he had little to protect him from falling under the Coronet's thrall. The very same calm congeniality that had gained Falmund the devotion of his friends lost him this battle. The seductive fog emanating from the Coronet wrapped itself about the strongman to become one with Falmund's soul.

Falmund stepped toward Josnah and dropped to one knee with his head bowed. "My lord," he spoke reverently.

"Falmund," said Josnah magnanimously – though only barely managing to conceal his glee. "You may rise."

Falmund rose as commanded and lifted his head to gaze in adoration at his liege.

Nazera cringed to view the strongman humbled. From where she stood, the witch could see the look in Falmund's eyes. Her stomach knotted in anguish and tears blurred her vision. What she saw in Falmund's expression was love, admiration, and utter, total devotion. So many times Nazera had wished to snare Falmund in her orbit, had wished to be the sun to his moon. And now she at last beheld all that she had ever longed for in those eyes. But once again it was not for her!

Nazera bit her lip and drew a ragged breath. "Watching him fawn over Thaedra was bad enough, but this..." she choked, "...this groveling before that fool Josnah and the damned Coronet... This *I cannot allow!*"

The Coronet might have released its grip on the witch, but now Nazera's own jealous nature took hold – now Nazera's own empty, aching, neediness dictated her actions just as surely as had the enchanted crown's entreaties. The witch's entire being seethed at the unfairness of Falmund's misplaced affections. All that mattered to her in that instant was to liberate Falmund from his bewitched state.

"I should have known that Falmund would fall under its spell with the others," Nazera muttered shaking her head, "but all I could hear was the voice of that accursed crown. But no more!" She would know Falmund's friendship again. Even if his affection never reached the kind of impassioned devotion that she had always craved, it would be better than the twisted tableau she saw before her.

"But how to break the spell?" Nazera wondered. She shuddered at the thought of grabbing the crown from Josnah's head only to have the Coronet's relentless pleadings begin anew in her temples. Nazera found herself in awe of the power and determination that Aza must have possessed to take the Coronet from Dargason and set it in its crypt so many eons ago. The crown's entreaties would have been reverberating through his skull all the while that he was locking it away.

Still, Nazera knew that her own powers were hardly insignificant, especially with so much of her ancestral magic crackling in the ether about her rather than entombed in the earth. Bathed as she was in the ancient magicks, Nazera realized that she had another option.

"I cannot fight the crown person by person," the witch mused, "nor dull its effects over a wide range. But I believe I can extend my immunity to a person or two of my choosing. And I choose Falmund!" It occurred to Nazera that her husband might deserve such consideration, too, but when the witch glanced at Hargot, he seemed to be holding his own. She returned her attentions to the strongman.

Nazera waved her hand, and Falmund's eyes cleared. She waved her hand again and withdrew the spell of protection that yet guarded Josnah. Nazera had given him what he wanted; now he would have to keep it on his own.

Warring emotions churned chaotically within the witch – regret, remorse, fear, love, loyalty, and longing – but it was envy that drove her now. Nazera watched with satisfaction as Falmund's eyes, eyes that had held such devotion for Josnah a moment earlier, narrowed in anger at his liege instead. Brief had been Falmund's subjugation; briefer still was the time it took him to regain his senses.

Silently, Nazera cheered the strongman on as Falmund slid his sword from its sheath threateningly. Josnah was her partner no longer. It was Falmund who had her allegiance.

"Take it off, Josnah," Falmund said coldly.

"What? A moment ago I was your lord!" Josnah's hand went instantly to his temple. Feeling the crown still secure upon him, he looked around him in bewilderment until his eyes fell on Nazera's smug half-smile. "What games do you play, witch?" he asked angrily.

"I brought you to the Raven Coronet," she answered slowly, relishing the power she had to defy him, relishing that she and Falmund were a team against the usurper. "I made no promise beyond that."

Seeing his former ally would be of no help, Josnah drew his own sword and turned to stave off Falmund. "I have no intention of removing the crown," Josnah said firmly to his adversary. "The Raven Coronet is mine. I paid for it with years of my life, and I shall reap its riches now."

"You *chose* to spend your life as you did. You should have enjoyed the days the gods gave you, not let them all slip by while you searched for some forbidden magic you thought would please you better!" insisted Falmund. "I say it again – return that accursed wreath to its tomb!"

Nazera saw Josnah glance at the other troupe members, saw him watch as Hargot and Thaedra's faces contorted with emotion in their struggles against the Coronet's influence. She knew that Hargot was drawing on every ounce of his magic to resist and that Thaedra was using years of mistrust to repel the wave of daughterly devotion that threatened to wash over her. Nonetheless, it was clear Josnah believed that time was on his side. Could the Coronet's chosen hold off the younger, more-fit Falmund in a sword fight until his soon-to-be allies joined in the fray?

Josnah made one more attempt to delay Falmund's attack. "But I *did* cherish what the gods gave! Every day that the sun rose on my beloved Thaney, I cherished to the depths of my soul," Josnah insisted. Then he went on bitterly: "But Thaney was taken from me, and even my little Thaedra turned away, and now I want – nay, I *demand* that if I am unable to have the love of the woman I want, then I shall have the love of all mankind instead!"

"You're a mad, selfish bastard," spat Falmund in disgust as he raised his sword to attack.

Josnah raised his own sword, as well, and for a brief moment the two former guardsmen stood eyeing each other and wondering whose skill with a sword would prove to be greater.

Grabbing the initiative, Falmund abruptly swept his sword in a narrow circle down and to his right, only to bring it up again angled toward Josnah's head as he endeavored to strike the Coronet from his opponent's brow. The move came close but never connected with the crown, for Josnah dodged to his own right. Raising his free hand to his left ear, Josnah felt the sticky warmth of first blood dripping from his earlobe.

With the failure of Falmund's attempt to dislodge the Coronet, the two men were resigned to a bloody battle that would leave one or both of them severely wounded, if not dead.

Falmund stole a worried glance at his wife and Hargot. Though Josnah seemed not to care, the two human bystanders remained in the center of the clearing; they were too focused on warding off the effect of the Coronet to step safely behind the tree line. It was obvious that, in this confined space, Falmund would have to be very careful not to lodge his sword in a tree – or in his friends.

Falmund swung again, this time for Josnah's sword arm. There was nothing fancy in the move, just a powerful downward stroke toward the older man's elbow. Josnah blocked the move expertly, bringing his sword up to knock Falmund's aside and continuing 'round to slash at his opponent's leather clothed thighs. The leather gave way and the tip of Josnah's sword drew blood of its own.

Suddenly Falmund fell to one knee, not because of the sword cut, but because the now-enthralled Hargot had just landed a sharp kick from behind to the tender hollow of Falmund's leg joint.

Falmund dared take only the briefest of looks over his shoulder, but the ensorcelled magic wielder towering behind him bore little resemblance to the Hargot he'd been traveling with these many months.

As Falmund turned back to parry Josnah's latest sword-swing, he winced at the stinging of sparks on the back of his neck, and those comrades standing nearby could smell his singed hair. These fiery nettles were not the pretty sparks of a circus show; these were flying embers designed to ignite clothing and hair alike.

Nazera raised her hand to intervene but Falmund was quicker than the still-distracted witch. Frantically, he dug the fingers of his free hand into the layer of twigs, pebbles, and earth that lay beneath this autumn's fallen leaves. Falmund flung this mixture over his shoulder into Hargot's face.

Mercifully, the fiery shower ceased – but relief came too late for Falmund. Hargot's attack had given Josnah the advantage he needed; the usurper's sword point was already at Falmund's throat.

CHAPTER 30

CONFLICT

Through all of this, Thaedra watched her lover's struggle helplessly. She saw Falmund trapped on one knee, saw Nazera pull Hargot aside and attempt to restrain him ere he could do more harm, but Thaedra herself could do nothing. Every fiber of her being strove to remain true to who she was, who she wanted to be – true to the woman she had fought all these years to become – and this endeavor took every ounce of her strength. She had nothing left to give Falmund.

In her mind, Thaedra could see the magic of the Coronet reaching to engulf her. Great wings appeared to be stretching out for her, ghostly wings of fog trailing flowing feathers of smoke. These servants of Morpheus sought to grasp her, to hold her, to woo her, to dull her mind and make her dream their sweet dreams of absolute devotion. Magic kissed her cheek and stroked her hair. Engulfed in the warmth of her wraith-like lover, Thaedra felt her resolve melting; she longed to breathe deeply of the comfort and rapture that were being offered her.

"No!" she railed against the spell. "You can't *make* me love you! Verin thought he could *make* me love him but he was *wrong*. I shall choose to whom I pledge myself!" Thaedra shook her head in anger; flying auburn curls broke apart the ethereal wings that clutched her, broke them apart into pale gray wisps of nothingness. The woman's eyes flashed, and her fists were clenched with determination.

Yet it was only seconds before the spell regrouped and the phantom feathers resumed their insistent caresses. Slowly, reluctantly, the grown woman began to give in to the voices that insisted she must love Josnah. Her shoulders drooped; her face went slack.

"No!" Thaedra cried aloud again as she jerked her head back up to stare at her beleaguered husband. It was *Falmund* she loved!

Falmund heard his wife's cry and bargained for time. "Would you kill your daughter's husband?" asked Falmund of Josnah.

Maliciously Josnah quipped, "She's had two husbands. I chose one; she chose one. She killed one..." He didn't bother to finish the sentence. Despite his words, Josnah appeared reluctant to wrong his stepdaughter again.

But inside Thaedra's head, her own thoughts betrayed her to complete Josnah's threat: "...and I shall kill the other!"

"I won't allow it," Thaedra snarled, more to the demons in her mind than to Josnah himself. She took a step closer to the combatants, as if to intervene. Josnah glanced at his daughter uncertainly. Would he have to strike her down, as well?

As Josnah wavered, Falmund managed to raise his own blade and knock his opponent's aside. Scrambling to his feet again, he circled around Josnah toward the crypt itself.

"Blast it, man," Josnah snapped, "can't you stay down? What tricks do you try now?"

In two quick strides, Falmund landed himself atop the crypt. From this elevated vantage point, he swung downward at Josnah's head. A ray of sunlight glinted off the polished metal as it powered viciously through empty air; Josnah had dodged just in time. Josnah slashed at Falmund's ankles. Again, leather split, and blood trickled through.

But before Josnah could complete his sword-stroke and raise it for another attack, Falmund launched himself off the crypt with his left foot, used Josnah's shoulder as a stepping-stone with his right, and landed on his feet in the leaves behind his opponent.

Josnah flinched at the impact on his shoulder and staggered. But he regained his balance before Falmund could take advantage. The older man whirled 'round and taunted: "Nice move. You should use it in your act. *If* you live to have one."

Josnah suddenly smiled. Unbeknownst to Falmund, that last move had brought Falmund within arm's reach of Thaedra. And Thaedra was clearly succumbing to the Coronet's urgings.

"*...And I shall kill the other...*" Thaedra whispered reluctantly next to Falmund's ear. Her hand fell on the hilt of the sword still sheathed at her waist.

With a start, Falmund realized his error and blurted out in panic, "*Thaedra, no!*"

At her husband's cry, Thaedra fought back once more against the Coronet's entreaties. "*Falmund must not die!*" she exclaimed.

Josnah used the moment to swing at Falmund's sword hand. Falmund moved belatedly to parry, but his grip was loose. The older man's blow knocked the sword to the ground. With his foe cornered weaponless before him, Josnah seemed in no rush to strike the final blow. Perhaps, in another moment or two, his daughter would join him to finish off this obstacle to the Coronet's ascendancy.

Thaedra yet resisted. "*...And I shall kill the other!*" The words were forcing their way into her consciousness.

"I shan't," she replied desperately. "*I love him.*" She fought the Coronet's power with images of Falmund's face in the glow of the cabin lamp the previous night, images of the battered and beautiful face of her husband hanging above her as they rediscovered each other.

Even as she tried to draw on last evening's memories, the images she called upon mutated. Now it was Josnah's face hanging over her own and soaking up the radiance of her love.

"Two can play this game of manipulation," Thaedra muttered in angry response. She summoned up more emotions from her past with which to defend herself as she declared with conviction: "You picked a poor way to warm my heart to your master, you foul crown!"

Determinedly, Thaedra forced herself to recall the *panting* and the *sweat* and the *disgust* of having Josnah on top of her. She remembered, too, the ice-cold lump of stone her heart had been then. The pain of her previous life came back with a force that took her breath away.

"Gods help me," she whispered, recoiling at the memories she had dredged up to use as weapons. Thaedra had freed her hurt and hatred from the dark corner of her heart in which they had been locked these many months, and the emotions flew at her with the wild abandon of the long-imprisoned. Now these evils churned unrestrained in her mind, churned relentlessly along with all the magicks of the Raven Coronet into a vile stew of anguish and deception. Exhausted and despairing, Thaedra allowed herself to at last slide into the sweet, faithless dreams the artifact offered its servants.

With her surrender, the world changed for Thaedra. Her stepfather became everything and her husband as if nothing. Bathed now in the Coronet's magic, she raised her arms longingly toward Josnah. The wall of distrust was gone; her battered face was again the relaxed face of a child.

Josnah glanced at Thaedra just then, as if seeking permission to widow her once more. But as he turned toward his daughter, she spoke.

"Papa?" Thaedra whispered, the years dropping away from her voice. There was no hate or sorrow in Thaedra's eyes now; instead they shone with pure love for her stepfather.

278

Memories seemed to bubble up out of nowhere. "*Papa, carry me, please?*" Little arms tight around Josnah's neck. The solemn words, "*I love you, Papa.*" All this the two remembered; all this father and daughter shared between them now. Josnah need only keep the Coronet to keep the unconditional love of Thaney's daughter. The Coronet must remain; Falmund must die.

But in those seconds of distraction, Falmund dove wildly for his sword. Grasping the hilt, he swung weakly at Josnah, still off-balance as he was, and cried out: "Thaedra! Get back!"

This time, Josnah also realized the danger to his daughter as the fight resumed. "Thaedra! He's right, get out of the way!"

But the bewitched woman kept trying to reach her beloved papa as the two opponents circled each other cautiously.

"Faylah!" Josnah commanded desperately. "Get Thaedra out of the way!"

Faylah stepped forward and took Thaedra's elbow. "Thaedra," she soothed in her honeyed voice, "come here with me. Your father and your husband have business to attend to without you in the way."

"Papa? And... and... My husband?" Thaedra looked questioningly at the creature beside her. She tried to remember. There was something important...something about her husband... something...

"Yes, Thaedra," Faylah reassured her, "your papa and your husband."

"My husband..." Thaedra murmured again wonderingly. "Verin?" A piece of the true Thaedra, a piece steeped in hatred, pierced the sweet, saccharine fog in her brain. "*That cruel bastard of a husband deserves to die!*" she spat disdainfully.

Embroiled in his swordfight with Josnah, Falmund heard only Thaedra's screamed curse and not the words that had come before. He had no idea she referred to Verin. Distraught at his wife's anguished condemnation, Falmund stumbled as he dodged

Josnah's latest swing. Again the strongman found himself kneeling in the autumn leaves at his father-in-law's feet.

Faylah made no move to help Falmund. Instead, she tugged again at Thaedra's arm. "No, Thaedra," Faylah explained. "It is not Verin to whom I refer. Verin is dead. Your husband is Falmund – it is Falmund who fights Josnah."

"Falmund?" Thaedra repeated. "*Falmund?*" She yanked her arm from Faylah's grip as if resenting this information.

Thaedra remembered cool water and warm kisses and longing – not the hollow, insatiable longing swirling in her head now for Josnah – but longing *fulfilled* by someone. Thaedra struggled to grasp the elusive memory.

"Falmund..." she sighed adoringly. A tiny wisp of Thaedra's own psyche made its way to the surface just in time to see Josnah raise his sword for the blow that would wipe Falmund's personage from the world for all time.

Summoning reserves Thaedra believed to be long depleted, she made one, last, valiant effort to sweep aside the numbing fog that enveloped her. As Thaedra pushed tenaciously toward freedom, the spell's resistance grew stronger; it felt as though a dozen men had suddenly thrown their weight upon her shoulders and sought to bring her to her knees. But her desperation gave her strength, and Thaedra forced herself to remain standing as she succeeded, temporarily at least, in throwing off the ancient enchantment.

Clumsily, frantically, ere Josnah could bring his sword down upon her lover, Thaedra lunged forward toward her husband. Off balance as she was, she nonetheless gained speed with each step, much in the same fashion that a drunk gains speed trying to bring his recalcitrant feet back under his center of gravity before he plows face first into the ground.

Startled by his daughter's charge, Josnah paused in his swing and let his sword hang uncertainly in the air.

"Thaedra? What..." Josnah stammered in confusion.

Falmund saw his chance. He rolled to one side and came up gripping his sword tightly. Falmund rose determinedly to his feet just as his wife reached him. Without sacrificing momentum, Thaedra placed her hands atop Falmund's own two-fisted grip on his sword-hilt. Together, the lovers swung their weapon in a deadly arc toward the usurper. The carefully honed sword bit into Josnah's neck and kept on going through flesh and bone.

In its defeat, the Raven Coronet lashed out again at Thaedra's mind and reclaimed her thoughts for a final wrenching moment. There was Josnah, her beloved papa, so close before her – *and Thaedra held the blade that was killing him!*

"*Papa!*" Thaedra screamed in unspeakable horror, her hands yet propelling the sword as it sliced through her stepfather's neck.

Panic-stricken and spattered with her stepfather's blood, Thaedra released her grip on the weapon – but the deed had been done. Thaedra and Falmund's combined blow had landed with such force that, as Josnah's gory corpse dropped to the ground, his head was thrown across the clearing to land eerily upright atop the crypt, its not-yet-sightless eyes still gazing at Thaedra, and the Raven Coronet still in place. But only for a fleeting sliver of time; then the visage that had been Josnah's rolled down the earthen mound to rest against a tree root, bloody and lifeless.

Except for Thaedra's forlorn, heart-rending sobs as she collapsed against her husband, there was stunned silence in the clearing. Suddenly, before anyone could collect their wits enough to speak, the sound of flapping wings filled the air all about them. The group looked around in confusion yet saw nothing.

"Look!" cried out Nazera. "The Coronet!" Everyone stared in the direction in which she pointed her finger.

The Coronet had risen from the head of its late regent and had begun to float, spinning, in mid-air. Within moments, the

281

source of the flapping noise became evident as dozens of ravens swooped down through the gap in the tree branches above. The birds however had neither feathers nor skin, tendons nor muscle, and only size and situation implied that they might once have been the large, black birds of legend. Though the skeletal creatures had wings of mere bone, they seemed to have no trouble staying aloft. And the sound they produced was that of feathers and flesh beating their way through the sky like any living bird.

Cawing angrily, these apparitions began pecking at the swirling crown. As each one pulled free a single feather of his choosing, he then abandoned what remained to his fellows and began circling over the heads of the onlookers. After a time, there were dozens of the specters traveling the perimeter of the clearing. Without warning, as the final feather was snatched up by its owner, the entire flock crumbled into dust. The dust in turn drifted away on soundless currents of air, until there was no sign left of either the Coronet or the ravens.

Just as the stunned witnesses to all this began to breathe normally again, Nazera fainted.

CHAPTER 31

PEACE

"Neesa! Wake up, honey. It's time to leave your dreams of that nasty old Coronet behind and get out of bed."

Little Neesa's eyes fluttered open, and she looked at her mother in bewildered awe. "How do you always know when the Coronet has been talking to me, Mama?"

Neesa's mother sat down on the bed next to her daughter and pushed the child's tousled hair out of the sleepy young eyes. "I remember what it was like to hear the Coronet's call all the time when I was your age. And you have to bear in mind that the women in our family are blessed with the ability to see more than most others can." The woman leaned forward and touched her index finger affectionately to the tip of her daughter's nose. "You never know just what a gifted seer like your mother can see going on inside that little head of yours!"

Neesa's eyes grew wide at the idea that Mama could read her mind – but then she caught sight of her mother's smile, and Neesa knew that she was being teased. "Oh, Mama!" the girl exclaimed, reaching up and drawing her mother down for a hug. In the midst of the embrace, the child realized she had a question for her mother, a question that suddenly seemed very important. Neesa released her parent and spoke: "Mama, I know all the awful things that might happen should someone find the Raven Coronet and wear it again, but what would happen if someone should find it and destroy it?"

283

"If someone should manage to destroy it then I, for one, would certainly rest easier. And you, I suspect, would have a little less magic in your life but a great deal more peace. Now, Nazera, it really is time for you get up and get on with the business of living!"

Nazera didn't want to get up. It felt so nice to close her eyes and feel her mother stroking her brow, feel the comforting arms about her, but the voice kept insisting, kept calling her name.

* * *

Nazera opened her eyes. It took her a moment to leave her dream behind and recognize the worried face that stared down at her as being that of her husband. Hargot's strong arms cradled her as she lay on the forest floor.

"Sweetheart?" Hargot asked, his voice filled with concern. Later he would have time enough to be angry, right now he just wanted to be sure his wife was all right.

Much like the child-Nazera of her dream, the witch reached up to pull her husband's face awkwardly down to her own. Hargot kissed his wife's cheek and tasted the salty dampness of the tears that lay there.

"I'm sorry, Hargot," she whispered softly in his ear. "So very, very sorry. Can you ever forgive me?"

Her husband simply held Nazera tighter and rocked her gently back and forth as if he were comforting a child.

The rest of the group turned away from the couple. Recriminations could wait. For now they would give Hargot time with his wife.

Thaedra leaned against Falmund and spoke tiredly. "Nazera is not the only one who could use a loving embrace at present." Thaedra was Thaedra once more, but it would be a long time before she would forget this day's horror.

"Aye, love, in that you are right," Falmund answered tenderly and drew his own wife into a long hug.

After a time, the centaur guard, who had stayed within the trees during the battle, stepped forward anxiously, his hooves producing a hushed crackle in the fallen leaves. "Excuse me, people, but there are yet things to be done here."

Thaedra pulled reluctantly away from Falmund and looked from her husband's clothes to her own in dismay. Suppressing a shudder at the spray of gore that covered them both, Thaedra deliberately directed her gaze away from Josnah's corpse and severed head to focus instead on the worried stallion.

"You are right, uh...?" Thaedra paused for the centaur to fill in a name.

"Terlow," the creature inserted helpfully.

"Terlow," she repeated. "You are right. We need to tend to our dead and remove ourselves from your woods. I must admit, even should I be whisked from here this very instant, it would not be soon enough for me!"

"Agreed," said Falmund wryly. "I believe my wise spouse speaks for all of us."

"Terlow," broke in Faylah, "I know that there are those of our race who consider the presence of humans in Faerwood to be sacrilege, but these are not just any humans. They have freed centaur-kind from the ancient vow to protect the Raven Coronet for all eternity. Surely my friends deserve a few minutes to catch their breath and some help from us in seeing to what remains of Josnah."

"Of course, Sister," assured Terlow. "It was not my intention to be disrespectful."

"Good," Faylah replied sharply. Turning her attention to her human friends, the centauress spoke more gently. "Thaedra, while I do not wish to put undue pressure upon you, you are Josnah's only family. The disposition of his body is for you to decide. Have you any suggestions?"

285

Thaedra sighed heavily and dragged her eyes over to look at the corpse in question. "I suppose we could carry him out of the forest and bury him in the meadow. It doesn't seem practical to lay him out as I did Verin – or as he himself did for my mother."

"Uh, Thaedra," Falmund interrupted, "do we really want to lug that..." he indicated the gory body, "...and that..." looking at the leaf- and blood-encrusted head, "all the way out of Faerwood?"

His wife looked helplessly about the clearing until her eyes fell upon the empty crypt. "Perhaps," she offered uncertainly, "if the centaurs don't mind, we could place Josnah's body in the tomb that he sought for so many years?"

Faylah and Terlow glanced at each other. Faylah nodded and spoke up. "It would seem fitting, and I believe the elders would have no objection. Perhaps we should ask Nazera if she is aware of any lingering spell that might make such a decision unwise." Faylah shifted her attention to the two magic-wielders where they yet sat on the ground. "Nazera?"

Nazera looked up at the imposing creature. Dirt from the tomb mingled with Nazera's tears to streak her face. "There is no magic left here," she spoke sorrowfully, "and precious little left within myself. The tomb is merely a hole in the ground now, a perfectly suitable place to lay a corpse."

"We seem to be in agreement then," said Faylah. "I'm afraid, Thaedra and Falmund, that the dirty work is up to you. Terlow and I cannot carry Josnah into the crypt; we are far too large to fit through the door. I believe Nazera is too weak to help, and I doubt Hargot wants to leave her side in order to assist."

"You are mistaken there, Faylah," Hargot spoke up as he tenderly disentangled himself from his wife. "I am as much a part of this as anyone." The wizard stood and removed the short, black cloak that he wore. He held the garment out to Thaedra and gave her a sad half-smile. "If you would wrap the head in this, it will make the task of placing it in its resting place a tad less objectionable."

Feeling as if he must somehow atone for his wife's misdeeds, Hargot then turned to Falmund. "If you, old friend, would take one side then I shall take the other and we can see our late traveling companion to his grave."

Steeling themselves for the unpleasant task, the three humans laid Josnah in the crypt without delay. The trio found themselves just as happy that their stomachs had had no food that morn.

"What of the door?" asked Thaedra. "Can we actually close the stone without Nazera's magic?"

"I may yet be able to help," the witch offered tentatively. "I believe I have enough power to levitate the door just a little so that the rest of you may force it closed."

Together, the group was able to bring the door to within a finger's width of being fully closed. Falmund and the centaurs suggested that they try once more to shut it completely but Thaedra shooed them away.

"Leave it as it is," she insisted. "If any of Josnah's spirit yet remains, 'tis better that it be free to leave the tomb than be trapped tight within the earth."

"As you wish," shrugged Faylah. She gazed distractedly off into the dark of the forest and caught sight of a flash of white as Crystal moved restlessly among the trees. Turning back to her companions, she spoke again. "'Tis time we took our leave of this place. Brother Terlow. thank you for your assistance. Give my respects to the elders."

With a nod of farewell to Terlow, the centauress stepped through the tree line and started along the route that would take them out of Faerwood. Behind her, Hargot shepherded Nazera out of the clearing, as well.

Falmund offered his hand to his own spouse but Thaedra hesitated. She stared instead at her stepfather's burial place and tried to understand just what it was that she felt now for the man who had raised her all those years. Patiently, Falmund stood at the edge of the glade and awaited his grieving wife.

Steadfastly ignoring the visions of Josnah's bloodied corpse that loomed at the edges of her consciousness, Thaedra imagined that her stepfather was yet whole and alive in front of her. Focusing on this image, she found that the years of anger and bitterness had dissipated with Josnah's death. Like the skeletal ravens who had reclaimed their tokens and crumbled to dust, her hatred had been claimed by the four winds to be tossed and tattered until nothing remained. She had only bittersweet sorrow for Josnah now. Sorrow, and a long list of questions that would never be answered.

Had Josnah really loved her mother so much that Thaney's death destroyed him? Or had he spent his whole life looking for some external bit of love or magic that would make him happy rather than turning to his own heart? Perhaps his marriage had simply been a raft to which he held fast in a sea of despair. What if her mother had lived? Would his fairy tale image of their union have survived the passage of the years?

Thaedra shook her head. She would never have been able to see eye-to-eye with her stepfather, even had they both lived to be a hundred. The type of love Josnah had clung to so feverishly seemed so very different from what she had with Falmund.

Resigned to live with such riddles, Thaedra turned toward her husband and reached out to take his hand. But once again she changed her mind. "Wait, I forgot something," she explained to Falmund as she stepped back toward the crypt.

Dropping to her knees at one side of the door, Thaedra began pawing through the layers of leaves so recently disturbed by the group's efforts to close the chamber. "Ah, here it is!" she announced elatedly as she gripped the obsidian box in which the Raven Coronet had slept for so long.

"It is indeed pretty, Lass," Falmund admitted, "but why would you want a reminder of such horrors as happened here today?"

"Ah, Falmund," Thaedra replied, "horrors there were to be sure, but true love triumphed over false in the end. And think of the tales we can tell with such a relic as evidence!" She opened the box to look inside, and a gust of wind blew the dust of what had once been enchanted velvet lining into Thaedra's face.

When the resulting fit of coughing had ceased, Thaedra grinned sheepishly at her husband. It occurred to her that the two of them, covered in dirt and blood and sweat as they were, were every bit as repulsive as they had been at their first meeting, perhaps more so. But she found herself loving the man more than ever.

Again Falmund extended his hand to his wife. "It might make a wonderful prop for a circus act at that, mightn't it?" he suggested with a chuckle.

This time she gripped the proffered hand firmly. Marveling at their love for each other, marveling at the human ability to find love and humor in the midst of death and grief and exhaustion, the pair hastened into the forest after their friends.

CHAPTER 32

NIGHTFALL

By the time the group had made their way out of Faerwood, the autumn sun was low in the sky. At the edge of the meadow they found Marcus struggling to dig a grave for his sweetheart.

"Here, Marcus," offered Falmund. "Let us help you with that." There was not a soul in the bunch with enthusiasm for the task, but they willingly found another shovel in one of the wagons, and all but Nazera took turns digging. Finally, as the sun touched the horizon, the hole reached a suitable size and depth in which to lay Desirée.

Thaedra gazed down uncomfortably at the corpse. "Surely we can spare a blanket in which to bury her? Or perhaps her gaily colored veils with which she claimed to 'paint the sky'?"

Marcus looked gratefully at the swordswoman. "Yes, you're right, I hadn't thought about a shroud." He managed a sad smile. "She would have liked to have her veils..." His voice trailed off as if trying to remember just where the veils might be.

Thaedra suddenly realized that all of Desirée's veils must be back in Marcus' wagon, back where they'd left it in the wee hours. Quickly she volunteered, "Actually, Marcus, I believe I have some lovely fabrics that she gave me some time ago that would be appropriate." Before Marcus could reply, Thaedra was on her way to her wagon.

When Thaedra returned with the delicate fabrics, she and Nazera spread them out on the ground so that the men could

291

place the dead woman upon the material. Carefully, Nazera and Thaedra wrapped and tucked the makeshift shroud as securely as they could about poor Desirée. Her young face was the last thing they covered.

Satisfied that the corpse was ready, Thaedra gestured for the men to place it in the grave. As Falmund and Hargot shoveled dirt into the hole, Marcus said quietly, "Sleep, my little flower. Perhaps when the meadow is abloom next spring your spirit will rise to paint the sky once more."

Thaedra watched silently and wondered how well the grieving assassin had ever really known his lover. Thaedra had always suspected Marcus of merely using young Desirée for his own pleasure and to soothe his aging ego, but now she saw that perhaps she had had it backwards. Perhaps it was Desirée who had been using the overly romantic, softhearted assassin to get to the Coronet. Or maybe they were each guilty of using the other; that seemed to be the way of so many couples.

When the last shovelful was in place, Thaedra looked at Faylah in the fading light. "Friend, is there a brook near here where we might wash today's doings from our skin and clothes? I seem to remember splashing through a stream with the wagon near the end of our frenzied journey this morning."

"You are right. There is one a very short distance from here. I, too, long to bathe." The centauress looked at the group of humans. "Who will join us?"

"The light is almost gone, and the chill of autumn has arrived," protested Nazera. "I shall make do with a change of clothes and water from the wagon to wash my face."

Hargot looked from his wife to Thaedra. "Even were it midwinter, there would be a certain appeal to Thaedra's suggestion, especially in such delightful company. But no, I shall follow my wife's example. Perhaps she and I might manage to concoct a dinner for us all while you are bathing."

Nazera's eyes flashed indignantly as she pulled her husband away from the others and towards their waiting wagon. "How dare you flirt with Thaedra like that!" they could hear her snap.

"But my darling," he replied naughtily, "it was your love spell that caused her to join us in our bed so recently! I can hardly be blamed for the fascinating ideas such a situation inspires!"

The couple's bickering grew quieter as the door to their wagon closed behind them. But even so, it was clear from the *force* with which the door closed that the fight far from over.

"Well," observed Thaedra, "at least things with them appear to be back to normal. One of these days, those two magic-wielders should come up with a spell that allows them each to spend a day in the other's shoes. Perhaps then they wouldn't be so quick to goad one another into a spat!"

"You realize," commented Falmund, "that Nazera was not present when you chose action over modesty this morning." He leered at his wife mischievously. "Since you mention goading, do you think we should inform Nazera that Hargot has seen you in all your goddess-given glory?"

Faylah snorted in amusement.

"If I weren't so tired," replied Thaedra to her husband, "I would smite you for that suggestion."

"Perhaps it's just as well you're tired then." Falmund put his arm around his wife. "I, of course, will be happy to join you and Faylah at the brook. Marcus? Will you come, too?"

Thaedra suddenly felt guilty at their display of playful affection in front of the anguished man. She pulled free of Falmund and turned to Marcus. "It might do you good to cleanse yourself of the touch of death. Won't you join us?"

Marcus shook his head. "All that I wish at this moment is to fall into bed and sleep for a very long time. Forgive me if I leave you for the evening."

Falmund and Thaedra looked at each other. "Marcus," Thaedra said gently, "in case you have forgotten, your wagon is back at the campsite we abandoned in our haste to get to Faerwood. But, if you would give Falmund and I just a few minutes to grab some things from our cabin, you are welcome to have our bed."

Her husband added, "Thaedra and I will be happy to spend the night under the stars. A little fire and a few blankets, and we'll be fine."

Marcus started to protest but then simply nodded his head gratefully.

Moments later, the two had retrieved blankets and clothes enough from their cabin to make themselves comfortable for the night. Thaedra had also used the opportunity to tuck the obsidian box safely away under their bed. As Marcus disappeared into the wagon, Thaedra turned again to Faylah.

"Shall we be off then? It appears it shall just be the three of us."

Faylah shook her head with a smile as she gazed off toward where the brook bubbled out of Faerwood. "Not three – four," the centauress murmured.

There, her white coat glowing in the twilight, stood Crystal.

Faylah continued: "It seems that there shall be two humans and two of the equine sort enjoying a moonlit swim this evening."

Taking a change of clothes and two of the blankets with them, the humans followed Faylah and the unicorn along the edge of the forest to the stream.

A melancholy sweetness permeated the group. The legendary Raven Coronet was gone forever, as were Josnah and Desirée, and the crisp fall air hinted at the coming ravages of winter. But there was hushed magic in the air all about them. To their right towered the tall, dark trees of Faerwood, ancient sentinels honoring the adventurers who had put an old wizard's threat to rest at last. Above the foursome, spreading across the sky to the horizon, were a billion stars twinkling and dancing before equine and human eyes alike.

Ahead of them, the group could hear the brook playing joyfully over the rocks in its path – yet, when they reached the waters, they saw only the glassy black obsidian of its ever-changing surface. In daylight, they would have seen every pebble within the clear water; by night, the stream was a mirror, secretive and mysterious about what lay below. Where moonlight struck the surface, specks of white light sparkled. And where the waters churned over a rock, the foam glowed as if illuminated from within.

"By the goddess," Thaedra breathed.

"Aye," agreed Falmund in hushed reverence for the wonder of the night enfolding them.

His wife shivered, either with cold or with the thrill of life itself. Falmund pulled her close to his side as they watched their four-legged companions slide soundlessly into the dark water; what little noise the fillies might have made was lost in the brook's own singing. Faylah and Crystal moved upstream and disappeared into the darkness of Faerwood.

Falmund put down the bundle of blankets and clothes he carried before looking questioningly at his wife. "Do they seek their own privacy or simply offer us ours?"

"Does it matter?" she replied softly, stepping out of his embrace to take his hand and slip fully clothed into the water. She drew her husband into the brook with her.

The water was bracing, the night air chilly, but their awe at the world around them and their memories of their first such swim dulled the autumn's frosty nip.

"I would seduce you, sirrah," Thaedra murmured, using wet fingers to wipe the dirt and blood from her lover's face, "but I fear this water is too cold for even our passion."

"Sweet Thaedra, thou art wise as always." He watched his wife's white blouse shine in the moonlight as it clung to her breasts before falling to float atop the water about her waist. "But I nonetheless swear that I shall strive my best to rub every bit of soil from that blouse of yours..." Falmund placed his hand lovingly on one mud-splattered breast, "...even if I must use my bare hands!"

Thaedra couldn't see her husband's grin in the darkness, but she was quite certain it was there. "Rub away then, sir. I shall bear what I must!" She raised her hand from the water to place it, palm outward, against her forehead, her movement throwing a spray of water on her husband.

"Was that bear – or *bare?*" inquired her husband hopefully before beginning a serious effort to remove the filth that covered both.

Getting down to the business, the pair cleaned up as best they could, shedding their clothes halfway through the process to better enable them to scrub both cloth and skin. When they were done, they climbed up the bank to put on the extra clothes they had brought along. Their wet things they left hanging from a branch to be retrieved in the morning.

"Shall we wait for Faylah before going back?" asked Thaedra as she wrapped one of the blankets about herself.

"Nay, she and Crystal will return when they're ready," answered Falmund.

The pair walked along together through the darkness to find that Hargot and Nazera, despite their differences, had managed to build a crackling fire and prepare a hearty vegetable soup for dinner. Thaedra noticed also that Windweaver had been unsaddled and was tethered near the recently unhitched mules. The woman felt a wave of pity for the poor beasts when she realized that they had been left to stand in their traces the long day through.

"Where's Marcus?" queried Falmund.

296

"We took him some soup in the cabin, and I believe he has gone back to sleep," replied Hargot. "What of Faylah?"

"She wandered off into Faerwood after showing us to the brook. I'm sure she'll be back in due time." Thaedra saw no need to say any more than that.

Dinner was a hurried and quiet affair, though Falmund and Hargot did spend some time debating in which direction the caravan should head come morning.

"I know we don't normally spend winter this far north," insisted Hargot, "but we need to rest and regroup now, not spend days and days making our way south. As far as I'm concerned, the season is over for this year."

Falmund replied thoughtfully, "I suppose one of the northern towns might offer us shelter until spring. We have to go back along the northern edge of the United Lands to retrieve the other two wagons anyway. Maybe Skylark? Or Cobbleton?"

Thaedra wrinkled her nose. "Cobbleton is still a ways from here, and I don't believe I would be comfortable spending months on end in my home town. Maybe someday. But at present there are too many sorry memories. I have no objection to one of the closer northern towns, though."

Faylah's alto tones broke in unexpectedly, for she had returned to the encampment without being noticed. "Winter is winter," the centauress declared. "The climate in the south is only marginally better than that in the north. Hargot is right. We're done performing for this year; we need time to heal our sorrows and reconfigure some of our acts. Skylark is still further away than I'd like. I vote to winter in Thistleseed, just two more towns west of where we left the wagons." She turned to the witch. "Nazera?"

"One town is as good as another, now that there is no Raven Coronet lying in Faerwood to torture my dreams," she admitted.

"I doubt Marcus cares at this point," observed Falmund, "and I'll not wake him to ask. So Thistleseed it is then."

"Good," spoke up Thaedra, "that much is settled. But right now it is all I can do to keep my eyes open. Can we *please* continue this discussion in the morning?"

There were murmurs of assent all around, and Falmund arose to join his wife in making a comfortable bed for the two of them near the fire. Nazera and Hargot retired to their wagon; Faylah disappeared into Faerwood to spend the night with Crystal at her side.

"Alone and cozy at last," sighed Thaedra as the two of them snuggled under their pile of blankets.

"And very, very tired," added Falmund sleepily.

"Did all of this really happen in only one day?" Thaedra marveled. Reviewing all that had occurred, she found the image of Falmund's sword slicing through Josnah's neck springing into her head again. She pushed it firmly aside and concentrated instead on Falmund's soothing presence.

"Aye, lass, one *very* long day."

"Falmund, my love, stay awake just one minute more," Thaedra pleaded. She feared the dreams that might come with sleep. But even more than that, she wanted to bathe in the peace of this instant just a few seconds longer.

"Yes?"

"You offered to sleep beneath the stars with me; will you not open your eyes to look at them in all their glory?"

Reluctantly, Falmund pried open his eyes. Above him, the heavens shone in radiant splendor. Next to him, his loving wife lay warm at his side. Falmund thought of their losses that day and cherished the moment all the more.

"You are right, my love," he admitted. "'Tis a wondrous sight. But even the heavens are nay as wondrous as my love for thee, nor as lofty as the promise of our future."

Allowing her husband and herself to at last drift into slumber, Thaedra murmured softly: "Thou art eloquent to the brink of absurdity as usual, husband. But, also as usual, thou art right, as well."

EPILOGUE

Trance-like, Nazera opened the obsidian box in Falmund's hands to remove the silver wreath from its resting-place. Behind her, each of her comrades moved to prepare for battle. Faylah reached for an arrow from her quiver; Thaedra went to draw her sword. Hargot extended his hands towards the witch as if to douse his opponent in flame, while Marcus gripped a dagger in each hand.

Nazera ignored them all and stared only at Falmund as she raised the crown high above his head. A gust of spring breeze whipped through the canvas to billow her sleeves dramatically and shape the fabric of the witch's robe tightly against her swollen belly.

In a voice that rang through the tent, Nazera intoned: "I, daughter of Aza, crown thee, my lord, with the legendary Raven Coronet."

The crowd gasped as Nazera lowered the coronet onto Falmund's head. The four players in back of the witch froze momentarily – before dropping their weapons and bowing their heads in submission to the wearer of the wreath.

Now Nazera shook her own head as if coming awake at last. She stepped questioningly from Thaedra to Faylah to Hargot to Marcus, but each ignored her in the midst of their supplication to Falmund.

Nazera suddenly whipped her head to one side to glare back over her shoulder at Falmund. Falmund simply smirked at her as he stood proudly with his arms folded. The witch turned back to

Thaedra and waved her hand over the swordswoman's head. This was Thaedra's cue to retrieve her sword and rise to challenge Falmund.

"Take it off," Thaedra commanded Falmund angrily for everyone to hear. She threw off her cloak to reveal a ridiculously skimpy suit of armor that would have been useless in a real battle. Nonetheless, her mail shimmered and jingled in a most eye-catching manner as she explained, more for the benefit of the onlookers than for Falmund: "The witch has regained her senses and freed me from the crown's spell. Now take off that accursed coronet!"

"Nay," proclaimed Falmund drawing his own sword. "The Raven Coronet is mine now. I shall slay you and the witch – and the whole world shall fall at my feet!" He gestured with his weapon at the others all standing helpless, as if to illustrate the power that he and the coronet possessed.

"Then prepare to die!" roared the swordswoman.

Thus began Falmund's and Thaedra's latest sword choreography. They had scripted in as many plot turns and twists as they could manage, including a little interference from Hargot as he sought to aid his "liege" by showering Thaedra with a colorful display of sparks. In the end, Falmund sank to his knees, and Thaedra raised her sword above him for the great blow that would sever head from neck. Just as she began her downward stroke, the tent was thrown into darkness. All around the ring, the crowd gasped.

In the darkness, a crystal orb began to glow, a crystal orb held by Nazera. With the dim light throwing its eerie illumination upon her face, the practiced storyteller offered her audience the rest of the tale in a hushed voice. When Nazera reached the description of the Coronet's destruction, a fog formed inside the sphere. This fog swirled and eddied within the globe and thus projected wavering gray shadows to flit mysteriously across both the tent canvas and the listeners' faces.

302

Standing off to the side with Falmund's arm about her waist, Thaedra spoke under her breath: "It seems our witch has lost little, if any, of her magic abilities. Impressive."

Falmund merely nodded his agreement.

Finally the story was done, and daylight returned. The entire troupe strode to the center of the ring to accept the crowd's accolades. Again and again the group bowed as the audience applauded enthusiastically. Eventually, the spectators left their seats to swarm about the performers.

"Ho there! Thaedra!" a voice called out.

Thaedra looked about at the sea of faces and spotted the source of the words. Thaedra had been a bit uneasy about unveiling their new act here in Cobbleton, given that there were sure to be old clients among the watchers, but this was one face Thaedra was delighted to see.

"Artella!" she shouted happily. Determinedly, Thaedra towed Falmund through the crowd to meet her former housemate.

"Thaedra, the show was wonderful!" Artella gushed. "Was the story about the Raven Coronet really true? Did you really do all that?"

"We took a few liberties with the plot," admitted Thaedra, "but basically that was how it happened. In truth, it is Falmund's role I play in the act."

Artella looked at Falmund admiringly. "Well, I guess you caught yourself quite a man then."

"I did indeed. Life had been very good to me lately – as has my husband," Thaedra explained with a grin.

"Oh," Artella responded in mock disappointment. "Does this mean we don't get to cut off his balls?"

"*Excuse me?*" Falmund exclaimed in bewildered outrage.

"Oh, my! I think not," replied Thaedra. "I like them just where they are!" Thaedra glanced at her husband's crotch with a leer every bit as lewd as Falmund's own best.

Falmund looked from one woman to the other with consternation until Artella and Thaedra both dissolved into laughter.

"I promise you, love," Falmund's wife assured him with a chuckle, "I shall explain it all later."

"I *am* jealous of you, Thaedra," insisted Artella. "You look so very happy now. You have not only escaped the brothel but have found a man who seems to have melted your heart completely."

"Perhaps you might join our troupe and make your own escape from Madame Calista's," Thaedra suggested, before adding with a wink, "provided you keep your hands off my husband!" More seriously she continued, "We are still short a person, and poor Faylah is trying to fill far too many roles by herself. *You* could assist Marcus with his knife-throwing act in Faylah's place, and I'm sure you'd make a fine exotic dancer, too. Your more delicate look would be a much needed balance to that of Faylah and myself."

"Ahem." Falmund cleared his throat. "I can just imagine what Nazera's response would be to adding one of your former co-workers to our little group. Her temperament may be more serene and her marriage more harmonious now that the Coronet no longer tugs at her, but she remains our dear, haughty, green-eyed Nazera."

"Nazera," Thaedra replied with a touch of irritation, "is going to have her hands too full when the baby comes to worry about Artella. Besides, an extra person around to help with both the show and the baby would be a good thing for everyone!"

"You may have a point there," Falmund agreed. "It is definitely worth discussing – if Artella's interested that is."

"Absolutely. I would be most interested," replied the courtesan.

"We shall get back to you then," assured Falmund. "Now, if you'll excuse us, my wife and I need to dampen our parched throats."

After giving Artella a quick hug, Thaedra followed Falmund from the tent. Out in the spring sunshine, she saw more familiar faces milling about. There were Arienne and her children waving to Thaedra. And there was one of her old fighting coaches, the blacksmith. Even a young man Thaedra had once thrown from the brothel greeted her cheerfully. Everyone she saw gave her a welcoming smile and a warm hello. Her newfound celebrity seemed to have erased her sins.

When Falmund and Thaedra were at last free of the crowd, Falmund turned proudly to his wife and said fondly: "Have I told you lately how much I love you?"

"Yes, you have," Thaedra replied, "but you may most certainly tell me again."

Falmund hugged her fiercely and exclaimed loudly: "I love you, woman!"

"And I, you," Thaedra answered, "with all my heart!"

Releasing her from the hug, Falmund took Thaedra's hand and towed her toward their wagon where he knew a cool draught of water to be waiting.

Smiling and silent, his wife followed obediently. But inside Thaedra's head, a little girl with tousled, chestnut locks and a nose that had never been broken skipped and giggled, warm and safe and happy again at last.

END

ABOUT THE AUTHOR

Christina Briley was born, raised, and still resides in the Greater Boston area. The third of four daughters, she grew up in a large, old house full of books and cats. Her professional resumé is an eclectic one; it includes wedding gowns, belly dancing, textiles, graphics, and making athletic shoe prototypes, as well as writing. An avid ballroom and folk dancer, she is currently working on a non-fiction book about the history of social dance during New England's Industrial Revolution entitled *Twirling Jennies*.

A few years back, Ms. Briley and her adored second husband downsized from their sprawling, antique, one-time brothel into a condo in a converted textile mill. They have three adult children and welcomed their second grandchild this past summer.